T0013148

PRAISE FOR *SO PRETTY*

'*So Pretty* is like Stephen King on crack; the most accomplished book I've read this year. Dark, gothic as hell, and genuinely scary, Turner has managed to portray loneliness, obsession and monster-worship in one neat little package. I dare you to open it ... Oh, and that curiosity shop is the stuff of nightmares' Michael Craven

'Dark, lyrical and intriguing' Fiona Cummins

'Twisted, toxic and deeply dark, this gives off mega *Needless Things* vibes – and that ending is just *perfect*. Brava' Lisa Hall

'What an incredible read. This book sucks you in from the first spine-tingling chapter and weaves a dark, twisted and compelling sense of foreboding. It will get under your skin. Brilliant' Claire Allan

'An utterly chilling psychological horror of modern-day witchcraft, possession, murder and madness. Who knew such evil could lurk in the heart of Rye?' Essie Fox

'Beautifully written and a real page-turner, this chilling gothic tale explores the dark corners of identity' C J Cooke

'So chilling, the nature/nurture debate is perfect for a contemporary Gothic thriller – the stuff of nightmares!' Anne Coates

'I read this book in almost one sitting. It had me completely rapt. Gothic, dark and fast-paced, it's a brooding thriller that had me asking new questions with every page-turn. Turner's prose is as delightful as it is dark, with beautiful turns of phrase that can be at once both buttery soft and sharp as a knife. I had a lot of fun reading this one!' Rheannah, Bookseller

'A dark, intense read that's intricately and beautifully written. This is a story that will creep under your skin and leave you desperately unnerved' Emma, Bookseller

'It was unsettling, it was unnerving, it was bloody brilliant'
From Belgium with Booklove

'Written with a classical nod and containing dark and beautifully observed pen portraits, *So Pretty* is startling and incredibly intense, and it engenders an atmosphere of fear and dread' Live & Deadly

'I'm shook. This book is a force ... a masterpiece' Emerald Reviews

SO PRETTY

ABOUT THE AUTHOR

Ronnie Turner grew up in Cornwall, the youngest in a large family. At an early age, she discovered a love of literature and dreamed of being a published author. Ronnie now lives in the South West with her family and three dogs. In her spare time, she reviews books on her blog and enjoys long walks on the coast. Ronnie is a Waterstones senior bookseller.

Follow Ronnie on Twitter @Ronnie__Turner, on Facebook at facebook.com/ronnie.turner.9022, and on Instagram @ronnieturner8702.

SO PRETTY

Ronnie Turner

ORENDA
BOOKS

Orenda Books
16 Carson Road
West Dulwich
London SE21 8HU
www.orendabooks.co.uk

First published in the United Kingdom by Orenda Books, 2023
Copyright © Ronnie Turner, 2023

Ronnie Turner has asserted her moral right to be identified as the author of this
work in accordance with the Copyright, Designs and Patents Act, 1988.

All Rights Reserved. No part of this publication may be reproduced in any form
or by any means without the written permission of the publishers.

*This is a work of fiction. Names, characters, places and incidents are either products of
the author's imagination or are used fictitiously. Any resemblance to actual events,
locales or persons, living or dead, is entirely coincidental.*

A catalogue record for this book is available from the British Library.

ISBN 978-1-914585-59-3
eISBN 978-1-914585-60-9

Typeset in Garamond by typesetter.org.uk
Printed and bound by CPI Group (UK) Ltd, Croydon CR0 4YY

*For sales and distribution, please contact info@orendabooks.co.uk or visit
www.orendabooks.co.uk.*

For Maggie

HELP WANTED

Berry & Vincent

Sales, stocktaking, general upkeep.
No experience required. Apply within.

Come to Berry & Vincent

TEDDY

Berry & Vincent

The shop stands apart from the rest, bent and misshapen. 'Keep clear,' its strange face seems to say. 'Keep away. We are closed to you.' Though, obviously, it is open.

A sign hangs above the door, tossed by the rain with a sound like: *begone, begone, begone*. Even this small thing does not care for my presence here.

Berry & Vincent
Ye Olde Antiques and Curios Shoppe
Purveyors of fine antiques, oddities and collectables.
Est. 1970

There is something malignant about the place. The blinds are up, its eyes are open, and I wonder if I have made a mistake in coming here.

'Oh,' I say to nothing. 'Oh.' *Have I?*

The best the shop window can boast are a fine, golden music box and a pair of emerald gloves in rich and buttery suede. A mask hangs there too, black eyes and waxy skin. I imagine it is made of some sort of rubber and I want to press my finger into its cheek and make it smile.

Drawing my woollen coat tighter, my reflection surprises me. The skin on my face seems loose, drooping like wax over the edge of a candle, an old man. A visual contradiction of my thirty-three years. The street is empty. The rain, the rain, I tell myself, it's because of the rain. It isn't because of me. I haven't frightened away everyone on my second day in Rye.

I look back at the mask...

But it's not a mask, it's a man.

He blinks, and I wheel back, heart stamping. *Courage, courage, Teddy*. I straighten my coat, run a hand through my hair.

A bell chimes as I push open the door. Black pillars quiver in front of my eyes, then they still and I realise they are towers of things. I worry I might stumble and break something.

Or something might break me.

The man from the window slithers forward. I wait for the inevitable jolt of recognition, the expression on people's faces when they look at me. It doesn't come. Perhaps he does not remember who my father was, perhaps he does not know this face I wear. My leg jigs. I take a breath, stick out my hand.

'Hello. My ... my name is Teddy Colne. You're Mr Vincent? It's nice to meet you.'

His hand is slick, and I must keep myself from wiping mine on my trousers. 'Thank you for accepting my application. I look forward to starting work.' Again, nothing.

'You have quite the place here. It must have taken a long time to build such a collection of ... things.'

He walks away. I follow, wringing my hands. Should I just slip out? Would it be so bad if I simply left? No. I can't. This is my fresh start. I sniff. Even if it isn't all that fresh.

'I don't think I've ever seen a shop like this before. It's ... impressive.' Compliments; the crutch of desperate men. 'This is my second day in Rye. Is it always this quiet? Perhaps it's the rain. It's a grim day. Heavy. Sends everyone indoors, doesn't it?'

How old is he? His hair is the colour of chalk, his body is bent, and sweat, sweet and sickly, wafts from his frayed clothes. I guess he is in his seventies.

'Gosh, I haven't seen one of those since I was a boy. Oh look!'
He does not look. 'Very impressive,' I mumble. 'Very impressive.'
But I am thinking, *Speak! Speak!*

The shop stretches back, a cavernous hallway bloated with
broken clocks, buckets, books, dolls with blue eyes, brown eyes,
black eyes, no eyes.

But there is more.

Shelves laden with curious curiosities. A tin brimming with
bodies, fleas, small as crumbs of bread. A stuffed terrier with two
noses. A human foetus lolling in a jar, half-formed eyes like five-
pence coins. Rubbery bodies and leathery faces in jars, in buckets,
in corners where I am afraid to step.

I see photographs on the wall. From the 1900s perhaps? Faces,
faces, so many faces, ivory pale, lips dark as a bruise. They watch
me. And I wish they would not. My feet clump to a stop. Their
eyes are glass, shiny and strange, almost as if ... I realise then. These
are photographs of the dead.

And.

'Are they childr—?'

But I have no words. They have run out of me.

🍎

Twice more, I consider fleeing, hoping some creature doesn't trip
me on my way. I wonder if he is a mute, Mr Vincent, some
voiceless, wordless little fish of a man. But I hear him mutter to
himself as he watches me complete my tasks, hear him curse my
clumsy hands, fury in his strange voice.

'Why will you not speak?' I ask him eventually, with more
courage than I know I have.

He looks at me. I apologise.

He speaks. So why doesn't he speak to me?

Will I find him tomorrow, tucked inside that shop, all the blood and bone gone from his body? A man with porcelain skin and a horsehair wig, grown into one of his many peculiar items?

Now, at home, shuffling out of my coat, I move with all the speed of a ninety-year-old man. My knees ache, arthritis swells them to melon-shaped bulbs. But it is not only this. I take a shaky breath. I feel thinned, stretched. I was only inside a shop. But the shop feels as if it is still inside me.

ADA

Curio and Curiosity

The first time I saw Berry & Vincent I told myself I wouldn't go inside. Its shadow spilled into the street, and I stepped back so it could not meet my shoe.

Albie's eyes were bright-blue saucers as he looked at the trinkets in the window. He dived inside, and I went after him, the single light casting a yellow haze that made the shadows blister, grow sharper. Sharp enough to cut. Albie reached for something and I snatched his hand back.

The shop extended, a black hole full to bursting with things I doubted I could even name. A man appeared, smiled, but it looked painful, as if the muscles had lost their ability to flex.

'This is Albie. I'm Ada. We've just moved into the town.'

He licked his lips. 'Miss.'

That was all he said. Yet I wanted to push that word back between his lips. A tremble rolled down my body, and I put a hand out to steady myself.

Albie tugged my hand, showed me a toy car. I nodded, aware there was only two pounds twenty in my pocket. The man refused the money. I pulled Albie out, the toy still tucked inside his fist, then we ran like the shop was a live thing and it could crack us between its teeth.

'Have you met him?'

'Who?'

'Teddy. He's just moved here. Works at Berry & Vincent. He'll come to regret it soon enough. There hasn't been an "assistant" in all the time I've lived here. Can't know what he's got himself in to.'

'He's really the first person to work there?'

'Yes. That place will put a rot in his belly. It will make him sick. You'll see.'

'Where's he from?'

'How am I supposed to know that?' She shakes her head. 'First newcomer since yourself. Two years you've been here now, isn't it?' A look, swift, scathing. There are two others in the grocer's; they look up when she mentions the newcomer, hands stilled on cans of soup and bags of apples. Now the women look away again.

'I wonder why he wants to work there,' I say, remembering the first time I saw Berry & Vincent.

'Where's that boy of yours?'

'He's home asleep. He's poorly. He could wake up any moment. I should go.'

Albie is just as I left him, curled up tight as a fist. I ease myself into bed. His eyes ping open.

'Hello, sweetheart. How do you feel? Any better?'

'My head hurts.'

'It's no better?'

'No.'

'Oh dear. It will be soon, I promise. I've got beans and toast for supper if you can manage it later?'

'Mrs James was worried about you.' A lie; she couldn't care less. 'She hopes you feel better soon. She told me that someone new has moved into the town. He's working at Berry & Vincent.'

He frowns, creases settling between his eyes. 'Who?'

'I think she said his name is Teddy. Like a bear.'

He smiles. 'Why does he work at Berry & Vincent?'

'He's the new assistant. He's going to help out in the shop. Come on.' I give him his glass of water. 'Have a little drink.'

After he's finished, he curls round me, sleeps. I keep as still as I can, but the silence is sharp, and I berate myself for wishing I had stayed longer in the grocer's because now I am back and I'm feeling the absence of a voice, anyone's voice, like a fist turning in my gut.

TEDDY

Riddles and Rye

There is more to the shop than I first thought. Before, it seemed to say, 'Keep clear. Keep away. We are closed to you.' Now it says, 'Come. Come now. Come inside.' And I do not think it will ever open its door for me to leave.

Strange shoals of things are spread throughout. A bowl of bezoars, casual as hard-boiled sweets: a skeleton of a two-headed baby; conjoined pups, pickled in a jar; leathery bodies of creatures I do not know the names of. Faces, faces, faces, all over the godforsaken shop.

I close my eyes to it all, turn to the master of it all, this strange civilisation. Close them again.

'How ... how did you come to have all this?' I ask, taking up a jar and polishing it. There is something inside, lumpen and small as a golf ball.

He turns and looks at me, but no answer comes. I try again.

'I've never heard of some of these things. Where did you find them?'

My voice is shaky. I swallow, tell myself to speak up. *Speak up!* Stop being such a fool.

'What was the last thing you sold?'

He turns, walks away. I stare at his back. It is moving, quivering. Is he laughing? I look down. The lump in the jar is a head. A baby's head, shrunken and brown as rock, three ivory thorns driven through its lips.

The café is full today, fit to bursting with townspeople. How long in Rye until they recognise me as my father's son?

I sit in the corner by the window, see the shop, see Mr Vincent moving around in there, this man who watches but never speaks.

I rub my hands together. Look away. Look back.

He's there.

In the window this time. Looking at me. I jump in my seat, knocking my coffee over. Across the street, a smile turns the corners of his lips.

The first smile of his I've seen.

Molly, the elderly proprietress places a hand on my shoulder. 'Can I get you anything else?'

'No thanks.'

Molly follows my gaze. 'It's bothering you, isn't it, Berry & Vincent?'

I push out a chair and gesture for her to sit down. She does so hesitantly. 'It's ... it's ... different.'

'We don't talk about the place. It keeps to itself. And we keep to ours.'

'I only arrived in Rye three days ago, but when I saw it ... I was drawn to it. It just, well, it looked unusual. I saw the poster in the window, put my CV through the door and I got the job. No interview. Nothing. I've still not quite adjusted to it though. It's not what I thought it was.'

'You shouldn't be working there.' She bites her lip, draws a single bead of blood before swiftly wiping it away.

This morning, countless townspeople threaded the street but not once did the door open nor its bell ring. And I realise now that they were all avoiding the shop.

But it wasn't because of me.

'What's ... what's the story behind the place?' I shuffle my seat closer, vaguely aware that four other people have done the same.

'We don't talk about the place, Mol. We don't.' One of the men shakes his head, fast, until I think it will come off his neck.

I look round, I see only aged faces turned to mine. Only aged faces all around this town. Everywhere I look.

'He should know what he's taken on, Phil.' Molly sighs, fiddling with salt on the table. 'It was a butcher's before it was Berry & Vincent. We'd all go there for our cuts of meat every Saturday, have a natter about the week. It was busier than the café some days. Old Bill Norton was a chatterbox, could talk your ear off in five minutes, but he was a sweet man. About fifty years ago, Old Bill had to sell. He moved from the village with his family, who were hankering for the big city.'

'London?'

'No, Hastings.'

'Anyway, one day, they turned up. Mr Berry and Mr Vincent.' She gestures to the shop. 'Opened the place two weeks later. Antiques and curios. The town was interested, naturally. It seemed like a good sort of place for the tourists, you know. The kids took a shine to it. All those toys tucked away in there.'

I think, *And now he has photographs of dead children on the wall.*

'What about Mr Berry? I haven't met him yet.'

'And you won't,' she says. 'He's long gone. He was here about a year, Berry, before he left.'

'He wasn't like the other one. Good man, Berry, good man.' We turn to see an elderly man shuffling his chair closer. 'He cared about us lot, he did. Every Saturday, he'd organise a treasure hunt for the kiddies. Hide toys round that shop and get them all involved.'

'Why did he leave?'

'No one knows. Not really.' Molly now. 'But we suspected that he was bought out—'

'Pushed out, more like.'

'What do you mean?'

'Vincent. He did it. Been infecting this place ever since. It was better before.' The elderly man's voice needles in my ears.

'Now, we've talked enough about that place. You're scaring the poor boy.' Molly, silencing the others with a look. 'Stop.'

I sit back, realising that the café is oddly still, the hum of voices has fallen away. Eyes watch me with sadness, fear ... pity. I shrink back from it, stumbling as I rise from the chair. 'I should probably go and explore the village. I've only seen a bit of it. It was nice to meet you all.' I laugh. Why am I laughing?

'If you need anything, anything at all, even if you just need someone to talk to, come to me. I'll help you.' Molly reaches for my hand, the salt on her fingers pressing deep into my skin.

With what?

'With him.'

I had not realised I'd spoken.

'Thanks.' I close the door behind me, but I feel these people looking at me as if there is a sickness already inside me.

ADA

Rotten and Pretty Things

'How long, do you think?'

'How long until what?'

'Until he runs.' The men walk by my living-room window, greasy chins thrust out. Their feet, thump, thump across the ground, as if they have heartbeats in their saggy boots. I watch them, Albie sleeping in my arms.

'A month, I'd say.'

'Won't be long. Poor lad. He'll turn. Like milk gone sour, stinking up the kitchen. It'll get him. That shop will get him.' There is sadness in his voice, and his words droop his shoulders a little further down his body.

'The wife's going to take him one of her lasagnes this evening.'

'Hmm.'

They are quiet then, pausing by my window, trying to look at each other without moving their heads. Eventually, the smaller one speaks, and it is a boy's voice from a man's mouth. I think how fear makes people small precisely when they need to be tall.

'I saw him standing outside Berry & Vincent the other day, you know. Just standing there, watching it. Like a lost thing.'

'He didn't go in?'

'No. When I asked, he told me it was his day off. But he went there anyway...'

'Why?'

'He said, the place was inside his head. And he couldn't find a way to get it out.'

I think of the shop then. Buttons, black, silken rolls of red ribbon. Hearts of hummingbirds in beaded purses; music boxes lined with whales' lung tissue; black and blue feathers from birds shivering above. The shop is asunder, a tangle of things, and you must watch your step, keep your breath in your body so you don't break anything and nothing breaks you.

When we arrived in Rye, the townspeople would not speak of the place.

'It's a curious box and a box of curiosities. We don't go inside Berry & Vincent,' they said.

'Why?'

'Don't go inside Berry & Vincent,' they said. 'There's a devil inside that place.'

Their lips pinched and they shook their heads. My questions about this strange shop, the strange shadow it poured across the street, went unanswered.

'It's an unkind place. Leave it be. And it will leave you be,' they said.

'But—'

'Leave Berry & Vincent be.'

TEDDY

Superstition and Suspicion

I can't remember what first drew me to Rye. Perhaps it was the Tudor cottages leaning like drunks down the slope of cobbled street, or a sense that here things could be hidden, forgotten.

The Mermaid Inn sits to my right, half-timbered with a sloping slate roof and mullioned windows. The place smells of chips and ale, a heady combination that makes my stomach roar. I find the bar and order lunch. 'This place is impressive.'

The elderly landlady grins. 'Thanks. We like it. We don't get many tourists in February so I'm going to take a punt and say you're that newcomer?'

'I am. I'm Teddy.'

'Charlotte. Heard there was fresh meat in town. How are you settling in?'

'It's ... a challenge. I've just started work at the antiques shop. Molly doesn't seem too keen on the place.'

'You won't find many who are.' She takes up a tea towel and picks at the thread. 'That place casts its own sort of shadow.'

'What do you mean?'

She shakes her head. 'Nothing. Ignore me, son.'

'Please.'

She studies my eyes, my lips, my nose. Panic threads itself though my chest, but finally she speaks and I breathe. 'It looks different now, feels different now. Parents warn their kiddies off going in there. We steer clear of it.' She pauses, eyes as wide as plates. 'No one knows much about Mr Vincent. He and Berry just arrived one day. Arrived with the rain. I remember because it was one of the driest summers on record. But that day it was like God was trying to drown the town.'

'Were they friends or just business partners?'

'Vincent used Berry, tricked him. He needed his money to get the shop. It was all calculated. They weren't friends. Barely business partners. Vincent hated him and Berry left a year later. Just disappeared. Haven't heard from him since. Came and went with the rain.'

'You have an idea why?'

'No. No one knows really. Vincent changed this place. We don't usually talk about him. Or Berry. It's best to leave it be, son.'

I detect a warning there, a glint of steel in her old eyes that bothers me. A pile of loose thread sits on the counter, a hole in the tea towel.

'I don't know why you want to work there. I don't know why he wanted you, he hasn't had an "assistant" the whole time he's been here. But can you do me a favour?'

I nod.

'Don't stir this up. There is a reason we keep from talking 'bout this.'

'What reason?'

She shrugs. 'Like I said, there's a rot in that man, like an infection that spreads from his body. But this is still our town and we choose to ignore it. It's the best way. Look, there are things you don't know. Don't stir it up. Please.'

Berry left only a year after the shop opened. But why? Why so suddenly abandon his business, all that he had built? And how has an entire village come to avoid one shop? One man?

But then must I really ask that? Don't I already know?

Charlotte keeps her eyes down. 'You're working there so you'll notice this soon enough. Don't think it's about you.'

'What?'

'Kids hold their breath when they pass the shop. As if they might catch something or as if it might take something from them.'

'Why though?'

'Watch, you'll see the children hold their breath when they pass by Berry & Vincent.'

ADA

Day and Night

I was in Sainsbury's toilets when I discovered I was pregnant. The lights were flickering over my head, and the smell of perfume and urine put a sickness in my throat. I remember hearing the woman in the next cubicle cursing as she tried to pull up her trousers.

I was twenty years old. The father, my first and last one-night stand, I have no name for. He was a quick distraction, one my three closest friends encouraged me to enjoy at a party. The next morning I left, thinking it wasn't worth the eleven pounds fifty I had to pay for a taxi to his place.

'Boy or girl?' A librarian asked once when I was in my first trimester, seeing the books I carried. 'I've always wanted a boy but I got four girls.' Like it was some snub from fate, dealing her duds.

'I – I – I don't know.'

'Have you thought of any names?'

I hadn't. 'No yet,' I said. In all honesty, I had forgotten about that part.

My body stretched, reaching new contours as I sprayed bottle after bottle of cheap perfume in the bathroom every morning to mask the smell of sickness. The skin on my stomach grew thin, scarred, I could follow the veins with my little finger, like some strange game of snakes and ladders.

I told everyone eventually, when my blister of a bump became too difficult to disguise. My mother's reaction was as I expected it to be. Her fury lasted a whole week – the air in the house was bursting with it and I took small breaths so I didn't choke.

'Get rid of it. You disgust me. Get rid of it!'

'No.'

'I shan't have it in my house. Your mistake, your problem. You're a fool, Ada Belling.'

'I'm not getting rid of it.'

'Disgusting!'

The word flew like spittle, smacked my cheek. I lifted my finger, pressed it to my face, but, of course, there was nothing there.

She packed my things, throwing the bags outside, the value of my life less than the empty bottles and balled-up wrappers she took such care to recycle.

Father was no help. I went to my aunt's after that, waited out my final trimester in the company of my three boisterous young cousins, who poked my bump until my aunt threatened them.

'I mean it, Andrew, stop poking her. Jesus. She's not your hamster.'

'God. Look. Her stomach just moved!'

'That's the baby kicking.'

'Sick!' said Andrew.

'That's just nasty,' said Patrick.

I did not see my mother again after that. She is cutting, nails always risen to harm. Even her bones have sharp edges. I recall standing at the bus stop, six years old. A boy my age was clinging to his mother like a monkey, soft young paws. But when I did the same, mother pinched my fingers. 'Don't do that.'

I sucked the redness, looked at the boy looking at me. I realised then I could not take love from a body.

TEDDY

Boy and Man

I see them. The children who hold their breath when they pass. Cheeks tomato bright. Feet quickening. I hold my own sometimes. Or have I just stopped breathing?

I have few responsibilities within the shop; these include cleaning and wiping down, pricing, occasionally helping Mr Vincent adjust some of the larger articles on display. I must not change the order of things, I must not rearrange or tamper without permission. If I should move a pen but an inch, he will move it back. I am not allowed to open the till although I am allowed to stand behind the counter.

I keep to these duties, I do not overstep.

'It's quiet. Almost wish it would rain. Something to listen to.' I am talking to myself because silence is a strange thing, it turns the mind in on itself. And he will not allow me to switch on the radio. 'Grim today. Always loved the sound of rain. My mum used to say God was in the rain. Never did understand that. Don't think she did either, really.'

I do not know where he is, where this peculiar person ends and the shop begins. They are bound together, as if with a crude row of stitches. Perhaps they really are one thing.

A book slips from my hand, and the binding cracks. Suddenly there is wool in my throat because I cannot breathe or speak. The shop has quietened, as if even it is alarmed by what I have done.

I bend, take it up, rise and, he is here.

A gasp slips from my lips. He snatches the book, his arm swinging back, and I think he is going to beat me with it. As my hands come up to my head, he turns, blends into the chaos. But the chaos in my chest will not calm.

🍎

It is quiet at home. Quiet there, quiet here. I like to press my fingers to my ears sometimes, until they throb, then I speak and I do not sound like myself. I sound like someone else. I unplug my ears, I plug them, and I am two people.

I have done this since I was a boy. It is a comfort to me. Because the radio and television do not listen, they do not respond. I close my eyes and I am back in my old flat, the first place I had of my own.

The carpet has a constellation of holes – moths, mice, I still do not know from which. There is a black fur on the wall, with each breath of mine it grows. And there is the quiet. I thrust a ready meal into the microwave. I own only one fork, one knife, one spoon. I do not need more. But tomorrow I might buy a new set. I might set the table, cook for two. The food will go cold, but I can tell myself it goes cold because someone is running late and not because there is no one coming at all.

I plug my ears:

'How was your day?'

'Rubbish. Yours?'

Yours?

I like how it sounds, someone asking after me.

Tomorrow I will pour wine, rub some red over the rim. There look! A woman has been here. Her lipstick, see ... see?

'I see,' I say. 'I really do.'

🍎

I am not a boy anymore. My skin is baggy, my hair thin, arthritis swells my knees, makes me walk with a tilt, as if I am always about to fall over. But now I am adept at becoming unknowable. I can pack up my homes in twenty minutes, I can fill my car, begin the run, to the next place, the next, leave those blinking faces in my rear-view.

They looked for it inside me – that rot. Sometimes it can take months, sometimes only a day, but in the end, I am recognised as his son. 'Don't watch his lips,' folk said of him. 'Watch his eyes. His eyes can't tell a lie.' And now they say it about me.

'There's a rust on you, boy. Red as the Devil's skin. I'm not letting any of that rust get on me. I might not get it off.'

🍎

He liked children. Little girls. Their innocence, their purity. He took them between the ages of six and twelve. Only they would do. My young foster 'brothers' used to call me Killer's Boy. They'd take their fork, stab it into my hand and the 'parents' would bluster at the blood on the tablecloth. I have no memories of my father, I did not know him, yet I am condemned for all he has done. Because, somehow, it is all that I have done too.

TEDDY

Birds and Bottles

My mother's mind wandered and it did not come back. When I was a child, her voice was always so clear and loud.

'Loud as a bell, Mum.'

'If you shake me, I'll ring,' she joked.

'I'm shaking you, Mum. I'm shaking.' My arms round her middle, moving us back and forth.

'Ring, ring.'

We laughed because it was funny. We could not imagine a time when it would not be.

But the years passed, folded in on us. Shame and guilt for my father's crimes quietened that bell. As a boy I did not know what tormented her, why she would go still during the day, like a wind-up toy stuttering to a stop. Or why she would run to me suddenly, faster than I had ever seen her run, gather me in her arms. So I kept still, breathing hard against the itchy wool of her jumper, tighter, tighter, but not wanting to ask her to stop.

🍎

There is a bird in a bell jar. With needle-thin feathers and a beak just a grain of rice. It's a blue tit; I know because my mother used to love watching the birds outside our home. As a boy I'd pad downstairs, find her hovering in the doorway, and she'd let me sip from her mug.

I run my finger over the domed glass. *Let him out, Teddy. He can't even stretch his wings. How would you feel? You'd feel trapped. Let the bird go.*

I can't, Mum. The bird doesn't belong to me.

The bird belongs to no one. Birds are free.

I do not know how long I have worked here. Days are months in Berry & Vincent. Time is an unfamiliar thing, it does not behave as it should. Mr Vincent. He is there when a moment ago he was not. I feel as if he'd like to take me apart, put my bones in neat piles, polish my skin, see my thoughts, like a cloth to a gritted window.

Who is he? And who am I to him?

I recall a conversation this morning with my neighbour:

'How are you settling in?'

'Very well, thanks.'

'Where are you from? I don't recognise your accent.'

'Reading.' A lie. I never tell anyone where I'm really from.

'I have a grandson who lives there. And how are you settling in Rye? How are you finding Berry & Vincent?' She spat its name.

I wiped my chin. 'It's … it's taking some getting used to.' What else could I say?

'I remember when he came to this town. I saw him once, you know, it must have been about five years ago now, through the shop window. He was talking. *But he never talks,* I said to myself. So I went for a close look. You know what I saw?'

I forced myself to smile.

'No one. Not a soul. The shop was empty. He was talking to his things. All those strange things tucked up inside there. Just talking.'

Brown bottles, copper pans, pocket watches on a bed of green velvet. Wax dolls, porcelain dolls with full pink lips, pursed to kiss. Or bite. Voodoo dolls stuffed with straw; a hand in a preserving jar, a lump of cancer across the thumb joint; shrunken tsantsas heads hanging together like strange baubles.

Why does he have all this? Why did he advertise for an assistant? And why hire *me*?

I move behind the counter, a barrier between myself and these questions, these strange faces inside the shop. There is a drawer open, cutting into my leg. Usually it is locked, the key kept somewhere on Mr Vincent's body. I wonder if he left it open for me. Or did he simply forget? Inside is a leather-bound book, heavy as a brick, curling at the edges. I open it and see hundreds of photographs, Mr Vincent's scrawl fanning around them. Everything in this place has been catalogued, studied. Revered.. This is not just a shop, this is a collection. His personal collection. I back away, my breath caught like a rock in my throat.

'Jesus!'

🍎

I'm slouched over a plate of fish and chips in The Mermaid, the salt and vinegar pricking my nostrils, but I can't stomach it. Sweat has dried on my skin, a covering of it that makes me itch. How does he afford his collection? How does he pay for the shop? Is he funding it with his own money? There are no customers.

Charlotte smiles at me from across the room. I wave and she reluctantly comes over, grey curls bouncing on her neck. I offer her a seat. 'Something the matter with your meal, son?'

'It's fine. Can I ask you about the shop?'

'No. Not about the shop. I've told you that already, son.'

I touch her hand, then snatch it back. I'm overstepping the mark but I am desperate. 'Please.'

She glares at me, folding her arms. 'Fine. Because I don't think you're fully aware of the job you've taken on.'

'I don't think I am either.'

'What do you want to know?'

'When was the last time you went in the shop?'

Her mouth pops open. 'It ... well, it was years ago.'

I lean closer to her. 'How many years ago?'

'Around the time Berry left. Why?'

'What was the shop like when Berry lived here? What was it like inside?'

'Well, it was just a shop. Lots of tat. It was a bit cramped. Stuff everywhere. Toys and old clothes. Jewellery, clocks, even had a unicycle. The kids used to go in there and mess with it, spin the wheel round and round. Berry thought it was hilarious. He'd let them do whatever they wanted, as long as they were careful.'

'Where was Mr Vincent?'

'He used to just stand behind the counter or disappear into the back room. He never spoke to us.'

'Do you remember anything odd inside? Anything that seemed like it didn't belong in a little junk shop in Rye?'

'What are you talking about? It was just full of crap. Stuff the kids liked and the tourists bought cheap.'

I nod. It changed after Berry left. That was when he must have started his collection. When the shop became his.

'You look very pale. Just a minute.' She goes to the bar. 'Here.' She passes me a glass of water, three fingers I wish were vodka. I gulp it down nevertheless, and suddenly there is an ocean inside of my stomach, waves roiling, curling, restless. It makes me sick.

'Thanks.'

'My old friend came to the town a few years back. To stay with me and my husband for the week. She wanted a break from the city.'

'London?'

'Hastings. Why do you keep asking that?'

'Sorry.'

'Anyway. She told me she went in the shop, but the whole time she just wanted to bolt. Said it creeped her out. When she went to pay, she said the man, the proprietor, was behaving weird. Kept fidgeting, twitching, sort of. She told me it was like he didn't want her to have the books. Like none of the stuff in there was for sale.'

It's not.

I suck in a breath, the tension built up over the morning making me feel lightheaded, winded. All my suspicions have been confirmed. 'Did your friend say anything else?'

'No. But I could tell it bothered her.' She pauses. 'Has ... has he ever behaved like that in front of you?'

'There have been no customers. How does he even keep the place open? He never sells anything.'

'Tourists. The summer season is always profitable for him. Apparently. He hasn't gone out of business, after all. Does it bother you? Working there?'

'I...'

'It's OK. You don't have to tell me. I was just wondering.'

I want to tell her everything – he watches me but never speaks – I don't, though because I don't know how to frame the words.

'I ... Well, I suppose I was taught to keep going, not to give up.' It's a weak answer and she knows it.

'Right, well, that's very noble of you, son.' She shakes her head, and I can't tell if she pities me or thinks I'm a fool. Both. She stands, glances at my untouched meal. 'I'll let you eat. Have a good day, Teddy.'

She heads to the bar. I want to call her back. I don't because then I would have to give her the truth: Berry & Vincent is a distraction. Beside the shop, I am a nonentity. No one spots the tell-tale clues in every line of my face, my father's face. How can I leave that? When I have been looking for anonymity for so long?

ADA

Everything and Nothing

I stand by the window and listen to the voices in the street:

'He shouldn't be here. Why has he come? Why work there? Of all the places.'

I know who they are speaking about. Come, come to the window, I think, I want to know more. But they do not.

'He's stirring things up. He's waking up a lot of ghosts.'

'And more besides.'

Berry & Vincent, of course. And the strange man arrived in Rye to work there. 'He must be strange,' one says. 'How can he not be, working there?'

'Oh but he's not strange. Not like that. He just doesn't know what he's got himself into. That's what Molly says. He will do soon enough.'

'What can he do all day in there? Has he said anything about him? Mr Vincent?'

'No.'

'I saw him the other day through the window. He was stood behind the counter. He looked frightened out of his wits. He was polishing a ... a—'

'What?'

Her face empties of expression. 'I don't know. I don't know what it was.'

'He should leave.'

'He should leave.'

TEDDY

Needle and Thread

She laughs when she squats and pisses against the wall. And when she holds a spoon to her eye, says, 'Look at this little fork.' Fat tears slosh onto her cheeks. There is much in her face, I do not recognise now.

Every morning, I bring her a cup of tea because I don't want her to feel glum when she wakes. 'Tea makes everything better, Teddy,' she used to say. She doesn't say it anymore.

'Morning, Mum. Good sleep?'

'Johnny, your bathwater was filthy last night. What were you doing while you were away?'

'Mum?'

'Soil. So much soil. I had to scrub that tub clean. Took ever so long. You been rolling round in flower beds?'

'No.'

She means the girls. Where he took the girls.

'I've made you tea: milk, three sugars. How you like it.'

'I have my tea black.'

'No you don't, Mum. You can't stand anything bitter. You've always taken it like this.'

She harrumphs. 'You've not answered my question. Where were you?'

'I was nowhere.'

'Well you must have been somewhere. They run you ragged with that job. All that driving. You hardly spend any time with your son. You're going to miss him growing up. I keep telling you this.'

'He wasn't delivering packages though, was he, Mum? Don't you remember? Why don't you have some tea and relax?'

'It's got to be black, Johnny. Never mind about the coffee now. Were you listenin—'

'Tea, Mum.'

'Do you want to miss your little boy's childhood delivering all these packages to God knows where? Hmm? Take some time off.'

'It's not coffee.' There is a lump in my throat, a lot like a coffee bean.

'You're going to miss it. You love Teddy. Be there for him.'

'Yes, Mum.'

'You love Teddy, don't you?'

I swallow the coffee bean, scratch at the tear on my cheek. 'Yes. I love Teddy very much.'

🍎

Lines appeared in my mother's skin, a restlessness sat deep inside her bones so she couldn't remain still. She'd walk back and forth – you could tell where she'd been by the worn tread in the carpet, then she'd hug me, drum her fingers against my spine.

'Teddy. Teddy. Teddy. Teddy.'

'I'm here. I'm here. I'm here.'

But those days didn't worry me. What did worry me were the quiet days, she could barely move, barely walk, and when she did, she would often come to a halt, I thought I could hear the grinding, like her bones were old machinery.

I found myself wondering if I would return home one day fetching milk from the corner shop and see her. Between one step and the next, dead yet still standing somehow.

'Mum?' I would say. 'Mum?'

But she wouldn't respond, she'd lived until finally she could stop. So I'd curl my arms round her body, still and solid, snuffling into her woollen jumper. And I would stay like that, with her. No one would find us because no one would be looking.

I hear him, in the home he keeps above the shop, tapping away. It's a typewriter. An old-fashioned one that lets off a ring at the end of each line. The noise breaks upon the shop. He has been typing all day, and I struggle not to burst out of the door and slam it shut.

I look at the death mask hanging in the corner, pinch myself to remind me I am real, and it is not. Would my father have liked these masks? That strange stranger. Would he have made little casts of all his little girls? A much more life-like memento than photographs. I glance at the ceiling. The tapping, it is getting louder.

Stop that! I would like to scream. *STOP making that noise!* If only I had the courage.

The police, the papers, the magazines and news anchors called my father the Hidden Devil because his handsome, kindly face could charm clutches of women with a word and a wink, but if you looked hard enough, you could glimpse the part of him that was bent, twisted up. Hidden.

'Johnny Colne, isn't he a looker?'

'He's handsome. Aren't they always, these murderers?'

'That's how they reel you in. Get you on side.'

'Isn't that the truth? I've always been a sucker for a pretty face.'

Stories and theories swirled round him, growing more sensational. Soon he was known in the US, Europe. Worldwide. Once, everyone knew my father's name.

I wish someone, anyone, would come. I pray the bell will ring. Earlier, in my desperation, I stood in the doorway, trying to draw walkers into the shop like a man on a market.

'Do you like birds, miss? We have flocks of them at Berry &

Vincent. Blue tits and black birds and robins and birds, exotic and rare. The brightest feathers I've ever seen. Would you like to see?'

'How about you? Do you like puzzles, mysteries? We have all sorts of mysteries inside Berry & Vincent. Care to solve one?'

Please, I am really saying. *Please. Come inside. Please. Let me talk to you. Talk to me.*

They did not come.

🍎

Darkness arrives in great swathes, unfurling across the shop. He is here, Mr Vincent. His silence is loud as a handclap. I am speaking suddenly, words sluicing into the air.

'It's dark out, isn't it? Very quiet. Everyone has gone home, haven't they?' I try not to look at the array of votives to my right, miniscule and repugnant. 'It's strange in here at night, isn't it?'

He looks at me.

'Do you ever mistake these faces for real ones? They seem very real to me? Where on earth did you get them?' Will they speak? When the lights are turned off, will they live? These strange creatures and odd, leering faces? Will they lift their eyes and gather? I pray they will not gather around me.

'You have a two-headed dog. It's quite frightening.' I laugh, nervous and high. 'It almost seems as if it's about to move.'

He does not speak. He does not speak. So I imagine words in his mouth:

'What happened to Berry?'

Questions are doors, they can open into something good, or something bad. Which door is yours?

'Why did you come to Rye?'

Why did you?

'They say you've put a rot in the town.'

Only dying things rot.

He is looking at me, when a moment ago he was not. Have I

been speaking this? I touch my lip. Check for words. No. No, I haven't but he is looking at me. My God, I think, he knows. He must know.

His lip twitches, and I want to take up a needle and thread, put a stitch in it so it will never move like that again.

TEDDY

Death and Co.

Two men walk ahead of me on my way home. I slow to listen in on their conversation. They are in their thirties, these men, balding heads and golden wedding bands. I wonder is this what I would look like if I wasn't me? If I was ordinary? Wife, ring; child, wrinkles. I like to think it would.

'He's a handsome little bugger. Like his dad,' says one smugly. A child.

'Sure. Emphasis on the "little". A smirk, a wink.

I would like a piece of this. I walk closely, and who's to say we are not three – three friends together. And I am a person like other people.

•

'You're Teddy?'

She knows, I think. She knows who I am. She is thin, birdy, this woman, standing outside my house. A gust and her coattails will flap and she will wing away.

'Yes.'

'What do you know about the man you work for?'

I scratch my neck, dig at the chill there. 'Only what the townspeople have told me.'

'Not much. They haven't told you much.' I want to pinch her wings down, pinch the answers from her lips.

The woman has hair the hue of straw, shadows under her eyes, dark enough to look like muck.

'Who are you?'

She lowers herself into the plastic outdoor chair, offers the seat beside her, even though she is on my property and I should be offering it to her. I join her, nevertheless.

'I've lived in Rye all my life. I remember when they came, Mr Berry and Mr Vincent. It rained so much that day. We put our furniture on stilts, packed our doors with sandbags. The way the rain hammered down, we wondered if it would ever stop. I imagine you've already been told that though. I wish it had washed those men away, out of Rye.'

'Why?'

She folds her fingers together, unfolds, folds. Carefully, as if she is trying to fold the fear in her into a neater, more manageable shape.

'The shop wasn't always like it is now. I imagine you've been told that too.'

'Who are you? What are you trying to tell me?'

She looks at me. 'You're young, Teddy. And this will knot you up. You should leave.'

'I'm not leaving,' I say. I'm not leaving because if it were not for this shop, your thoughts would now turn to my face, the familiarity of it. It is a thin guise but it is one I cannot tear through. 'Tell me.'

'Nobody knows him. Not really. But he has become a bad story.'

I want to rest my hands on hers, make them still. 'Tell me what you do know about him.'

She sucks in a breath, blustery and loud, and I wonder how her small body can fit all that air inside. 'He was always such a silent, strange man. Berry knew it.' She pauses, then says, 'It happened outside the shop. Twenty years ago now.'

'What did?'

'It was all so quick. Quicker than it is to say out loud, "She's dead. That child is dead."'

I scratch my neck, driving my nails into the skin at my hairline. I only stop when I feel blood. 'The child is—?'

'She was always so fast, bounding about like a mountain goat. We used to say, "Slow, down, slow down, you'll hurt yourself." I watched it all happen. She was running down the street. And as she passed the shop, she saw something. Her head swivelled round and her mouth pinged open. It was strange, how fast and slow it all seemed.'

'And she...'

'She died. Her head hit the cobbles. I remember her skinny arm hooked over her head, her little bare foot poking through the door of Berry & Vincent. We couldn't find her shoe.'

'She couldn't be saved?'

The woman shakes her head. 'No. It was instant. I went to her, tried to help her. Everyone was indoors, no one heard me. But he did. Mr Vincent, he watched from his window. I screamed at him to help me, but he just stood there, watching.'

I grit my teeth. There is a sickness in my throat, rising.

'I couldn't make him move. He just watched.' Tears are in the eyes of this woman I do not know the name of. 'I scrubbed and scrubbed to fetch the blood from the cobbles after she was taken away. And still he watched, like it was simply mud on my fingers and what happened hadn't happened at all. We don't know what frightened her so much, what she saw in that place. We don't know who he is, but we know he brought something bad into Rye.'

'I ... I ...' I cannot speak.

She rises, moves away, turns back. 'I tell you this because you're young. I tell you it because I don't think you know what it is you've found.'

'The girl...'

'We do not go inside Berry & Vincent. We leave it alone now. We do not speak about it.' She looks at me, and I want to look away. 'The next day, her shoe appeared in his shop window, all red and crusted. He put her little shoe in his shop window.'

ADA

Missing and Found

'You've had it, then?' The first words my mother said to me.

'Yes – yes, this – this is Albie.'

She inched forward, eyes skimming over him. This was the first time I had been invited back to my childhood home. But I was already wishing I'd refused. I tried to catch my father's eye.

Look at me, I wanted to say. Look at me! But he wouldn't. We stood in silence. And then:

'What's wrong with him?'

These four words were delivered calmly, without a trace of hesitation yet they smacked me in the chest, four swift blows.

'What did you do? Did you sit on him? Did you drop him?'

'Stop it!'

'You must have done something. Look at him. His ear. He's broken.'

Tears gathered on my cheeks, but I couldn't feel them. My father put a hand on her shoulder, hesitant, but it was an attempt to help all the same. She shrugged him off.

'He looks like a little monster.'

'Stop it!' It was louder than I intended, and Albie woke, began to cry. I left, struggling to get the pushchair through the door, tripping, smacking my knees on the ground.

🍎

The street is empty. Regardless of their cutting words, I wish the townspeople would come, speak with me. In the beginning, I used to call out:

'Nice weather we're having!'

'Horrible weather!'

'Hope the weather cheers up soon.'

'Glad the weather has cheered up.'

'Well, we were lucky for a while, weren't we?'

In the beginning, they would come to me with light, curious voices. Then they stopped, they saw a single mother, a poor and lonely mother, and that's all they saw. They would purse their lips, nod, they did not speak, they moved on. And the days moved on too.

The kettle is boiled. I pour myself a cup of tea, milk, two sugars. I go to the window. There is no one. I take a sip, look. Look! Is that someone? No. It is a paper bag, not a brown shoe. I sip. I check on Albie. I return to the window, look again. No one. My bones are humming with silence. I look. I return to the kitchen. I pour my still hot tea away. I boil the kettle. I make another.

TEDDY

Devils and Hanging Men

'You'll get scars, scratching like that,' she says.

There is a bloody corona round my thumbnail, the skin split into strips. I rub, rub, until they are threads.

'Your dad used to do the same.' But what she is really saying is, You are like him and it is hurting me.

I suck in a breath, blow out my cheeks.

'He did that too.'

You are hurting me. You are hurting me.

'You have your dad's hands. Fine-boned, feminine. You'd never think hands like his could do what they did.' I know who he is, all that he did, so I wear gloves, day and night, to ease her.

'I used to wonder why he got through so many shirts.' She sighs, decades of weary in one breath. 'Then I knew and I wished I didn't. I wished I could get rid of those thoughts, bleach them from my mind. It works on grease you know, bleach. Not much good on anything else.

'No one told your daddy it's cold water that gets blood out. Breaks down the proteins. All those good shirts gone. Wonder if he buried them with the girls. Wonder if when they dug them up, there was any white left in them.'

I could drink gallons.

'What gets the blood out, Mum?'

I could fill my body up.

'Water.'

But will it get it out of me?

She hid my father's crimes, protected my childhood, but then her mind went and it flooded out. 'Those girls, those girls, those girls.' Again and again until the words stuck to my skin. 'Teddy, those girls. Those poor girls.'

'Mum, it's not your fault.'

'They were just little girls. Why did he have to hurt them? And they are just the ones we are aware of. What about when he was young? What he had in him must have been there all along.'

'Maybe.'

'Secrets belong to God, the Devil and the dead.' She patted my chest. 'Well, your daddy is the Devil and the dead. God isn't going to tell us now, is he, Ted?

When I was two years old, she found pictures and tufts of their hair balled up in my father's socks. She held the phone with shaking fingers, dropped it twice as she dialled. As police picked our home apart, the family liaison officer said, 'Where is he? Your little boy?'

'He's safe. He's safe.'

'But where is he?'

My mother pulled back the blanket draped round her shoulders, revealed a boy no bigger than a loaf. She held me for another three hours.

'I have him. I have him. I have him.'

My father was found on his second morning in prison, just a pint of blood left in his veins. The news of his death filled the papers for weeks. His was the name on everyone's lips. The Devil! The Devil is dead. As for my mother, she blamed herself for not having discovered it all sooner. Hers was a mind too heavy with guilt to be lifted.

I stand outside the shop. I look at the window, the man inside, and cold curls between my bones. I must enter, begin my shift, but I am afraid to. At night, all I have heard sits in my head, heavy, so much so I cannot lift it from my pillow. I am standing in the same place I stood when I arrived in Rye, drawn to this strange shop. How different I feel now.

'You OK, Teddy?' Molly stops beside me, worry in her face.

'Fine. I ... Fine ... I'm...'

She pats my arm. 'I know.'

We do not speak. We watch the shop window. He has not noticed us. What will happen when he does?

'Does it get better?' I ask quietly, and I do not think she has heard.

'No,' she says finally. 'No. I've lived here all my life. I remember when he came fifty years ago. And in those fifty years, it hasn't gotten any better.

'I'd like to take the ears off that man. Cut them clean from his head. Like a butcher with a pig. He'd hear nothing then, know nothing. And wouldn't we be better for it?'

'What do you mean?'

'Three years back one of our older residents died. I wish I could say it was natural causes, but he had something weighing on him, you see. His son was killed by thugs in Hastings about two months before. Dick was broken, lost, back bent so low so you could see his spine poking through his coat. Three years ago, he hung himself with his son's belt.'

'I'm sorry.'

'He was a good man, Dick. My friend. His burial was sad, subdued. We returned home, passing Berry & Vincent as we must every day. And I'll never forget what I saw. There in that window, hung these figures, 'bout the size of your thumb. Some made of wax, others of felt and wool, all of them with a piece of brown twine tied round their slim little necks. Belts ... Belts.'

'Jesus.'

'We stood there, rows of us, breath misting up the window. Suppose that's what he wanted. Charlotte was sick; her husband had to clean it up. I screamed at him to take them down. But he wouldn't. They hung there for a whole month. And every time I passed, he'd tap, tap, and make one of those poor figures swing.'

'That's ... that's...'

She shakes her head. 'He's the devil, that man. I hope he dies. I hope he does.' She pats me on the arm, shakes her head again. 'Be mindful of your devil, boy.'

TEDDY

Rare Books and Oddities

I am in the shop and he is upstairs again, fingers flying over his typewriter. The ringing. Oh, the ringing, it bounces off the porcelain dolls' faces, the brass pots and glass vases. I clamp my hands over my ears, but I can still hear it. When will it stop? Does he know how it hurts me? This noise.

I imagine screaming at him through the ceiling. I have worked in the shop less than two weeks yet the place keeps me awake at night, tapping at the corners of my mind, trying to get in.

Or is it already in?

'Please stop, please stop!'

I think of the girl who died outside the shop, of her shoe in his window. I shake my head, move cracked pens and odds scraps of paper round the counter, move them back. Move them. Move them back.

Where is he? Where is he?

The shop is silent, and I think it curious how that silence can make such a racket.

Where has he gone?

I take the closest thing, rub a cloth over it, all the while I am looking.

He's here. He must be.

I am holding a glass jar. Inside, a heart, a human heart. Real and rubbery thing. A heart upside down.

Thump, thump, thump.

It beats again. It moves.

No it isn't this heart, it is my heart.

No.

It is not.

Thump. Thump, thump.

It is him. I listen to his footsteps, close my eyes, pretend I am not holding a heart in my hands, pretend he is not here and Berry & Vincent is a shop like any other.

ADA

Rumour and Rope

The woman has butter-blonde hair and eyes like blue marble. Her smile is even, bright, and I wonder, does she look in the mirror at that smile and feel pleased to have it? Mine is askew, slipping, as if it is being tugged by a string. One day it might even be halfway down my chin. I wonder what it is like to have a smile like hers.

She is new to this area, or so I've overheard. Sometimes she comes here to let her son stamp his feet into the spongy sand and laugh at the gulls. I've wanted to talk to her but words are strange, slippery, right when you don't want them to be.

I tuck Albie's hand in mine, the warm, sweaty shell of it, and go to her.

'Hello. My name's Ada. I live in town, thought I'd come say hello.' I've said that word twice now, and I bite my tongue. The iron taste of blood slinks down my throat and I feel as if I've just swallowed a penny. It's cold and hard in my stomach.

The woman smiles. 'Oh! Oh, hello. Nice to meet you. I'm Margot. This is my son, Charlie.'

'This is Albie. Bean, can you say hello to Charlie and Margot?'

He burrows into me, fear striping down his face, and Charlie runs off, bored, shells crunching under his feet. 'You've a shy one?'

I nod. 'You?'

She shakes her head, and that buttery mane swings. 'No. I wish I did have sometimes, though. Charlie can be a beast.' Her laugh is high, crunching, like she has a Scrabble piece stuck in her throat.

'How old?'

'Six. How old is this big guy?' She kneels, and Albie runs off in the opposite direction. I sigh, deep, and I feel it at the bottom of my spine. 'Sorry. He's four.'

'That's OK. I get it. So you live in Rye?'

'Yes.'

'I'm in the next town. Still getting used to it – we only moved in a few weeks ago. Charlie loves this beach, demands we come every day. Even if it's raining. Even if I've just sat down with my carafe of wine and my book in the evening. I think he saves the question up all day, for that exact moment.' She is laughing again. Hock-hock-hocking at that Scrabble piece. 'He fixes me with those little eyes, and I can't say no. Of course he knows that.'

'Albie loves it here too. Gets a kick out of rolling round in the sand. I'm brushing it off him for hours afterward.'

'I just stick Charlie under a hose. Gets the job done.'

'I'll try that.' I am laughing, then I'm thinking, *We are talking, she is talking to me. I hope she does not stop.*

'How long have you lived in Rye?'

'Two years. Where did you move from?'

'London.'

Albie is fishing through the flotsam and jetsam, bottle caps, tampon wrappers, curls of seaweed and cigars of driftwood. He looks up, thieving glimpses of Charlie.

Margot follows my eyes. 'Is he shy because of his ear? I hope you don't think I'm prying. I couldn't help but notice.'

'He's self-conscious. Kids can be pretty blunt, can't they?'

'Yep. I wish they had a stop button sometimes. Wouldn't that be nice? Charlie could do with one. He says the first thing that comes into his head.'

I look at her son. He is swinging his fingers through the sand, pink stub of a tongue stuck between his teeth. 'Life with kids.'

'Life with kids. God help us.'

'Gives the days some colour though, doesn't it?'

She nods. 'Got that right. Can't remember the last time I wore a white shirt. Little life-ruiners.'

'I miss white shirts.'

'I miss my drawer full of chocolate.'

'You don't let him have chocolate?'

'No. He has all of it. All *my* bloody chocolate. Thieving bugger.'

We walk, watching our sons. 'Do you think you'll go back to London when Charlie's older?'

She shrugs, and her hair drips down her shoulders in perfect blonde rivers. I pull my lumpen hat down my head, cover my oily scalp. There is a delicate shard of crisp above my ear. Why is there a crisp above my ear?

'I think so, yeah, when he's older. We love it here though. We're getting used to everyone, trying to fit in, you know.'

I know.

'It's not always easy in places like this.'

'How do you mean?'

'It can be quite insular. There are no other people our age here. And ... well, they can be old-fashioned. Cliquey. If you don't fit in, you don't belong.'

She nods. I look at my son, and then I look at hers.

'Will you have more kids?' I ask.

'Oh, God, no. One will do me just fine. I'm still trying to get rid of this muffin top. What about you? Second helpings?'

I shake my head, hold my stomach. 'No. Not for me.'

She laughs. I laugh. Then I laugh because we are laughing together.

'Listen, I'd better run. But it was nice to meet you.' She touches my arm. 'Maybe I'll see you again?'

'Sure.'

She collects her son and his bounty of driftwood, hair flapping like coattails as she marches into Rye.

Two townswomen walk on the opposite side of the street, tucked into each other as if they are one person not two. I listen from my doorstep, rubbing sand from between my fingers, stamping my shoes clean.

'He can't know what Mr Vincent is like.'

'He wouldn't stay if he did.'

'Why would he want that boy?'

'Nothing good. Nothing good. I've got that feeling again.'

'What feeling?'

She sucks in a breath, suck, suck. 'Fifty years ago, there was a shaking in my bones. Then those men came to Rye, and Berry & Vincent opened its doors. It's happening again now. My bones are shaking so it's like they're coming loose.'

'Dear, oh dear, that boy better watch his back. Those who get close to Vincent risk a bad end.'

I am looking without looking like I'm looking. I wish they would come over. I savoured those words shared with Margot on the beach, but now the silence is back. And I feel emptied.

If these passers-by would just come over, we could discuss the shop together. I could offer tea and we could wonder about this man Teddy over steaming cups cradled in chill fingers.

TEDDY

Sirens and Spent Hearts

My mother's mind wandered, and I would rest my head in the warm hollow between her neck and shoulder, know that just a few fingers down was her heart, this thing that still moved but was slower, different now.

She died one evening without noise or fight. Just a breath. One. Quietly. Before the life left her aged face and the fear arrived in mine. For an hour I sat with her, tapped her chest with my finger, put movement back where there was none.

When I called 999, I said, 'She's not here. She's not here.' And I wondered if I could not be here too.

They took my mother, put a blanket over her body, but it was frayed and too small so I could still see her eyes. The social worker, Nina, put a stiff hand on my shoulder and asked: 'Is this OK? Are you alright with this? I think this would be best, don't you? Let's do this, shall we? Hmm?'

But those questions sounded like they already had answers, so I didn't say a word. It was decided I would be put into the care system even though I was seventeen, technically an adult. 'Special circumstances.' There I met my first set of foster-siblings. I didn't react to their salted words because I had *her* voice, always her voice, in my head, willing me to be better.

She died young, my mother. Her bones were dry and loose, so when she moved, you could almost hear them rattle. And then there was the rattle in her lungs too. I remember the weight and shape of her in my arms. She did not feel like a young woman, she felt emptied. Her body bared of life. If a body could be, while it was still living. She was my father's final victim. He didn't mean for her to be. But he killed her all the same.

●

My mind is full of her today, busy. But this room is empty. And I wish it was not so. My clothes are piled on the settee, lumpen and still. I arrange the shirts above the trousers, shoes lined up on the floor. I imagine they belong to friends, who come over, kicking back with beers. Three sets, three people. My people.

The coat I bought before the move is smart. If I were to wear it, I would look sharp. But it is not for me. I hang it by the front door, and I will look at it tonight, think for a moment there is someone else in this house. I will close my eyes, see a figure rushing about, keys, phone, ah! coat. They will snatch it up, swing out the door. And this silence, it will last only as long as it takes for them to return.

'Nearly forgot. Be freezing my balls off later. HA!'

'Don't want that, do we?'

'Nah, I'd rather keep 'em. See you later, mate.' Me. I'm 'mate'.

ADA

Pen and Pencil

My skin is not clear, it does not shine. My features are only pleasant from a distance (ten feet I've been told). Sometimes I pinch my nose into a straight line but always it snaps back, with more determination than any nose should have.

Carrying Albie has put a stoop in my walk; when I straighten my back, my bones chirp and crack, as if there are birds inside me, flocks of them. I will never have a face to make women pine or make smart men stupid. I do not, nor will I ever, have quick wits. My mind is not much of anything.

'Dull as a penny in a pocket.' That is what my mother has said.

I cannot even blush 'well'. Pink fills my face, whole rose bushes under my skin. When I was young, she pasted cream over it. But the make-up was thick and always too light. 'Better this than that pink. Look like a pig! Don't wipe it off. Don't touch it until we get home. Understand, Penny?'

Dull. Penny. Dull. Penny.

'It itches.'

'Leave it. LEAVE IT!'

Her voice cracked across my ears, making me shrink, making my fingers heavy, fall still to my lap.

One morning when I was twelve I woke to find my knickers red-spotted. I screamed because I thought my body was leaking, and soon all those strange, swollen shapes inside me would run out. Father came to me, swallowed, mumbled, 'Perfectly natural,' called my mother, left. She did not come.

I stuffed toilet paper between my legs, wobbled to school. Mother would not let me change when I returned. The blood grew cold, put a chill inside my bones. And in the morning, it looked like I was wearing red velvet trousers.

'You're disgusting, Ada Belling. Look what you've done to your trousers. And your bed. Clean them up. I won't. I won't let your father. This is your mess.'

'Darling, please. I'll do it. Let's not be too hard on her. Hmm? It's not her fault. Please now.'

'Quiet!'

Father taught me to read and write, but Mother taught me to write well; 'Stick inside the lines. Stick inside the LINES.' The tail of a comma swooping over and she would Sharpie a whole word on my wrist: *WRONG*.

This is the first word I knew how to write. I copied the letters on my skin, made my writing look like hers. *WRONG. WRONG.*

TEDDY

Red and Black

There are many hearts in this shop; a constellation of them hung with string, some dried and used up; others red and plump, as if they have this moment been taken from their persons. Where you'd least expect a heart, there one will be. Stitched into purses, inside the toes of old shoes, between your fingers when you reach for a pencil.

I hold one to my eye. It is small, lumpen, and I wonder if it looks like my own. Turning it in my hands, I am back in the alley behind my childhood home, piss, human and feline, a fug near my nostrils. I remember the boys, four of them, a fury inside them that was too old for their young faces.

'Oy! Killer's Boy!'

I did not need much time to consider; I began to run.

Five steps and I plummeted, legs tangled in a ginger tabby cat who was taking a shit. The boys came, and I thought their feet sounded an awful lot like thunder.

'Killer's Boy. That's what you're called. I got a kid sister. You gonna take her, fuck her up. That's what your daddy did, isn't it?'

He had a swatch of red hair, this boy, a swatch of ugly hair on his lip. 'That's not my name.'

'Your mum should have drowned you. Nasty, filthy little fucker. My folks say she's just as bad as he was. She must have known what he was, she must have helped him. She should be dead too, that's what they think.'

The smell of piss was in my lungs, I worried it would never clear.
'He looks like him, don't he? Johnny Colne,' says one of the boys.

A round of grunts.

'Yeah. Face like that. Makes me sick.' The red boy sent a kick
sailing into my chest. 'My folks say when your daddy bled out in
there, his blood was black. Cuz his heart was rotten and it stank
the place up so bad, they couldn't get rid of it. Couldn't get it out
the floor. Sour, dirty, that's what they say.'

'Kick him, Dill, kick him.'

The cat looked pleased.

'You smell the same. Wonder if your blood is all black too. Let's
have a look.'

I kept my eyes on the cat until they had done and gone. There
was blood on my fingers, and I was surprised it was warm. I'd half
expected it to be cold.

That cat watched me rise for home, sixteen-year-old boy with
a red face, running.

🍎

Later, I lifted my shirt, examined the marks, shapeless masses on
the right side of my chest. They had aimed for a heart that wasn't
there. I heard my mother's words then, as I poked and blundered
at the red, and when it hurt, I did it harder.

'You've got it too, that strange heart he had.' She touched my
chest, the left side of it. 'Not here,' she said. 'Here.' And touched
the right. 'It isn't where it's supposed to be.'

'Can I move it? Doesn't it need to be in its proper place?'

'No. It's rare, this heart condition, but it will do you no harm.
When you were born, the nurses were all in a fluster because they
couldn't hear it.' She smiles. 'You'll not find it there. On the right!
I said. On the right! Like his Daddy's.'

'Like ... like his...?'

'Do you know what those nurses said to me later?'

I shook my head.

'Said that a baby is equal parts of its parents. But with a heart like that, you must be more of your daddy.' She shakes her head. 'I laughed at the time, thought it was the funniest thing I'd ever heard. Only makes me sad now.'

'Why?'

'Because I wonder to myself if that's why he never harmed you. Not because you were a boy, but because he saw himself in you, and no man ever wants to harm himself, does he?'

She tapped my heart with her finger, and I wanted to take it out.

I wanted to take it out in the bathroom after the boys had tried to stop it.

I want to take it out now.

There is a tapping again, I open my eyes and half expect to see my mother.

It is Mr Vincent, his finger, stiff as a root, on my chest. Not the left, the right.

ADA

Salt and Stitching

'Do you love me?'

There is no answer, at least not in words. Simply a finger pointed like a gun.

'What? What is it, Mummy?'

'You look like me.' That same finger to my hair, my hands, my mouth. 'These are mine.'

I know this is my answer, and that answer is no. It was a no before I was born. Still, I try. 'You love me, don't you?' I am pushing, pushing always for love from an empty body.

She lifts her shirt, taps the pale puckered line across her abdomen; next come the stretch marks like rows of stitching across her legs, the weak, fatty skin round her arms and middle, like soggy bread, I used to think.

'This is what you are.'

'What am I?'

'Faults.'

🍎

'Do you love me?'

When my son asks this question, eyes big, cheeks reddened by the sharp sea air. I am reminded of my mother. I lift my shirt like she did, show him the silvery lines across my stomach, my arms, the fatty pockets no number of salads can rid me of.

'Yes. I even love these lines because you made them. You're quite the artist.' I grin. 'I love everything you are.' I throw it out, this affection, submerge him. Show him that this body of mine is not empty of love, not like my mother's. It is full.

We sit on the beach, and when he throws himself into my arms, sand flies into my hair. I hold him a little longer than usual, until he wriggles and grumbles to be free.

'Mummy!'

I laugh. 'Alright. Alright!'

He pulls me up and we run to the shoreline. As he stamps through the water, I look back toward the slipway. 'Margot? Margot!'

She and Molly are turned in to one another, their backs to me, the breeze making strange shapes with their hair.

'She's an odd one, isn't she – Ada?' Margot says, and I stop. They don't see me. They don't look over their shoulders.

'She always has been. And that little boy with his ear. I wonder how it happened. Do you think she dropped him as a baby? Or hit him?' Molly is speaking now, tucking her scarf round her neck to hide the wrinkles from the younger woman. 'He's a sad little picture, Albie.'

I want to take that name out of her mouth, button it up. They think I hit him? They think I would ever?

Molly says, 'I keep my grandkids away from him when they come here to visit. They are only young, and a little timid. That ear would frighten them silly.'

'Does Ada not want to get him corrected? Fixed?' Margot asks.

Him, she says. Not 'it', him.

'No, I don't think so. All you ever see is her wandering round town with him on her shoulders like some sort of bird. His little shoes swinging. He has holes in his coat too. Have you noticed?' Molly sighs. 'It's sad, very sad. Ada has never really fit in here. We are cut from different cloth, you see. She can come across as a little desperate. '

Albie kicks a piece of driftwood. Its edges like a gun. It's a shame it is only wood. Because I have bullets for both of them. Their backs are tall pillars, hard and smooth as stone. I have never been welcome here. They say I am strange. But I do not feel strange. They say I do not belong here. They agree on this.

Perhaps I agree too.

I lift my mobile to my face, see my reflection with their eyes. Inkpots of shadow upended below my eyes, bursts of red spilling across my chin and forehead from too much chocolate, hair crusty and stiff as roots. After bathing Albie, I have no energy left for me.

Margot frowns. 'I think she is lonely.'

'Hmm, I feel bad for Albie, he hasn't got any friends. He must be lonely too. His mother has made him lonely. She shouldn't have taken him away from his family, his grandparents,' Molly says.

There is a pain in my middle, as if my stomach has teeth and it is eating every other part of me.

Molly touches the buttery cloth of Margot's coat. Wealth in every neat and organised stitch. 'If she bothers you again, just ignore her. That's what the rest of us do. She doesn't fit in this town. She never has.'

Margot nods. And I turn my feet away from their tall backs. My heart has teeth, my thoughts too. Biting through. There are so many cuts, I expect blood. I tap my fingers to my head, my chest, my middle. Checking I am whole. I do not feel whole. But there is nothing. No red to mark the wound.

I cover my eyes and catch fat, salt tears. Albie comes to me, wraps his arms round my sides. I draw him up, hold him tight, too tight, so he complains. 'Sorry, bean.'

'What's wrong, Mummy?'

'Nothing. I'm alright. Salty air makes my eyes a bit dry, that's all.' He tucks his head into my neck. I carry him home, that silence like wool inside my ears.

TEDDY

Earth and Sky

He's in the house. This time I'm sure of it. He must have followed me home, crept in after me. What does he want? A door opens and closes, and I jolt up in bed, sweat gumming my forehead. He is in the spare room. My heart jackhammers, and I pray he can't hear it. Can he hear it? He must. Easing back the covers, I tread as lightly as I can to the door. Then it starts.

The tapping.

'Why are you here? What do you want?!'

Tap, tap tap.

'Stop it! Tell me what you want!'

My hands are shaking. No. My body is shaking.

'Please. Just tell me what you want...'

No answer. Just more of that noise. Before I can lose my nerve, I dive for the door and throw it open. It swings and scrapes across the wall. I shrink back, my feet like blocks. The room is empty.

'But...'

Tap, tap, tap.

I scramble downstairs, barrelling my way through the black. *Tap, tap, tap.*

'STOP IT!'

But it doesn't. It only gets louder.

I trip and land heavily on my side, the breath shucked from my lungs. Gritting my teeth, I fight my way to a standing position and crash through the door, scanning the lounge and kitchen, expecting to see his small, stooped figure.

Nothing. Silence.

The tapping has stopped. I swing round, cupping my head in my hands. 'But – but – but.' The one word runs from my lips. I check behind the sofa, I check the bathroom, the cupboard. But he is not here. There is a cut on my hand, deep, the bits of skin around it flayed. I stuff my hand under my arm and open the front door. Without another thought, I begin to run.

Moonlight stitches the earth with fine silver threads. The cobbles are ice beneath my bare feet. The street is empty. I skid to a stop outside the shop. The shapes in the window are gaunt. I wait, sweat soaking into my shirt. I need to know. I have to know.

Then I see him, his outline behind the blind, and I bend double, struggling to fill my lungs. It is hard to breathe, to take in this air. I watch the blood drip from my hand until I am calm, watch my blood run into nothing.

TEDDY

Broken and Whole

Earlier, he wafted in like a wraith, stood by my side, close, closer, until his sour breath stung my nostrils. I paced, like a trapped rat, had to keep myself from stuffing a piece of rope between my teeth and biting.

'What ... why do you do that?' I asked. 'You stand so close. Why?'

His face, barren, lips too thin to form any words

'You *can* speak. I know you can. Please!'

Again, nothing.

A scrap will do. A word.

'They say you've never had an assistant before. So why did you put that poster in the window? Did you just want someone to terrorise? Tell me. Come on. And why did you hire *me*? Why did you want *me* to work for you?' My voice rose. There was a fire in my belly. 'Speak. Speak, man!'

He came to me. I wanted to drive my hand between his teeth, drag out the words. 'Speak. Speak!'

He sucked in a breath as if he was trying to breathe me down. And, dear God, I felt thinned out.

Now he stands by the window, watching the street. I move as quietly as I can, slipping through the storage-room door and up the stairs. A tattered bed shoved into a corner, a single armchair and hardback book. Its spine is broken. This brief glimpse into his life tells me nothing.

I move on to the next room.

A desk is crouched in the corner with a typewriter. There is a name written on the wall. *Teddy*, it says. And I think, *Why is my name on the wall?* I see it again, ink on paper, a newspaper cutting this time. Then again, And again. So many Teddys.

I see a photograph of me as a boy, cheeks flushed, chubby as peaches, the scar on my face still fresh and red. I must be three? Four?

I see that little boy as a young man now, standing by the graveside of his mother, hands shaking so hard, the picture has blurred them into orbs.

I see myself older, the age I am now. Walking from the grocer, my finger piercing the flesh of an orange. That is me, I think. Why am I in this room? Why has he put me here?

I run my eyes across the photographs, the articles, the charts. Boy to man. A blueprint of my life.

A noise starts at the back of my throat and gums up my teeth. There is blood on my fingers, cuts in the meat of my palms like half-moons. I look away, look back, to be sure, to be certain this is real.

All this time, he has been mapping out my life, writing a narrative on his wall. Above my very head. I feel invaded, splintered. A chill climbs my body, and I think in a moment I will shiver into pieces.

I tell myself this cannot be happening. Not here.

But it is. I see a timeline, pictures of me as a boy, as a teenager, as an adult. I see pictures of my father. The girls, over thirty of them taken, but not all of them found. I see names. So many names.

Elissa.

Jane.

Mary.

Poppy.

Sarah.

Verity.

Emily.

I remember Emily. I remember her picture. Seeing it as a young boy. I knew something of death then, its shape and weight. My mother ripped the newspaper from my hands. 'Oh, don't be looking at that, Ted. Don't fill you mind with all that sadness.' Always protecting me from my father, even when he was dead.

I stumble forward, legs rubber, drag the paper from the typewriter barrel:

Edward (Teddy) Colne

Thirty-three years of age.
Son to infamous serial killer, Johnny
Norris, and Betty Colne.

Description:
Brown hair. Black eyes. Sharp nose and
jaw. Broad shoulders, fine-boned fingers.
5'10" in height. Sharing strong
similarities with father.

Mannerisms:
Compulsively scratches his neck (A tic
perhaps? A family trait perhaps?) Stirs
his coffee with a pen. Walks with a
slight impediment due to arthritis in
both knees, despite young age.

Other Notes:
Appears lonely. Craves company but is
simultaneously weary of close contact.

There are more. Hundreds of pages. One dedicated entirely to my hands.

The tapping, all day, every day. He has been writing about me.

My legs give out, and I land awkwardly on my side. A noise burbles up from my lips. The whole of Rye will hear. He will hear. He will come to me, as he always does.

I was never simply an assistant, an employee. I might as well sit on a shelf, stuffed like his animals, skin shined with spit and a patch of cloth. I am the son of Johnny Colne, an anomaly. A prime acquisition.

I am a rare piece in his collection.

I am a *living* piece in his collection.

TEDDY

Questions and Answers

It has been hours since I barrelled out of the shop, but still I think of him, of the pieces of my life he has collected and put together. Sickness rises in my belly, and I must bite my lip.

My online searches hang in tabs at the top of the screen, a trail of my broken thoughts. There is nothing of any use, regarding either Old Berry or Mr Vincent. No social-media pages, no shop website. No trace of their existence. I keep scrolling nevertheless.

'Vincent & Stallis Burns to Ground in Tragic Accident'

I see a black-and-white photograph of a striped big-top tent, its left side collapsed inward. Men with singed waistcoats and women with blood-spotted ballerina shoes walk amid the chaos, eyes to the floor, searching for leftover remnants.

At 6.30pm on 5 November, Vincent & Stallis Circus burned down in a tragic accident. The fire is believed to have started in the menagerie tent, caused by a dropped candle, killing well over forty animals and two men, one of whom was co-founder and ringmaster Peter Vincent. He leaves behind a young family. More than a hundred circus hands have lost their livelihoods and homes. Mr Stallis stated he has no plans to revive the business. And so it seems that after thirty years, Vincent and Stallis Circus has come to its end.

I keep scanning the images on the screen, of the tents, no more than husks of some idea; of the ash being swept and bagged. I skim past it all, my heart tapping, see a photograph of the Vincent & Stallis welcome sign being unhooked from its posts.

'Where are you?'

A crowd is gathered round it, with sadness and handkerchiefs. But it isn't them I'm looking at. It's him.

The young boy in the background. With Mr Vincent's face.

Was it him?

I tell myself, no, it cannot have been. It was an accident, a tragedy. I tell myself I am being foolish. My mind is running away with me.

But I have seen that smile before.

He is Peter Vincent's son. A circus boy. Could he really have set that tent alight? Killed two men, including his father? Why would he do that? I glance at the picture again. That smile. That smile.

It was no accident.

I recall a conversation with Molly, her hand pressed to my chest; I had just come from the shop; the place was inside my skin, and I couldn't be still.

'Why are you still here?'

But really she was asking: *Why is* he *still here?*

'What do you say to him?' *Does* he *say anything to you?*

'I...'

'Why won't you leave?' *Why won't* he *leave?*

'Do you know why Berry left?'

Has he told you? What did he do to him?

She picked at her fingernail, smearing blood into her cuff. I ducked back into the shop, found the tissue I'd left on the counter, offered it. She shook her head. She would take nothing from the shop.

'I can't leave,' I said.

It's always been about my father. The fans and admirers who latched on to him like ticks. But this is different. This is about me.

I snatch a knife from the kitchen drawer and stuff it into my coat pocket. The sky is dark, rain clouds smudges of black paint over Rye. The odd townsperson wanders the street, head tucked into their scarf.

I push open the door, face him, and he smiles. That smile. That smile. That smile.

'Why—?'

The bell chimes overhead. I spin round. It's a woman, with a threadbare jacket and a stripe of red lipstick that has missed most of her bottom lip. A boy grips her hand. They edge past me, head into the bowels of the shop, as if they have done it a hundred times. But I have not seen them before.

I turn to Mr Vincent, open my mouth to speak, demand answers, close it. He isn't looking at me. He's looking at her.

Suddenly he leaps forward, and I shrink back, arms raised. He stops her, puts a gentle hand on her shoulder.

And speaks.

'Hello, Ada. Hello Albie.'

ADA

Fire and Ice

The shop is as resolute as the rain. In the beginning, I felt as if it could swallow me down, that it wanted to. It took me months to tease and pluck its past from the lips of the elderly townspeople. Even longer to set foot in there

For fifty years the proprietor has not left his shop. Not once have they seen him put even a foot across the threshold. The place turned rotten, an apple left too long in the heat, they said. They don't go inside the shop now. They don't dare.

'Keep away,' they told their children. The children told their children. 'Keep away from Berry & Vincent.'

'Tell me about it?' I asked them.

'You don't need to know,' they said, bullets in their old eyes. 'Don't take your boy in there. That's all there is to it.'

But I resisted, kept on until they gave in. I could see the memories bottled inside them like poison. The elderly here would have been boys and girls when Berry & Vincent opened fifty years ago. Time has slowed their feet, worn thin their skin, but memories keep.

'A few years after Berry left, you'd hardly recognise it. By then the place cast such a shadow, you could feel it touch your skin as you walked past.'

'Why though?'

'It changed. That's it.'

They had hoped it would close, the proprietor would be put

out of business. But tourists came each summer with full pockets and it clung on and the open sign did not turn.

🍎

The air between Mr Vincent and the newcomer is brittle, I might crack it like an egg if I wished. The man, Teddy, can only be in his early thirties, but his face is full of lines, like matchsticks. His hands are shaking. Why are they shaking? I want to make them still.

'Hello. My name's Ada. You must be Mr Vincent's new assistant?'

His mouth opens, closes, opens. 'I ... yes—but—he—' Finally he says, 'Yes. I'm Teddy.' But he will not look at me. He will only look at Mr Vincent.

The air bites at my neck. What has happened between them? I wish we had not come into the shop. I swing Albie into my arms, leave. Passing, I see their shapes through the glass: still and unyielding, as if they have forgotten how to move. And then the man, Teddy, speaks, and I wonder what he says.

TEDDY

Ada and Albie

She is back. The girl.

She greets us with a polite nod of the head, before guiding the boy deeper into the shop. Mr Vincent stands behind the counter, fiddling with his buttons. What is it? What makes her so important? She is no beauty – her eyes are too close together, her noise crooked at its tip. How has he become this? A nervous, fumbling image? A man with words. But only words for her.

Yesterday I planned to confront him and leave this town behind. Yet when I returned home, I couldn't. Because I must have all the pieces before I can have the whole picture.

And it begins with her.

I straighten my shirt. 'Erm ... hi, it's Ada, isn't it? We met the other day. I'm Teddy.'

She blinks but a smile is not forthcoming.

I offer my hand. 'I'm sorry if I was rude when we met. You caught me at a bad moment.'

'It's OK. We all have off days. How are you settling in Rye?'

I garble a reply. I have forgotten how to speak after so long in silent company. 'It's taking some getting used to. How long have you lived here?'

'Two years.'

I nod, glance at the boy crouched on the floor. 'Who's this fella?'

She perches him on her hip. 'This is Albie. Albie, bean, can you say hello for me?'

The boy struggles in her arms. I pluck a toy car from the box. 'Do you like this one?'

A shake of the head. 'Which ones do you like?' I hold the box out for him. He rummages through it, shows me a green car. 'This one? It's nice. Do you think it's very fast?'

His eyes widen, sweet, pale pebbles.

'My mother gave me one just like this when I was your age. I used to make it go so fast round the kitchen floor she'd scream that a mouse had gotten in.'

'She must have been a saint,' Ada says.

I pretend to laugh. Mr Vincent is still watching. 'I've got my break coming up. Would you like to get a bite to eat with me? You could tell me a bit about the town.'

'Sure. We'd love to.'

As we leave the shop, I throw a glance over my shoulder, bite my tongue so I don't cry out.

He's no longer looking at her. He's looking at me.

🍎

'What brought you to Rye?'

'Fresh start, I wanted to try somewhere new. I came across Rye by accident. It seemed like a nice place.' She takes an over-large bite of her sandwich. A flush creeps up her cheeks. 'Crap. Sorry.'

'No problem. Made the same mistake many a time,' I say, and she smiles.

'Can I ask you a question?'

'Of course.'

'Why that shop? Why Berry & Vincent?'

Her expression has turned stony. I stop.

'It's ... it's difficult to explain. The day I arrived, the shop was closed. The blind was down. But I saw the *Help Wanted* poster, and I felt drawn to it. I supposed I thought I could lose myself in there.'

'Why would you want to lose yourself?'

I shrug.

'And how do you feel about it now?'

'Why do you ask?'

She has her head turned away so I cannot see her expression. 'When we arrived in Rye, we were told to leave the place be.'

'I was too. Do you believe them? About the girl who died outside.'

Ada nods. 'Yes. As soon as I set foot in there, I hated it.'

'But?'

'I got used to it. I mean, it's not swallowed me down yet, has it?' But I sense there is more to it than that.

ADA

Mr Berry and Mrs Berry

There is an apple core on the ground. Black, rotten. Teddy sits on the bench, fingers at his neck, between his teeth, at his neck again. Then he rises, crushes the apple under his boot, picks off the mulch. I pause to watch. He tilts to the left as if he is being pulled with string. I look at the swollen bulbs of his kneecaps, puckering the cloth. He sniffs his finger then, and I think he would cut it off if he could.

I smile, continue. 'Don't like apples?'

He shakes his head. 'Hate them.'

'I've never known anyone who hates apples.'

He is digging round his neck. 'Too sweet.'

'Oh.'

'How do you stand the smell?' Teddy asks.

'The smell? It's not that ba—'

'Makes me sick.'

There is blood on his neck. I take his hand, hold it down. He smiles. 'Thank you,' he says quietly.

'You'll get scars, scratching like that, Teddy.'

He looks at me with far-away eyes. 'I know. I've been told that before.'

I nod. 'How is work?'

'The same. Very quiet.'

I nod. I wonder if he will ask again why I return to the shop, why rumour and suspicion has not put lead in my feet and stilled my hand on the doorknob. I do not want to admit to my poor motivation that this one small act rattles the people of Rye, like dolls shaking in their dollhouses. And that, after how they have behaved toward me, I enjoy it, I cannot help it.

'It must be strange, all that quiet, all the time.'

He nods. Looks at me or looks through me, I cannot tell which.

'I'd love to know what happened to Berry all those years ago.' I say. 'What made him leave Rye? The townspeople say Mr Vincent pushed him out, did something to him. But rumours are like rot here, they spread. And then you can't tell what's rumour and what isn't.'

'I don't know. Did he have family?' Teddy asks.

'Yes. He had a wife and daughter. I think the girl was about twelve. The townspeople say she was very warm and sweet-natured. It's a bad habit but I listen in on a lot of conversations.' I wink. And he smiles.

'So you don't believe Mr Vincent drove him out?' he asks.

'No. I can't see any reason why he would. He started a business with him, after all.'

'Maybe he needed his money.'

I shrug. 'Fair point.'

'What did she look like?' Teddy asks.

'Who?'

'Berry's daughter.'

'I ... I'm not sure. She was a redhead I think, fair-skinned. There's a picture of the family in The Mermaid. Why do you ask?'

'Just curious.'

'Hmm.'

We watch Albie play, a smile on his lips, the mud between his fingers might as well be gold. Teddy is stiff, his hand rising then falling, part way between his neck and waist.

'What is it? You look funny,' I say.

'Just wondering about Berry and the girl.'

'Long time ago now. She'll be all grown up. Berry might even be dead.' I sigh. 'Can I ask? What does Mr Vincent have you do in there all day?'

'Not much. I clean – it's repetitive but it keeps me moving. If he could nail me to the wall, I think he would.'

I laugh, but his face tells me it was not intended as a joke. 'Why do you think that?'

'It doesn't matter. Not anymore.'

'But it did before...?'

'I know him a little better now. I understand him.'

'Really?'

'Yes.'

'So why do you think he'd like to hang you on the wall? Do you remind him of someone? Have you asked him?'

'I mean something to him,' Teddy says.

'In what way?' I am stiff from so much digging.

'Because he's got nothing else like me in his shop.'

🍎

Because he's got nothing else like me in his shop.

I consider what I know about Teddy Colne and realise I do not know much.

TEDDY

Wife and Daughter

The photograph is on the wall just as she said. The Berry family pose proudly, arms looped round each other; Berry, rake thin with a robust moustache that looks like something from the 1920s; his wife, plump, dumplings for cheeks; and their daughter, tall, with thick red hair and neat features. She is a beauty. No boy could resist. Nor a few men.

I tap my finger against the glass. 'Charlotte, do you have any other photographs of the Berry family?'

'Yeah. Why?'

'Can I see them?'

A sigh. 'If you like. I'll dig them out.'

Moments later, she deposits a pile on the table. 'Here. Quite a few. He was only here a year, but we loved him and his family. Not often you can say that about newcomers. What are you looking for?'

'When was this one taken?' I ask.

'A week before he left.'

In the photograph, he stands with his family in front of Berry & Vincent. I search the windows for that pale moon of a face, but it is not there. Then I see their expressions. Withdrawn, grim caverns, each of them. The wife is thin now, Berry thinner. And the girl, no one would look at her twice.

'What was bothering the girl?'

'How'd you...? Gilly was a bit quiet, that's all. Figured she was just being a teenager. Berry and Mag were stressed. Didn't say about what.'

'Did she go into the shop often?'

'Of course. Her dad worked there. He used to call her his "Gilly Bird".'

'What about on his days off?'

Charlotte frowns. 'Yeah, I suppose she did. Why?'

'Just curious. Thanks Charlotte, for showing me these.' I rise, squeeze her arm, leave before she can ask again.

🍎

The girl. It was the girl. I am certain. Perhaps Mr Vincent had focused on her, perhaps he had threatened her. Or perhaps he liked her, lured to her. Was she like Ada? Was there just something about her? Regardless, she would have been the most efficient tool to shuck Berry from the shop, from Rye.

I return to work. He is behind the counter. He is familiar to me now. I take out Charlotte's picture, lay it down for him. 'Gilly,' I say. 'Gilly.' And this is all.

I know I am right.

🍎

His room is just as I remember. Though now there is a golden patch in the centre of his bed, like the yolk of an egg. I bite my tongue to keep the sickness in my stomach. Mr Vincent is downstairs, dressing the window. I know it will keep him distracted long enough for me to search.

'There must be something here.' I am talking. To nothing. To myself. 'Gilly. Gilly.' As if I am calling her to me. 'There must be something left of you.'

I look under the bed, a piece of bread swollen with green mould. No family photographs. No personal treasures. I leave the room and its stink. Open the second door. It's all there still, my history, a map of my movements through the world. A thick wodge of paper has been added to the pile on the desk. He is still writing about me.

I pull a box from under the desk, listen for him downstairs. He could appear any moment. Inside the box, are two old tapes, some notes, a diary with a cracked spine, its pages thin as old skin. There are photographs too, faded, peoples' skin bleached to bone. But I recognise them. The Berry family, standing before the shop. They are smiling. I bundle it all into my pocket. Are these reminders? Trophies? Did Gilly mean as much to him as I do?

A bell rings below my feet and I quickly throw the box back under the desk, return to the shop floor. Ada.

She is smiling at Mr Vincent. I shout a hello, then she is smiling at me. His knees bang together, anger inside his bones. He thinks I have taken something from him, a thief of her smiles. I am. I shoot them down, like birds. She is kind to me. She is my *friend*. She does not know him like I do. I hope she never has to.

'Hello, Teddy. How are you?'

'Good, good.'

'How about you, Mr Vincent?'

I ruffle Albie's hair, bring her eyes back to me. Back to me now. And some fearless thing inside me rises.

'I was thinking today we could go to the beach? What do you think to that, fella?' I say.

'Yes. Yes. Yes!'

'Yes?'

'Yes!'

'Well, alright then. That OK, Ada? I don't think I've even been down there yet. I'd like to see it.'

'Sure. That would be nice.'

Mr Vincent tries to reclaim her attention, pulling trinkets from his pocket like a cheap magician. A golden cotton reel, a golden watch face, a golden necklace. Bright as honey. She does not care for fancy things. He tries the boy. But he isn't interested. He wants the beach.

As we leave, I hear the ring of the bell and imagine the bang of his angry kneecaps snapping together.

🍎

I insert the tape into the VCR. The image is peppered with black marks like cigarette burns. The machine is old, rusted in places, but it functions, moaning the longer I ask it to play the tape. I discern Berry's face. Mags'. Mr Vincent's. More importantly, I see Gilly.

The four of them stand outside the shop. A banner is tacked over the window, and scrawled in a youthful hand, are the words:

OPENING DAY
Berry & Vincent
welcomes you

There is paper confetti in the air. Paper rain. It sticks to licked lips and oily noses. Gilly is throwing fistfuls from a sack at her hip, smiling, smiling. As innocent as a babe. Townspeople flood through the shop door, a stream of bell-bottomed jeans and bubble sleeves, hair high and unmoving. It is strange to see bodies in there. There is no sound, but I imagine the voices, the children calling for toys to be bought.

Gilly remains outside, talking to a girl. Mr Vincent watches them. He is younger, he has a little more hair on his head, a few less wrinkles, but for the most part, he is the same. The same predatory stillness, the same coal-blackness in his eyes. The same sense that he is not a man like other men.

He watches Gilly. Where did he hide the camera to tape this? I want to reach through the colourless image, withdraw her so he cannot hurt her. Mr Vincent moves toward Gilly, picks confetti from her hair.

Her lips move, Thank you, Mr Vincent. I think the shop has had a good turnout, don't you?

He does not speak. Continues to pick at her hair.

The people seem nice here, don't they?

She yelps as he pulls a few strands from her scalp. He makes no apology, only tucks them into his collar.

That hurt. I think you'd better stop.

His hand is up again, digging into her hair. She bats him away, and I want to tell her to move. MOVE! Go to your father. But this was fifty years ago. It happened already.

Mr Vincent, I don't like that. Stop please.

There it is.

I see it in her eyes. Fear. The grainy image cannot hide it. She is wondering about him, about the things inside his head.

This is the beginning of it. I wish someone had noticed them. Had taken Gilly clear from this town, which was already turning, like a tooth to rot. All that she had coming. What did she have coming?

ADA

Bruised and Smudged

I glimpse Teddy inside Berry & Vincent as we pass on the way to the grocery shop. His head is bent, back too, shadows under his eyes like ink thumbed onto his skin. Mr Vincent is nowhere to be seen.

Albie tugs on my hand, impatient for the sweets I've promised him. 'Just a minute. Just a minute.'

Something in Teddy's face stops my feet, holds me where I am. He has a cloth in his hand. He is dragging it over the dolls, the dust and grit on their faces.

'A minute, Albie.'

Teddy looks over his shoulder, furtive, then his hand shoots out and violently grates over the dolls. They are bruised now, ruined now. Mr Vincent will be angry.

'Mm.'

'What, Mummy?'

'I don't like the dolls either.'

Albie and I move on, but my thoughts stay with Teddy. Inevitably, attention follows him wherever he goes in Rye. The townspeople watch him, lips puckered, as if there is a bad taste there. They wonder why he is still here. They wonder how long it will be before the shop sours in his belly and he runs from this place. If something inside him hasn't already begun to turn.

I hope he does not leave.

We meet every day now. It is mechanical, a new routine of sorts.

There is much he keeps to himself, but I do not mind because I enjoy his voice, the break in the silence. It is a balm to me, even if it is coarse, flayed with a sadness I cannot identify.

'Albie, what do you think of Teddy?'

'He's nice.'

'Do ... do you think he's upset about something?'

A shrug. 'He doesn't like Mr Vincent.'

Not many people do.

'What about us? Do you think he likes us?'

He nods, smiles to himself. 'Yes.'

I want to ask Teddy what is wrong, what is putting this sadness and fury in his body. At times, I worry he'll draw away from us like Margot, rubbing his cuff as if we've left a stain there. Because we are different. But he doesn't.

Later on, we do call in, and he lets out a deep breath. 'When's your break? Fancy lunch in the park?' I lift a bag of homemade sandwiches but they have gone soft so I quickly tuck them behind my leg.

'The park sounds good.'

His nails tear at his hairline. Fresh blood beads along the previous crusted shore. I get a faint whiff of blood, and something else too. It is rough, sharp, like a pin in my throat. I breathe his sadness. His body is stiff, cold, even though the day is fine and the sun is warm velvet on our backs.

'Are you OK?' I ask.

'Yes. I'm fine.'

'You seem ... I don't know, anxious, upset. Do you have something on your mind?'

'I was thinking about Mr Vincent.'

'Oh?'

'And Berry, his wife. Their daughter,' Teddy says.

'What about them?'

'The reason they left Rye. You told me about a photograph in The Mermaid, but there were more that Charlotte showed me. One was taken a few weeks before they left. They did not look like people, they looked hollow. As if someone had stripped them clean.'

'Of what?'

'Of life.'

'Do you know what happened to them?' Is this really what is bothering him, some old town mystery?

He does not respond. I do not force him to.

'You don't have long left. We'd better start walking back?'

'Not yet. Let's have a few more minutes.'

The iron tang of blood is sour in my nose. I take his hand – fingernails red and sticky – hold it still. He looks at me, smiles, grateful, and I smile too.

TEDDY

Birds and Paint

Hello?

She looks different now. Gilly. In the second tape, there is darkness under her eyes, smudges of shadow, her cheeks are pale, sagged. Her lips move, and I move closer to the image, I don't want to drop even one word.

Hello? Dad, is that you?

Gilly is in the shop. The blinds are drawn. There are no customers. She stands by the counter, and from the angle of the camera, I suspect it is hidden amongst the shelf of dolls. She does not know it's there. She does not know he's filming her.

She looks ahead, searching. I want to tell her to leave. Her father is not there. Four steps from where she stands to the door. Take them. Those steps. They are not many. Just leave. But she does not. Continues, calling, Dad? Dad?

I have stood where she stood, I have breathed down the stink of this shop. It hurt her. It has hurt me too. I have stood in its stomach and wanted to rip it down, I have lit a match in my mind, held it to the eaves.

She knew then what I have come to know now.

He and the shop. They are the same. He is its breath, its lungs. *He* needs that match. To his heart I would touch it.

I see him, his strange, curled-up figure at the edge of the frame. He goes to her, a beast with a bird, his slow lips are moving, stretching. What is he saying?

Gilly steps back. Three more, I think. Just three.

Where's my dad?

He paws at her waist, lower. Lips moving, slow, slower.

Stop. Stop it. Leave me alone!

He takes a coil of red hair between his fingers. She throws herself forward, bites his thumb. He stumbles back, then launches his body at hers, gathering her hair into a rope, holding her as a child would a doll. She hits at him, but her fists are coins bouncing off a wall. He shakes, and her head wriggles on her thin neck.

The film is running out. I do not want to leave her. Mr Vincent holds her head to his chest, his lips still moving. What is he saying?

I try to hear his words even though there are no words to be heard. Gilly is crying, her bony, bird-like legs quivering. Her arms are up, between their bodies, to keep his heart from touching hers.

I cover my face but I can still see them, ghosts inside my eyes. Then my hands slip away and I look at Mr Vincent and realise.

He is singing to her.

🍎

The diary is crumbling, pages coming away in my hands. It was pink once. Now it has lost its colour, like a body rotted inside the shop. I open it, carefully, as if its insides might dribble out, hurt me. My heart bangs when I see a messy scrawl, innocence in every curl and strike. I breathe in the damp of the pages, steady myself, begin to read.

Diary of Gilly Berry
Thoughts, observations and random things.
__PRIVATE!!!!__

Something strange happened to me today. I don't know if there are words to describe it. If there are, I certainly don't know them. All I've got is Bad. Something Bad happened to me today. Bad Bad Bad.

It's not the shop. The opening was good. The kids roared, flooded the place like water. Berry & Vincent is part of their childhood now, and he hopes they'll look back on it with a smile.

I haven't told Dad about what happened. I don't know what to say. Perhaps there is nothing to say. He was in the shop at the time, so was Mum, they did not see Mr Vincent come to me and start pulling at the confetti in my hair.

I thought he was helping. But then it started hurting.

When I asked him to stop, he wouldn't. Mum's said that if a boy is ever bothering me, I should kick his 'pieces'. Is it different with grown-ups? I don't know. Perhaps I didn't say stop loud enough. His face was strange. His lips were smiling plenty but his eyes weren't. His eyes made my stomach sore.

My scalp is sore too. And it hurts to touch it.

I can't have said it loud enough.

🍎

He's started following me round. I tried to kick him in his 'pieces' yesterday, but he moved and I fell. Dad didn't see. He was busy with the customers.

I will try again tomorrow. Perhaps then he will leave me alone. I'll be louder, clearer. I'll make him stop.

🍎

It's getting worse. He's getting worse. I kicked him when he tried to touch me this time. It was a definite 'clear off' message, but it was one I don't think he understood. He got angry. That smile turned into something else. I could see his teeth still, but it looked different. Animal.

He likes my hair. He grabs it in fistfuls so I can't move. Sometimes he brushes it with his fingers, and I feel like there are mice inside my skin. I put it up today, brushed it tight to my scalp. He ripped the red ribbon out, my head spun, and I worried for a moment it would spin off my neck. My mind went blurry, like the corner of a window when your breath mists it over. All I could think was, Please don't let my head spin away from me.

🍎

He's moving my things. My lunchbox, my rucksack, vanish, and I look and look but I can't find them. He sees me looking. Smiles. And I wish I could take that smile from him like he takes my things.

I'm careful in the shop now, to keep my distance from him. But sometimes I have to go into the store room and he follows me. Yesterday, I threw a pocket watch at his face. He pinched my arm. Hard. Because I hurt him. But I wasn't having that, so I pinched him back. He didn't like that.

Today he is different. Sharp. At least that's how it feels in my stomach. Like it is full of screws. The hairs on my arms rise, I press them back down with my fingers. I am not scared. I'm not. He should be scared of me.

🍎

I wondered how the birds had got inside.

There were so many, swinging, twirling, above my head. Their eyes were like chips of coal. The sunlight filled their feathers with colours I only wished I could paint with. I heard hums in their little throats, and I thought to myself, Did they come through the window? Through the door? How did all these songbirds find their way inside Berry & Vincent?

Then I realised something.

The birds were dead.

I thought I might fall, top over bottom. I saw the strings, trapping their little bodies to the ceiling, the stitching too, the shoots of wool. I heard their wings, their voices, but they'd only been inside my head.

Hummingbirds, lovebirds, birds I could fit in my fist they were so small. I wanted to call for Dad, but I knew he wouldn't be able to hear me from the café across the street. Did he know they were here? They shouldn't be. Dad didn't like stuffed things. I didn't either.

Something fluttered to my right. I thought, One is still alive, maybe I could free it, maybe I could save it. *But it wasn't a bird. I saw him and then my own insides felt woollen. He smiled at me. That smile, that smile. Opened the store-room door, back and forth, back and forth. Cool air wafted across my face, then something hit me. A drop on my cheek. I touched it, it was red.*

The birds were moving now. They were flying, the wind putting life back inside their bodies. Wind and rain. Red rain. I felt it on my skin, my hair. And when I looked up again, I screamed. Their wings were dripping.

The birds were bleeding.

I ran then. I ran with my woollen legs, fast as I could make them go. I did not stop until I was home. My heart hurt. It was like there was thunder in my chest. Tears were on my cheeks, they'd run into the red, and it looked like my eyes were bleeding. I pushed my finger through, sniffed it. It was paint. Only paint.

Paint, paint, paint.

I wiped it off, the tears too. I did not go back to the shop for three days, and when I returned, the birds were gone. I looked for them. I looked all over the shop. It was as if they'd flown away again. I knew they had not. I knew he must have taken them down. I know it was real because of the red-stained tissue bubbling over the sink. But also because of the shake in my fingers. They're shaking now. They won't stop.

Why won't they stop?

🍎

The birds are here. I stand in the shop and wait for their wings to start dripping red. He must have put them back up when the

Berry family left Rye. He likes his birds, Mr Vincent. Perhaps this is why.

I think of Gilly, wet-faced, red-faced, of Mr Vincent swinging that door to make them fly. He must have known the nickname Berry had for his daughter. He must have heard him call to her: Gilly Bird, Gilly Bird, where are you?

I feel cold rivers inside my body. I want Ada, my friend, my only friend, to come into the shop, calm me, warm me.

As I step onto a rickety old chair, I catch a bird, a robin, in my hand, run my finger along its back. Dried paint. Red paint.

Poor Gilly.

ADA

Love and Duty

'Ada, darling!'

'Jerry? Oh my God. What are you doing here?'

'We'll get to that. Now, don't just stand there. Give me a hug, I need it. I've just sat next to an old man with onion breath for three hours.' My aunt stands outside my door, fanning her face. 'Three hours! Of him talking about his misshapen bollock, his divorce with a "fat old grub" – his words not mine – and his bowel movements. Irregular, in case you were wondering, and I know you must have been, because it's pretty thrilling shit.'

I laugh, throw my arms around her. Her hair is neatly pressed, swirling up to her crown, yellow like old paper. My cousins say it looks like she has a swan sat on her head.

'Woah, woah. Steady on, girl. Don't break me. I love you too.'

'I – I can't believe you're here. Are you alright? Are the boys OK?'

'Of course they are.' She closes the door behind her, sniffs the air, scrunches her nose and heads to the kitchen. 'Smells of damp. Fancy a cup of tea? I'll make them. You're a very talented person, Ada, darling, but you're terrible at tea.' She winks, and I hug her again.

'Why are you here?'

'I've come to see you. I've come to talk about a few things.'

'Things?' I ask.

'Don't look so worried. We'll get to that. Where's Albie?'

'He's upstairs.' I leave her in the kitchen, call him down.

Albie rockets himself into her arms.

'Hello, hello.' My aunt swings him up, kisses his cheeks, his head, his fingers. 'Oh my goodness me, I've missed you. You've gotten so big. So big!'

Albie squeals. 'I'm four now.'

'I know. You're a little man, aren't you? I brought you some pressies. Go and have a rummage in my bag.'

He rockets back out of the kitchen. Jerry smiles. 'A few puzzles and books. I think he'll enjoy them. He smells gorgeous. I love that sweet smell babies and little kids have. You're so lucky. My boys just smell of shit now.'

'How's Phil?'

'He's still Phil, so he's a lazy bastard. But, yes, he's good.'

'How did you get the time off?'

'Blackmailed my boss.'

'Should have guessed.'

She shrugs. 'Had to be done.'

'How long are you staying? Can you stay for the week?'

She shakes her head. 'I'm sorry, darling. I have to leave tonight. I've only got a few hours with you.'

'Oh.'

'But we can make them count, can't we?'

'Yes.'

'Tea, tea!' she says.

Two years have chalked some grey into her hair, drawn a few wrinkles under her eyes. But otherwise, she is much the same. During my pregnancy, she was the one with a bottomless supply of mints and salted crackers in her pockets, the one who guarded me from *her* poking, and from questioning boys, and who let me live in her home rent free.

'Here we are.' She presses a mug into my hand. 'Eighty percent milk, twenty percent sugar. Just how you like it.'

'Thanks.'

'That's a serial-killer's tea, that. It's frightening, "screw-loose" tea.'

I laugh. 'I like it. Milky and sweet.'

She shivers. 'It's not even proper tea, just sweetened milk. A thimble, that's all I can take. Pinch of sugar. Half a pinch.'

We look at one another.

'I love that you're here. I do. But you're here for a reason. You have a family, you have a busy life. You taking time off is unheard of.'

She sighs, pats my hand. 'We're getting straight into it, are we? Alright. I spoke to your dad. He thinks you're lonely. That you need help.'

There are roses in my cheeks, a cold screw burrowing into my gut. 'We're ... alright.'

'He told me you're finding it difficult with Albie.'

'I wish he hadn't done that.'

'Why? I'm your aunt, aren't I?'

'It's not that, Jerry, and you know it. Did he tell you he refused to take Albie? A grandad who wouldn't have his grandson for a sleepover. Because of her.'

'Yes, he did.' She taps my finger, makes me look at her. 'But that's part of the reason I'm here. Your mother.'

'What do you mean?'

She knocks her mug and a creosote wave of tea laps at the rim. 'Oh! Shit. Sorry.'

'It's fine.' I mop up the spillage with a tissue. Check on Albie in the next room, close the door.

'Your parents wouldn't want me to tell you any of this. I feel like I'm breaking their trust. But I've thought you should know for a long time now. It might help you understand.'

'You're being really obscure.'

'The last time you spoke to your dad, you asked him why your mum is the way she is. He told you that she had a difficult upbringing. That's all he'll ever tell you?'

'That's right.'

'He tries to be honest with you because he loves you, Ada, darling. So much.'

'Just tell me, Jerry.'

She gulps in a breath, and her body grows, then shrinks as she exhales. 'I don't know the whole story, your dad kept a lot of it back. He's protective of her. Private. But he told me a long time ago that your mother was abused as a girl.'

My left hand is shaking suddenly, so I stuff it under the table. 'She...' My other hand starts, and I stuff that under too. 'By who?'

'Her father. He was a devil. No sense in holding back with you, darling. Your grandfather was a devil.'

'What did he do?'

She leans back, face older than it looked before. The grey in her hair is paler, the wrinkles under her eyes deeper, brushstrokes in her skin. 'He abused her, sexually, psychologically.'

'Oh my God.'

She takes my hand; her fingers are damp. 'The very bones of that man were bad. You know, when a woman would walk by him, he'd lick his lips, like there was sauce on his chin he couldn't reach, like he wanted to eat her up. That's what your dad told me. He put a fear inside women.

'None more so than your mother. He played terrible games with her mind. He made her doubt her own thoughts, her own perception. "What's this?" he would say and hold up an orange. She told him, and he would hit her, stop the breath in her throat, "No, it's an apple." He did it so often, she started to believe it. An orange was an apple. An apple was an orange.

'She was bent up inside. So much so, she started to mirror his behaviour. Your grandfather would fold up a cigarette, suck fallen tobacco off his fingers, and she would stick her fingers in her mouth too. He would fiddle with his earlobe, pick at the piercing, so would she. And when a woman walked into the room, she would lick her lips, looking for sauce.'

There are tears in my eyes and on my lips, between my fingers, sliding between hers. 'Mum never let me have any oranges. She wouldn't have them in the house. So Dad would sometimes buy me one at the market on Saturdays.'

She smiles sadly. 'There are reasons for everything. Your dad told me that when she was a girl, she'd cover bruises on her face with paint. Pink paint she found in the shed behind her house. She used to say it looked like she was blushing.'

I touch my cheek. Roses.

'No one knew? No one helped them?'

'Your dad met your mother in a grocer's. He was smitten. He helped her, guided her, and eventually, he took her away. He had to wait for her to be ready though. Your dad is a kind man.'

'What happened then?'

She sighs. 'With your mum's permission, your dad rang the police. More than enough evidence. The man was arrested.'

'I feel … I feel sick.'

She pushes the mug into my hand. 'Drink. Come on. You have it so sweet, darling, get some of that sugar into your body.' I close my eyes and her hands are holding the mug to my lips, they are stroking my head, they are firm and strong on my shoulders. 'Another sip, darling. Come on.'

I breathe, wait for the sickness to fall away. Then I open my eyes. 'Thanks.'

'It's OK. It's a lot to take in. You're getting some colour back now.'

'I … I … didn't know any of this. Why didn't they tell me?'

'Your mother doesn't speak of it. Ever. And your father promised her when she was fifteen that he wouldn't breathe a word. And he hasn't. Except to me. Still hates himself for it.'

'Why did he tell you?'

'He couldn't keep in. It was a lot to carry. I think he just reached his breaking point.'

'What happened? After they left?'

'Your dad persuaded her to see a doctor, a professional who could help. As you can imagine, it was ... difficult for them. Your mum had been severely abused for many years. It takes twice as long to be mended than it does to be broken. If ever.' There are tears in her eyes. She smothers them with the back of her hand. 'Eventually, bits of that man faded, and bits of her came back. She studied. She passed her exams. She was a smart bean, your mum. Still is.'

'But...?'

'But she's still got all that inside of her, Ada. To this day, when a woman walks by, she'll lick her lips. She won't have oranges in the house. There are things ... left over.'

'Why is she this way with me though? She doesn't love me. She never has, despite what Dad says, but why be so...?'

'She does love you. She just doesn't know how to use it, how to show it.'

'When I was a kid, she'd kiss me. But it wasn't a kiss, not really. She'd just touch her cheek to mine, as if it was too intimate, too personal for her. I used to think I tasted bad.'

'And what do you think about that now I've told you all this?' Jerry sighs. 'Your grandfather wasn't kind when he kissed your mother as a child. He was not gentle. Perhaps, Ada, she was worried she would hurt you. After all, all the affection she has ever known has hurt her.'

I nod. 'I hadn't thought about it like that.'

'I remember when you were five, you and your mother were dancing in the garden, twirling, twirling, I lost count of all your circles. Your mother didn't smile, she just watched.' Jerry rubs the veins in her wrist, tracing each river with the nail of her finger, eyes changed, as if she is far away from herself.

'I don't remember this.'

'Your father and I wondered why she didn't smile. You held your stomach so tight, as if you thought all that happiness would spill right out of you.

'You fell, cut yourself deep. I remember a single spot of blood landing on your mother's white sock. You cried and cried, your little hands on either of her shoes, trying to remind her you were there. But she wouldn't be moved. She watched the sky as if she was seeing strange birds. As if her legs were roots in the earth. She wouldn't calm, you, she wouldn't say a word.'

She stops, gulps in a breath, her face pale as chalk.

'And then she slapped you.'

'What?'

Jerry nods, opens her hands. 'It wasn't hard but you fell on your back and started screaming. You father rushed over to you and your mother walked away.'

'I ... I don't remember any of this.'

'I saw something in your mother's face, Ada, after you fell. And I've never been able to get it out of my mind.'

'What?'

'Confusion.'

'What do you mean?'

She pats my wrist, looks at the veins there, deep inside my skin, as if she wonders how and why she is old. 'She didn't know what to do, Ada. I could see it as she watched those birds. No one had ever comforted her when she was a child and she hurt herself. She didn't know what it looked like, or how it felt, or what words to use. So she did what her father might have done.'

'She hurt me.'

'Yes.'

'What happened after?'

'I followed her into the kitchen. She was eating a biscuit, boiling the kettle for tea. I asked her why she hit you. She said she thought that was what she was supposed to do.'

I nod. 'I think I understand.'

She pats my wrist again. 'When you were young, you gave your mother so much love, and she didn't know what to do with it. How to manage it, shape it into something she could hold and could carry. Parental love reminded her of her father and so naturally you reminded her of him too. Of unkind love that spills into violence.'

'What did Dad say?'

'He was furious. He didn't speak to her for days. But I explained what I'd seen to him and he knew it was the truth. He knew already, deep down, your father. He forgives your mother everything, because she needs him to. She is afraid and confused and angry with herself for not being able to be a mother.'

'Did she realised what she'd done was wrong?'

'Yes, afterwards. She never touched you like that again.'

'She has so many sharp edges.'

'She sharpened them herself when she was a girl. To cut her father's fingers.'

'I wonder what it's like. To feel how she feels all the time.' My fingers are numb, I pick at the skin round my nails until I meet blood. But I do not feel the sore.

'I imagine it must feel like tiredness.' She looks at the blood coating my nails, mops it up with a tissue. 'I have a video tape from when you were young. It's short, barely a minute long, but you might like to see it.'

'What is it of?'

'You and your mother. But I think it will help you understand some of those edges.'

'Why are you telling me now?'

'Your dad told me he wouldn't take Albie for a sleepover, and I could imagine how that made you feel. When you have kids, things cut in a different way. Someone rejecting your son hurts more than someone rejecting you. I've wanted to tell you for years, Ada, darling. But I told myself I couldn't because it wasn't my truth, and I didn't want to break your dad's trust.'

'You're right.'

'About?'

'It hurting more because of Albie.'

'Perhaps I shouldn't have left it this long. I'm sorry, I am.'

'Thank you for telling me. I needed to know.'

She kisses my forehead when we part. We wipe our eyes, we smile.

'I used to take her cups of tea, you know, when I was about seven. I would get Dad to help me pour the kettle. I knew exactly how she liked it. Strong, dark. No milk. Half a spoon of sugar. She never drank it though. Not if it was from me. Full teacups, gone cold outside the office door.

'One night, I asked her to read me a story, but she refused, so I sat by her bed and read one to *her*. Do you know what she did?'

'No.'

'She said to Dad, "Get her out. Move her. Now. And lock the door or she'll try to get back in."'

'Perhaps she did that because she was frightened. She didn't know how to be with you. What did your dad do?'

'He did as he was told. But I understand now. Why he does what he does.'

'Oof.' She sits up straight and her back cracks. 'Bloody old age, that. It's a musical. Popping bones, wet farts, coughs, moans. My own orchestra.'

I smile. 'I've really missed you.'

'Only right. Now, I haven't got long. Why don't we go and play with that little boy in the next room? I expect he's found those Polos I had hidden in my bag.'

TEDDY

Bones and Stones

I take a breath, open Gilly's diary and begin to read. Almost instantly I want to close it again.

I thought I could made him stop. I can't. I need help. But I don't want to tell Dad. He and Mum are so happy. And I am happy they are happy. If I tell them this, things will change.

There's something about the shop now that's just not ... right. I'm in there, and I smell something, lick my lips, my teeth: death. The shop tastes of death, of something that has turned. No one else seems to notice it. Only me, which makes me wonder if it's only in my head.

I wonder if it's all in my head but, no, it's not. I know because of the ache in my body. Fear, such a short word, such a light word on the lips. But inside my bones, it is heavy, and when I wake in the morning, I struggle to move. I tell my heart to move, move! But it is full of stones. I even think I can hear them sometimes.

Yesterday, Dad had me pricing a new batch of books. I used to like the yellowed pages, the greasy thumb prints and annotations, often too messy for me to translate. As if it was a secret language, which only the characters and reader were privy to. I don't read them now, not since Mr Vincent started moving those nice old books to his bedroom. A trail up the stairs, especially for me. I do not follow it, but seeing those books, used like that, hurts my insides.

Then he appeared as if my mind has called out to him. Dropped down next to me, his knees touching mine. His hand was touching mine. It was touching my hair, looping it round his fist, his wrist. It seemed like he had more hands than he ought to have. They were everywhere, all over me, then they were near that private place of mine.

My mind emptied, thoughts falling like buttons from a jar. It took me a moment to understand what was happening, what it meant. I heard Mum's voice, so close in the back room, I wondered how she did not hear me, my heart full of rocks, thumping.

I leapt up, ran. From the shop, from him.

And that night, my pillow was soggy with tears and shame and fear. I could still feel his fingers digging, rifling through my clothes, looking for that part of me.

I don't want to leave Rye. But I don't want to stay either.

🍎

He's following me. He followed me to the park yesterday. No one saw. He's careful. I don't know what to do.

What do I do?

🍎

When he presses himself into me, I want to scrape his parts off mine. I want to scream and scream, but I don't. I bite my tongue and swallow the screams down with the blood. They sit in my stomach then, I can feel them there, rattling like pennies. What will happen when my body is full and I cannot bite another one down?

Well, I will scream. For days. I will stand in the shop, and scream, emptying my body of all this noise.

🍎

Oh God. He's doing it to Mum. He's started on Mum.

I don't know what to do. I don't know what to do.

Mum's face has changed. Like mine did. She is quiet. Withdrawn. Her eyes are open but they are empty. Sometimes my heart jumps because I think she has died. I touch her chest, look for her own beat, and she panics, asks me what the Hell I'm doing. I say nothing.

She's hiding it from me. I'm hiding it from her. And we're hiding it from Dad.

I've told them. I've told them everything. That in the beginning what he did to me was so much simpler than what he does now. Pulling my hair, poking at my neck, pinching my arms. Like a boy. A silly boy. But when a man does boy things, you have to wonder who it really is in there. And what he will do next.

I've told them about opening day. And everything since.

Mum cried. Roared, is a better word. I've never heard her roar before. It was a wild noise. Not a scream like those in my belly. It was something else. Dad went all quiet. It took him a minute to come to terms with it. Then Mum told us her secret, admitted it finally. I already knew. I guessed. I'd seen things. I'd just not known what to do.

Mum held me. And I screamed those screams. It felt good to clear out my body like that. Our bones went soft, we slipped to the floor. And Dad held us until our bones were bones again.

He's gone to the shop. Dad.

He didn't ask us why we'd hidden it for so long, each with the same secret. And I'm glad he didn't. Because I wouldn't know how to answer. Confusion, fear, denial, anger, shame. Take these strong words, perhaps they'll give you an idea. But I think, mostly, we were trying to protect each other, from his 'rot'. It's like those webs – Mum calls them spider silks – that catch you as you walk through a doorway. You feel them wrap round your head, search and search but you can never find them with your fingers. That is what Mr Vincent has done to us. We are bound up, but we cannot get these bonds off our bodies.

He's gone to the shop. Dad. Why did he have to go to the shop?

🍎

Dad came back different. There was wind in his bones before, blustering, fury. I thought his feet might lift from the ground. His face was red, like a tomato. All that wind in there, trying to get out. But when he came back, all the wind had gone out of him. He was pale, pale as bone. His back was curved, like a safety pin. And his skin seemed to hang off his body.

I put a blanket round his shoulders. Then Mum told me to leave the room. And I did, but I listened through the keyhole. They talked. Mum was shaking, then Dad started shaking, as if he'd caught it from her. He said we should leave Rye. But Mum said no, we stay. We will not be run out of our home, like mice running from a fox. Dad blames himself. For not having guessed. For being blind. But I don't think he's blind. How can someone ever know all the parts to another person?

🍎

Dad has to stay in the shop, keep it open, keep it running. He says we need the money. Mum keeps me indoors all day. Not that it makes much difference. Mr Vincent only stands outside, peering in. He's got that dreadful eye on me. Only me now.

Sometimes I go upstairs, lay on my bed so I don't have to see him. He's careful. He never does anything to raise suspicion from the people here. Mum says he's evil. And I think he is.

I'd like to swing a book at his head, I'd like to see it come off. I'd like to have his blood on my fingers, I'd like to know he is dead and I am free. I've never thought about killing someone before. I wonder about it now.

And then I wonder about killing me.

●

I sleep in Mum and Dad's bed now. Between them. My sentinels. Once I might have been embarrassed about that, but not now. I cannot sleep without them. They cannot sleep without me. The bed is too small, and often Dad falls out. But he doesn't care. They hold me tight. And I wake with finger-marks in my skin. I am glad there are finger-marks there.

●

He came in last night. I don't know how. Mum says he must have picked the lock. Things had moved downstairs. The phone, a pile of books. We know it was him because we could smell him on them. Dad has put a bolt across the front door, and tonight we're going to pull the wardrobe across, trap ourselves in the bedroom. Mum doesn't want me to know but she's got a kitchen knife under the bed.

I don't think a knife could stop Mr Vincent.

●

Mum and Dad look different now. I do too.

You can see the bones under our skin. My ribs poke out, so much so they almost look like the strange, slim spines of books. We look odd. We do not look like ourselves. We look like the dolls in the shop, vacant, emptied. We sit together in the evenings but we do not watch the telly-box. We do not talk. We just sit. Sit and breathe.

Sometimes we stop, air catches like gristle in our throats, so we will tap the inside of each other's wrist where that forest of veins grows. A reminder, a comfort. Breathe, Mum says to Dad. Breathe, Dad says to me.

And we listen to the breathing, draw in, blow out. Draw in, blow out. Hear that? We're alive.

🍎

I don't think I'm going to write in here anymore. It makes me sad. And I can't hold the pen properly. My fingers shake like there are little earthquakes inside them. I wish I'd stopped sooner but I needed a way to keep my mind straight over the last year. I'll leave it here. And say:

We are not people. My mother is shrunken, changed. My father too. I wonder if it is my fault. And this is something I have done to them. It's me Mr Vincent has his eye on. That awful eye. I hope it is not my fault. Please don't let it be my fault.

Sometimes I look at them, and I think, I'm sorry.

They are paper. I've cut them into a strange shape. Mum doesn't smile anymore, at me or Dad, or anyone. She does not read snippets to us from Jackie *mag. She does not brush blush onto her cheeks in the morning as she always loved to do. She does not dance ditties or sing silly songs. She is smaller, and sometimes she pinches her hand in the evening, and I think it's to prove to herself that she still feels. You're alive, Mum. You're alive. I think.*

Dad is gone too. His colour dribbled away. His character emptied. There is nothing there anymore. In his eyes. He used to laugh, my dad, at anything. But usually at himself. Now he laughs at nothing.

They are different. I am too. I am not me.

My dad used to call me Gilly Bird. He doesn't call me Gilly Bird anymore.

ADA

Mother and Child

Albie and I are hooked round each other, the shape of us like strange runes. His warm, tacky breath makes strands of my hair shiver. His eyes are closed, and his sleeping noises are all there is to mark the hours that pass. This and the greasy, fetid air that has grown in the bedroom. Since my aunt left yesterday, my bones have silvered, turned to steel, and I can motivate myself to do no more than feed and bathe Albie.

I look at him now, face innocent and young, feel emptied, as if something has been taken out of my body. Then I see pieces of my mother in him, the arch of his brows, the dimple in his chin, but I wonder if they are not really from her but from him. Grandfather. They are in me too. Somewhere. Perhaps they are not in my face, nowhere the light can reach, but somewhere. Yes. They must be.

Before she wrangled Albie's hands from her sweet-strewn bag and left, Jerry asked me if I was alright, if I would be alright. I nodded. But I am not alright.

I hear her voice in my head, words I know she would say: *Your mother loves you. But it's a fractured love. Not a simple one. She can't help it, darling.*

Albie turns, drapes a short arm over my face. I smile, kiss his wrist. He grumbles, like a wolf. I kiss his wrist again, and he grumbles louder.

Tears are on my cheeks, I notice them when I move Albie's wrist away. I call my aunt, but I know she will be at work, she will be busy. Tonight too, when she will have to cook and clean up after the boys.

A piece of me would like to tell Teddy. But I do not know him. Not properly. And he does not know me. Lately, he's always itching at his neck, so I hold his hand down. Something troubles him. I wonder if it is really about Gilly. About why they left. It is just an old town mystery.

Later, I will rub some life into my legs, these bones will become bones again. I'll blow the tired air out of this room, take Albie to the beach. I will pat this sadness down, meet Teddy, hold his hand if he needs me to. Smile.

But now I do not smile. Now, I close my eyes, breathe and curl myself into a rune once more.

TEDDY

Green Shutters and Brown Bags

'You seem quiet today,' Ada says.

'I'm alright. I just have a lot on my mind.'

'Like what?'

We are in the park, sitting close. Albie is playing with a ball, crop of hair bouncing over his strange little ear; he does not wear a hat as often now. His confidence has grown since he met me, and I am glad.

'I was thinking about the Berry family,' I say.

'Still?'

'I found some old photographs, notes, things they left behind.'

'What did the notes say?' she asks, rummaging through her bag, withdrawing two pieces of toffee. She gives one to me and puts the other inside her mouth. Her cheek bulges, and I poke it with my finger. She frowns at me, quickly chews and swallows.

'They were about Gilly.'

The family were surviving, just. So what made them leave? What made them run?

Ada's brown eyes are wide as fifty-pence coins. 'Oh?'

'Something happened to the family fifty years ago. Berry and his wife started writing notes on scraps of paper, about how to help Gilly, protect her. What to do about their problem. They were afraid. They were all afraid. Gilly kept a diary too, full of sadness.'

Ada is chewing on her lip. I want to tell her to stop. She'll make it bleed. Something is bothering her. I knew it as soon as I saw her this morning. I wonder what it is.

'Jesus. What happened? What was wrong her?' she asks.

'She...'

'What is it? Teddy?'

It is the woman. The bird woman from before. She is walking through the park, that brown bag of a coat lumpen and flapping. Her head is down, her fingers twisting together.

'Excuse me a minute.' I rise, run across to her, my arthritis making every step awkward and unbalanced. 'Wait, please. Wait! I need to speak to you.'

She stops, eyes widening. 'You're still here then.'

'Yes. You remember me?'

'Of course I do, Teddy.'

'I – I wondered if I could ask you a few questions. About the Berry family.'

Her face changes then, the sharp plains of it rising, sharper, the hollows sinking, deeper. It is alarming, the sight of it.

'Gilly. You want to know about Gilly.'

'Yes,' I say.

She sighs. 'Suppose you should know. You're working with *him*. And you're not leaving, are you?'

I glance at Ada. 'No,' I say.

'Fine. Come to my house this evening. I'll tell you about Gilly. I'm on the outskirts of the town. Green shutters. You can't miss it.' She wraps the brown bag tight round her body, walks away. I watch her go. I still do not know her name.

🍎

The cottage is hunched like its mistress, curved inward as if it cannot bear to look at the world. Something drips from the windowsills, puddles by the door, sadness is wrapped around the place. I take another step, and it slicks onto my shoes.

She appears behind the door, still wearing that brown bag, only now it is tied round her waist with a man's scarf. On her feet are oversized leather boots. They look like boats. She smells of smoke.

'Hello, Teddy. Come in.'

I follow her into a small box of a room. Neat piles of books, cushions neatly pressed onto the sofa. But the sadness is here too, stitched into seams, trodden into the rust-red carpet. I walk and it sucks at my feet like mud. I sit and feel it pressing against my spine. It is everywhere. And it is inside me now, as I breathe her air. She brings me tea, spilling it over into the china saucer.

'I'd hoped you'd leave. Pack up and get out. You seem like a nice boy...' She pauses, taps my temple with one long, bony finger. 'But I see it's knotting you up, like I said it would.'

'I'm fine.'

'A "fine" man wouldn't be here picking at that scab on their thumb like it's dried gum.'

I shrug.

'Drink your tea.'

I do as I am told. 'I ... I don't see you much round town.'

'Is that a question? It's not a very good one. Try again, properly.'

'Why don't I see you round the town?'

'I prefer my own company. I got a dog after my husband died. Philip. I needed another heartbeat round the place, you see. But he died when he was a pup. Got hit by a car.'

'I'm sorry.'

She sighs, that great big sigh that makes me wonder how she fits all the air inside. 'You're not here to hear my sad stories. You want to hear about Gilly. I'm not sure where to start.'

'Start at the beginning.'

She nods. But she does not speak. I realise the coat, the scarf, the boots – they must have belonged to her husband. 'Catch a glimpse of myself in the mirror and I think I'm him. Isn't that daft?' she says.

'No. It's not.'

Tears have come to her eyes. They puddle into her wrinkles. She wipes them with her sleeve. 'The Berry family left after a year. But Berry wasn't Berry. And that little girl left a different girl from the one who came to Rye.' She dips her finger into the cup of milky-white tea. Winces, sucks it dry. 'If she hadn't started coming to my house. I would have just assumed it was teenage angst, boy trouble, peer pressure, you know.'

'She came to see you?' This was not mentioned in the diary.

'We were neighbours, you see. I was friends with her mother. She was such a bright girl. Curious. By the end, she wasn't curious about anything.'

'How did Berry meet Vincent?'

'They met at an auction. They both got outbid on some curio they wanted. Berry could be so naive. He thought when he went into business with Vincent it would be a partnership. But Vincent was calculating. He used Berry for his money, to open the shop, to make the payments. He was just another puppet.'

'What happened to Gilly?'

'It started when the shop opened. It was the small things at first. But as the year wore on, it only got worse. He started playing games, "mind tricks" she called them.'

I see him sniffing at Ada then, and I bite my tongue. She sticks a cigarette between her lips, *pup-pup-pups* on it.

'She came round, I don't remember why. Postman delivered a package to the wrong house maybe.' The cigarette is a wet, soggy stump. 'We talked, and she fell asleep in this chair. A while later she left without saying a word. The pillow was covered in her hair. It was falling out, you see. Stress.'

'Then one night I saw Berry storm out of the house. His feet might have been on fire, he moved so fast. After that, the family changed. The mother and father started to look a lot like the daughter. Thin, emptied out, willowing. Like bodies with nothing inside them.'

'What happened that night?'

'He went to the shop, and Vincent attacked him. In more ways than one.' She sighs. 'Berry was a good man but he hadn't always made good business choices – he was gullible, you see, and those choices should have put him behind bars. Vincent blackmailed him, threatened him with his past. So when he left, he had a lump on his skull the size of a peach, and he was bound like a man for the noose.'

'What then?'

'He tried to fight back, I think. Tried to play Mr Vincent at his own game. But it didn't work.'

'Why didn't he just call the police?'

'He did. They laughed in his face. You see, they had no proof. That's the clever thing about Mr Vincent, he gives you wounds no one can see.' She taps her temples. 'He wounds this.'

I nod. I know.

'Why did they stay here then?'

'They'd spent all their savings on that godforsaken shop. They had nowhere else to go. But, boy, they ran in the end.'

'Something happened, didn't it, toward the end?' This is it. This what I need to know.

She crunches her cigarette into an ash tray, lights another, her lips *pup-pup-pupping* at it. There is a clot of spit in the corner of her mouth. She sees me looking and wipes it away.

'Yes.'

'Tell me.'

'She went to the shop looking for her dad one night. But her dad wasn't there. Only Mr Vincent.'

I think of that second recording. Of the girl calling for her father.

'In those days the shop had these shelves, tall things, taller than you, heavy. They were unstable, dangerous. Berry had wanted to get rid of them. Vincent didn't let him. And that night he packed those shelves full, cut the legs and pushed. Looked like an accident, didn't it?

'Berry found her. Underneath it all. She was such a small thing by then. She looked like a doll, thrown on the ground by a child. Her legs were crumpled. And all those things, they'd put bruises in her skin.'

'Was she alright?'

'If you mean, did she survive, then yes. She did, but she had lost something important. That little girl never really came out of the shop that night.'

TEDDY

Songs and Sorrow

'He tried to kill her.'

The words are between us, and I want to collect them up, put them back in my mouth.

'Berry rushed her to the hospital. She had a lot of broken bones, some internal bleeding. They fixed the body. But it was *just* the body they fixed. When she came home, she wasn't Gilly anymore.'

'Did anyone know? The townspeople?'

'No. Berry carried her out the back to his car. He brought her home a week later. No one ever knew anything. Except me. Mags told me what had happened.'

'And then?'

'They left. Left the night she got back from the hospital. Packed up their things. Posted the keys through their front door. It was raining, I remember looking at Mags' shoes as she said goodbye. I remember watching the water roll off them. I don't know why I remember that.'

'Where did they go? Did they tell you?' I ask.

'No. Rye woke the next morning, and the Berry family wasn't there anymore. Came and went with the rain. Vincent tried to kill Gilly, and so they ran as fast as their feet could manage. I don't know where they are now. I don't know if that girl ever came back to herself.'

I sit back, breathe. The moments pass. I watch them on the clock. She does not say anything. She breathes too.

Eventually, she says, 'It was all about the shop, you know. That shop.'

'He wanted it for himself? Used Berry to fund it?'

She nods. 'He waited until it was open then he started on Gilly. This – this campaign began then.'

'Jesus.'

She looks at me, long and deep. The hairs on my skin rise, and I think, there are thoughts in that head of hers I don't want to be there.

'Teddy ... why do you stay working for that man? I'd like to know, I'd like to understand this. Because it's been niggling away at me.'

I swallow, the lump that hurts my throat, sinks and begins to hurt my gut. If she knew why, she would say that the shop is gathering devils to its door. And isn't it the truth, in a way?

'I don't know. I don't know.' I wanted to keep my anonymity, thought the shop could hide me, then I wanted to understand Mr Vincent, what happened with Gilly. And now? I see Ada in my mind.

'You think she's alive? You think any of them are?' I ask.

'What do you mean?'

I shrug, recalling that page in the girl's diary. 'Trauma is a greedy beast. Eats you up, doesn't it?'

'Oh. Oh. I see what you mean.' She wraps her brown bag tighter still, as if she is trying to squeeze the sad out of her bones, like water from a dishcloth.

'Everyone says the shop changed after Berry left. The town too. But it started changing long before that, didn't it?'

'Mm, I remember Gilly telling me that she'd started seeing things in there. Strange things. Bones and faces and twisted bodies They frightened her. Are they still there, Teddy?'

I nod. 'They're there.'

Then, 'You know, Gilly was afraid of the dark as a child, and she would only be able to sleep if the duvet was pulled right up over her head, nose sticking out through a hole. Berry used to sing to her. He sang every night for a whole year. The same nursery rhyme. She started sleeping on her own, she stopped covering her head, it comforted her.'

I smile. 'Did Mags tell you that?'

'No,' she says. 'She did. Gilly. And then she told me that *he'd* started singing to her. Vincent. He'd sing her dad's song. Right into her ear.' The biscuit turns to carpet in my mouth. The recording. The singing. Berry's song.

'How did he know? How does he know so much?' I ask.

She shrugs. 'He listens more than other people do. Picks up details they drop. He's a collector, isn't he? Stores up secrets, spins them into knives.'

We are silent. The air is thick with all our words. She does not move, and I think she has fallen asleep. Then her voices rises:

'Lavender's blue, dilly, dilly
Lavender's green
When I am King, dilly, dilly
You shall be Queen!

Call up your men, dilly, dilly
Set them to work
Some to the plough, dilly, dilly
And some to the pond.'

'I should go. Thank you, thank you for what you've told me.'

'I've never told anyone else, but I think Gilly would have wanted you to know.'

I nod. 'What's your name?'

Her face empties of expression. 'I've not heard someone say my name in fifty years. Funny ... that.'

'Would you like to hear someone say it now?'

'It's Birdy.'

I smile. 'It suits you, Birdy.'

'Gilly used to say I reminded her of a blackbird. She used to say she liked to imagine me flying.'

'That's nice.'

'Her dad called her Gilly Bird, you know. We were two birds together. When she was sad, crumbling biscuits in her fingers, I said, "Why don't we close our eyes and pretend we have wings." I like to think of her now, off flying somewhere. Somewhere far from Rye.'

🍎

The North Devon Gazette
Obituaries

Gillian 'Gilly' Berry passed away 3rd January 1999, aged forty-two, following a brief illness.

Miss Berry was institutionalised aged nineteen, after the death of her parents in a vehicle collision, caused by damage to the brakes of their car.

Miss Berry will be missed by many at North Devon's Mental Health Hospital.

Miss Berry will be buried in the family plot in Mortehoe Cemetery.

🍎

I wonder if a part of her is still inside this place. Like Birdy said. If a part of her never left, even in death.

I see her moving through the aisles, flapping her arms like they have feathers. I see her full of words, of movement. Then I see her changed, emptied, of smiles, of innocence. I see her shrinking, bones thrusting through her skin, hair falling from her head, trails of it on the floor. I see her eyes, large, like button holes, stretched and empty.

Then I see Mr Vincent. Think of all that he has done, her diary
in his trophy room. He dismantled her. Precise, efficient, savage.
She was only a girl. Couldn't he have aimed his weapons at Berry?
No. Because Gilly was his knife, and she was sharp, she could cut
into her father like butter.

His back is to me. I say, 'Gilly Bird,' and he turns.

'Was it all just about Berry? About forcing him away? Or was
there more? Did you like her? You did, didn't you?'

He smiles. It is not just me who has been hurt by that smile.

'How did you meet him – Berry? Some people say you used to
work together – at an undertakers. Some people say you met at
an auction? You were on your best behaviour, weren't you? Poor
Berry, trusting, so trusting. He didn't stand a chance.'

He is smiling still.

'You tried to kill her.'

His face shivers into a confusion.

'You didn't know I knew that, did you, you fucking bastard!
Well I do. They left after that. Berry tried to stand up to you, fight
you, but he couldn't. You messed with those brakes, didn't you?
You killed them, you murdered them. Gilly lost her parents, then
she lost her mind. And the people here, you've had them like
playthings ever since.'

He rummages in his coat pocket, withdraws a ball of red wire,
or is it twine? He lifts it to his nose, breathes deeply, flicking it
softly with the spear of his tongue. The wire is thick, red as rust,
stitching through the air. But it isn't wire or twine. It is something
else. Her hair.

I swing my arm, suddenly, furiously, and he stumbles back. The
hair is brittle, thick. I withdraw a lighter from my pocket, watch
it burn.

'Gilly doesn't want to be in your pocket anymore.'

ADA

Smoke and String

The package is addressed to both Albie and I. I let him open it, fingers suddenly like claws as he tears through the brown paper. Inside is a single disc and a packet of jelly babies. 'Those, I think, are for you, Bean. From your auntie Jerry.'

He laughs. 'I'll share...' Bites his lip. 'One, you can have one.'

'Generous. Very generous.'

He upends the pack, pours half into my hands, then runs out the door with the rest. I smile, insert the disc into the laptop and watch the screen come to life. I see a bedroom, my old bedroom, books covering every surface. I see photographs on the walls, of my father, my aunt, my family. I do not see my mother.

But there she is suddenly, in the middle of the screen. I am asleep in her arms, curled into a shell. I must be three or four. My mother is younger, there are fewer lines in her skin, twists of hair tumble round her face. She lowers me onto the bed, tucks me a little too tight into the sheets. She isn't gentle. Her hands don't know how to be, I realise now.

'Goodnight, Ada.'

She turns, switches off the light, but then she pauses, comes back to me. She doesn't smile. Not like other mothers would. But she puts one finger softly to the point of my nose. For a count of five seconds. Then she leaves.

It is brief, the video. But it is enough. I watch it again and again, until her shape is a ghost in my eyes and I can feel that touch on my skin. Then I close the screen and take a breath.

Take another.

And another.

TEDDY

Pocket Watches and Tarot Cards

The window changes.

From silver pocket watches and silken neckties, to bell jars and oil-painted tarot cards. I cannot predict what will be next. Saturday evenings, the blinds are drawn against the dark, the sill is emptied, a body without embellishments. Sunday mornings, and it is full. There is no rhythm or design I can comprehend. Things are simply there, when yesterday they were not.

Today there are apples, red and green, soft with bruises. They hang from the ceiling, blistered orbs. There are apples of wool, stitched and dyed; apples made of wood, painted, propped. There are so many of them, and I cannot tell which are real and which are not. I think he must have had barrels hidden in his rooms upstairs.

I touch my finger to one through the glass, see underneath it, a newspaper cutting, it is old, the ink has smudged, but no matter, I know what it says. I have seen it before. It is about my father, the apples, the girls. I can just make out his picture, the point of his chin, very much like my own.

'You could open a tin can with a chin like that.' That is what the people said.

Something pale shifts behind the glass, and I draw back. Mr Vincent.

Is this a ploy to make me lose my balance? Is he trying to hurt me because I burnt Gilly's hair? Well, doesn't he know, I never had any balance? I have not been steady since I came to Rye.

I look over my shoulder. Has anyone seen this? Has this jolted anyone's memory? The street is empty. I breathe. Then I open the door, step inside.

His smile nearly makes me sick on my shoes.

'Why have you done this?'

He does not speak. Of course, he doesn't. Not to me. I snatch the sodden newspaper cutting from the display, tuck it inside my pocket. It soaks into the fabric. And I smell them all, the apples. It's what my mother said my father smelt like. Sweet, rotting.

There is a heat in my belly. My palms are wet, I wipe them on my trousers. 'Sickly, isn't it? The smell. Turns your stomach after a while. It will make you ill, sitting in your nose. You won't eat an apple ever again. I haven't had one since I was a boy. Before my mother told me about him.'

Him.

Him.

Mr Vincent shifts, his eyes bright screws. You liked that, I think.

The heat is in my chest now, this fearless thing rises. I lift an apple, hold it to my nose. I feel bold so I take a bite. He is looking at me as if he would like to put me in his pocket. I give him the apple, hope he takes a bite too and chokes, and say, 'You'll not be able to get the smell out of this place for weeks. Believe me, I know.'

TEDDY
Boil and Burn

He is waiting for me.

Yesterday, I walked out, left him to breathe down the stink of the apples, to think on his words. Today, they still hang in the window. Only now, that round moon of a face hangs in the window with them. I remember the first time I stood here, in this street, and thought he wasn't a man but a mask. It feels like such a long time ago. Time is endless.

He is smiling. Why is he smiling?

'What have you done?' I demand, as I enter.

He strokes the backs of my knuckles, and I shiver. He is looking at me, fire in his eyes. Then he takes a photograph from his pocket, and I lose my footing. It is of my mother. It's the only photograph I have of her, and it should be in my home.

'How did you...?'

'You don't look like your mother. Not even a bit,' he says, and he wags it in front of my face, his voice deep and strange to me. 'You look like him.'

'You'll put that back.'

'When she looked at you, did it feel like she was looking at him? Were her smiles ever meant for *you*?' He is trying to nudge something out of me. To clear a path, to allow something to come through. He will write this down later. He will write: *Teddy comes undone.*

And I do.

I take the photograph, put it safely inside my pocket, then my fingers spill into his collar, and I shake. I shake until his head rocks on his neck, his feet kick out and his black eyes water red.

If this man died, I would dance. For the longest time, my body has felt strange to me, stretched, unfamiliar. As if he stepped into it, the seams puckering, the pockets sagging. Now it returns to me, it is too tight in some places, too loose in others. This is what he has done to me, what fear has done to me. Is this how Gilly felt too?

He wanted me for his shop – a curio, a piece for his collection. And I have fitted well. But not anymore.

I stayed here, working in this shop, to hide, to conceal my identity. Then I met Ada, and I stayed for her. All the while Mr Vincent has watched every footstep, heard every breath. But no longer. He has stepped out of my skin and now my body is my own again. Fear is falling off my bones, away, away. I am not a thing with strings to be drawn and stretched. Not by his hands. Not anymore.

ADA

Men and Devils

'Did you hear the news last night?' I ask.

'What news?' Teddy says.

'A man was found dead in his home not far from here. "Suspicious circumstances." That means murder, doesn't it?'

'I always think so.'

'I wonder why someone wanted to kill him. Perhaps it was revenge or something.'

'It's not always so clear cut,' he says.

'What do you mean?'

He looks at me. 'There are crimes of passion, yes. There are those that are premeditated, thought-through, analytical. But there are others. Simpler, baser.'

'Explain.'

'Some people want eggs and coffee in the morning, others want something else.'

'I'm sorry but you've lost me.' What is he trying to say?

'I'm saying that some are driven by a compulsion. The same compulsion that leads you to go to the fridge, take out your breakfast. It's powerful. It's a need, a necessity.'

'What? Killing?' I ask.

'Yes.'

'I see.'

'Some crimes are simple, calm, easy as cracking an egg into a frying pan. One man wakes, thinks of what to put in his stomach.

Another man wakes and thinks of something different. Something else that will fill him up.'

'I've never thought of it like that. Jesus.'

'My mother once said: "There are no monsters, Ted. Monsters are imagination. But humans are life. And isn't that worse?"'

'Is there anything people won't do?' I ask.

He responds, 'There is nothing people won't do.'

TEDDY

Nature and Nurture

We are together more than we are apart, and I marvel at the parentheses I once lived my life between: quiet breakfasts to start the day, quiet suppers to end, voices made in the back of my throat for company, meals prepared for two, though there was only one.

Now these spaces have been filled.

We walk, and sometimes we do not know where it is we are going. The town might be made of paper, we do not see it. It is thin, insubstantial. It falls away. She tells me of her son. His birth, his deformity, his four years of existence. Four years. Not much, but it is the only portion of her life that has mattered.

'He had the sweetest nose, a mushroom, soft and so kissable. Every time he'd sleep, I'd run my finger down the bridge of it, and he'd sigh. And I'd sigh. It was the happiest I've ever been.'

'That's nice.'

'What's the happiest you've been?' Ada asks me.

I do not know. I do not remember.

'What about a holiday? Family gatherings? Special occasions?' she says.

I look at her. 'Family gatherings?'

Her bottom lip twitches. 'Yeah.'

'We didn't have them.'

There was no family to gather.

'Oh.'

Suddenly I am polishing my mother's glasses with a fold of my shirt, returning them to her nose. *I know she does not see me, or much of anything; I do this because her old self wouldn't have wanted to view the world through smudged glass.*

'Where are my glasses, Teddy?'

'On your nose, Mum.'

'Fetch them for me. They're soaking in the sink.'

'OK.' *I am making a theatre of fetching them, shaking them dry.* 'Here you are.' *I'm lifting her hand to her nose.* 'Feel them?'

'Thanks, Johnny.'

'I'm Teddy.'

'Oh.' *She is smiling.* 'Teddy, fetch me my glasses please. They're in the sink.'

'OK, Mum.'

'You're looking blank. Where did you go?' Ada asks.

'I'm fine. Just remembering something.' I pause. I cannot tell her the truth. 'My seventh birthday. My mum baked a cake so big, it only just fit in the oven. I ate too much and I was sick. Swore I'd never eat cake again. The next morning I was eating the leftovers for breakfast.'

She laughs. She really laughs.

🍎

We take the boy to the park. I nudge words from his lips because I know Ada likes me to. I play with him, I bolster him, and when he puffs out his chest, begins to chitter like a monkey, Ada pats my arm in thanks. I do it for this.

I like her fingernails, the clean pink shells of them, cut precise and efficient. I like the hangnail on her thumb; I imagine twisting it off with my teeth. I like the mole behind her ear. It juts out, small as a nut.

There are finer things too, that I find, collect up:

Her left brow risen a fraction higher than her right; her freckles like a splattering of mud over her neck, chaotic and perfect; the hair behind her ears always oily because she is always patting it back; her face, wrinkled, screwed up when she tries to suck crumbs from her teeth.

🍎

'They say all daughters become their mothers, and all sons become their fathers. I hope I do not become mine.'

There is a bubble of laughter in my throat. I have heard these words, in some shape, every day for thirty-three years. 'I hope I don't become my father either.'

She looks at me. A deep, invasive gaze. I want to take her chin between my fingers and turn her head away. I am not someone you want to look at too closely. If I tell her about my mother, and what she kept in the toes of her slippers, would she rise, pinch Albie to her chest, run? I wonder how fast and how far she would go before she felt safe enough to stop. I sit on my hands.

'Why do you say that?'

I shrug. 'Lots of reasons. What is your mother like?'

'Cold. Nothing can warm her up. Not even a baby. Although I think that's what my father hoped for.' She pauses, scratching her temple; she is hiding her eyes. 'But she's that way for a reason. There's always a reason.'

'I'm sorry.' I attempt to hold her hand but it is more like a poke I withdraw mine so quickly. 'You have a difficult relationship?'

'Yes. And you? With your father?'

'Some people shouldn't be parents. They are broken, then they break their children. They can't always help it. But some can.'

Her brows ping into her hairline. 'Does that mean we are broken?

'It means I am. Troubled parents make troubled children.'

She pokes my hand, pointedly. 'So, un-trouble yourself.'

ADA

Splinter and Bee Sting

'I used to take things when I was a child. Collect things,' Teddy says.

'What sort of things?'

'All sort of things. Pens, bits of paper my mother had written on. Pieces of string or cotton. Paperclips, books, gel washing tablets. One burst in my eye once. My mother panicked herself silly.'

'Why did you want those?' He is pinching his neck again.

He shrugs, shakes his head.

'Tell me.' It comes out as a command rather than a question, and I bite my lip. 'That sounded really rude. I'm sorry.'

He is smiling, he has stopped touching his neck. 'That's OK. I don't know. I just liked it. It made me feel good ... for a while anyway. My father liked to collect too. I stopped when I released that.'

'What sort of things?'

'"Things"?'

'Yes.'

His mouth opens, closes. 'He didn't collect ... "things".'

'I'm confused.'

'My mum used to say the house was making mischief,' he says, and I feel as if I have missed a step. 'A pen would go missing, or her shoe or a bottle of shampoo, and she'd find me, put her hands on her hips like this and sigh, a great gust of air. I wondered how she fit all of that air inside her. Then she'd say, "Ted, I think this house is making mischief again. It's taking all our things. Where do you suppose it's putting them? They've got to be somewhere. Shall we look for them?"'

'She didn't know?'

'Oh, she knew. But she wanted me to have the chance to give them back.'

'She's sounds very fair.' I think my own mother would not have been so fair.

'I'd fetch the bottle of shampoo or the napkin ring, and she'd always say, "Good old house. It's returned them to us, hasn't it? It's always best to be honest, you see, Ted? Return the things you take. It's always better to be good".'

'Why make out it was the house though?'

'Perhaps she liked to pretend it wasn't me, that this thing I did, didn't happen. She must have seen so much of my father in me then. Perhaps she was just trying to teach away his habits. But I'm not like my father. Not really. Not in the ways that matter.'

'We all have parts of our parents in us. We can't help it.'

He looks at me. 'What about you?'

'What about me?'

'How do you match up to your parents?'

'I'd like to say I don't but I know I do. I take too-large bites like my father. I can't leave a crumb on my plate. If I do, I have to go back and eat it, even if it's stale. I don't know why. It sounds strange, but we don't have any choice in what we inherit.'

'And your mother?'

I fish in my bag for nothing in particular, offer him one of Albie's sweets. He smiles, takes it, and I see a small brown hair stuck to its side, say, 'Oh!' He drops it in his mouth, and I turn away, cringe.

'Well? Your mother?'

'She is smart, my mother, smarter than my father, than me, than anyone. I don't think I've ever really seen her properly. She lived through something when she was a girl. And it has left some pretty deep marks.'

'MUMMY!'

Albie is on the floor, a stripe of blood on his arm, fat tears bobbing on his cheeks. I am there, rising, moving between breaths.

'It's OK, bean. It's alright. Just a little cut. It's all better now.'

I do not make his pale face red with a slap, like mother; I do not rage, a sting on my tongue and teeth; I am not her. I am not her. I soften his cries, clean his arm, keep him until he is ready to go again.

I am not her. I am not her.

🍎

Teddy returns to the shop. We return to our endless route round the town. I try to spear words from the lips of the people we meet on the way but they are solid and I cannot move them.

On our way home, I pause outside Berry & Vincent. I check on Teddy. But I do not see a frightened man anymore. And so I go on my way. The sight of the two of them filling my eyes:

Proprietor and assistant stood shoulder to shoulder. Vincent pressing closer, closer, as if breathing Teddy down. Teddy, wooden, hand pushing him back. But there is force there too now. And I wonder if Teddy's hand will leave splinters.

TEDDY

Watchful and Wanting Men

I look for her. I tell myself I am not, but I am. My body thrums, hot and sharp, as if there is glass in my skin. People are in the street. I'd like to blot them out with my finger so I am able to spot her more easily. Mr Vincent stands by me. There is a noise in the air. I touch my lips, and there it is, the plea I make for her to visit me.

'Come. Come. Come to Berry & Vincent.'

🍎

'Speak to me. Speak to me.'

She goes to the bakery, buys a chocolate tart for the boy. I watch. Up and down the street she goes. The bookshop, the café, the bakery again. Up and down, up again. She does it because she must.

'Speak to me. Speak to me.' That is what she is thinking. I know. I recognise that look on her face. I've worn it myself. She is lonely.

'Speak to me. Speak to me.' I used to think it too.

She avoided the shop yesterday and today, carried on to The Mermaid. Why? Perhaps she is worried I will tire of her, shrug off her friendship. But I won't. I followed her, I couldn't help it.

She has so many questions. How can I tell her that every job I have ever had ends in only one way: colleagues sniffing out my history like dogs with their noses to the earth. I look too much like my father, walk like him. What if I collect children like him too? And so I had to go.

We are similar, she and I. Up and down the street she goes, hoping someone will come to her, nudge back the silence. 'Speak to me. Speak to me.'

Mr Vincent stands behind me. He looks at her like she is a bird. He looked at Gilly the same way. But Ada is not Gilly. She will not be bent by his fingers and stuffed into his pocket. She will not. I will not let it happen. She is my friend.

I am stiff, wooden, then I see her, and I am human, my body becomes what a body should be. Always, I'm holding my breath, like the children do when they pass the shop, then I hear her voice, and I breathe. In. Breathe. In. Breathe. Her. In.

'Why her? Why Ada?' I ask.

He will not speak. I glance round, see a smile on his thin lips, wolfish. My fingers twitch, begin to shake

I step in front of him, blotting out his view of her.

She is not his bird. She is my bird.

TEDDY

Coffee and Apples

'Your dad used to have this smile, the corner of his mouth twitching like something was under his skin. When he smiled like that, I knew he was thinking about something bad. Of course, I never knew what, Teddy.'

Today, her eyes are clear. We are sat together at the dining table. A blanket is ruched round her hips. Her hair is a mess of tangles so I take a brush and tidy it up. Pick the tough spittle-balls apart with my nails.

'I remember those quiet evenings, with his arms around me, my head on his chest. I used to feel his heart bob under my cheek. I used to like it, tickling my skin. I didn't know what sort of heart it was then.'

I do not speak. I let her speak. It is better for her to throw out her memories instead of clutching them inside her head.

'Johnny'd sit ever so quiet. He didn't fidget. Used to bug me, made me feel like a child who couldn't get comfortable.' She strokes my hand. 'I'd glance up sometimes and his eyes would be wide open, but he was looking at something inside his own head. And, Heaven help me, that mouth of his would twitch and twitch. That's the smile he kept for his girls.'

'I'm glad you don't have that smile, Ted.' She rubs her finger across my lips. 'Don't think I could bear to see it on you. Promise me you'll never have that smile?'

'I promise, Mum.'

'Good. Good boy. You're not like him.' She looks at me, into me, like fingers burrowing deep into the earth. She does this more and more. Searches for that bad thing he had inside him.

Sometimes, I take myself to the mirror. I search my face, stretch it into different shapes. I pull back the silky eyelids, open my mouth wide, look, look. As if that bad thing will be at the back of my throat. Like a slice of apple, rotten. I check my ears, I check under the pink shells of my nails. I cannot see anything. I am just me.

She points to an ant that has crept under the skirting, its legs like bits of cotton, its body no bigger than the eye of a needle. 'Stand on that for me? I hate ants. Creepy little things. Kill it. Quick! Get it.'

'I don't want to kill it.'

She smiles then. 'Good boy.'

She has done this before. It is a new habit of hers. Two weeks ago, a bird, a blackbird, landed on her windowsill, looked in on us, as if it pitied us with its marble eyes. Mum cried, 'Teddy. Teddy! My shoe. Hit it with my shoe. Quick. Get it quick!'

'I can't do that, Mum,' I said. And she smiled, like this was exactly what she wanted me to say. I realised afterwards, that this was her looking inside me again.

She squeezes toothpaste over her cereal, pours in apple juice. In a moment, she will forget what both are called. 'He's not there.'

But her voice sounds weak. I want her to say it again, this time stronger, like she is sure. 'He's not.'

'He's not.'

'A few of the papers called him Johnny Appletree. Like that man from the history books. The years passed, and mums and dads would say to their children, "You be quiet now, you go to sleep or I'll call for him." A warning, a cautionary tale.' Her cheeks are red, dimpled with tears. 'Call him three times, "Johnny Appletree, Johnny Appletree, Johnny Appletree, come to me." And his ghost would put naughty children in his sack of apples, take them to the orchard. Bury them. Deep.'

'You haven't told me this before.'

'Made me sick.'

'Don't let it make you sick anymore.'

I don't think she hears me though. She is retreating, running back into herself. I see it in her face. 'Mum?'

'Go and fetch me some coffee, Teddy.'

'You don't drink coffee, Mum.'

'I do. You're wrong. Stop trying to confuse me. I know what I like. I know!' Tears fall and dab the cuff of her shirt. 'Get out. Get out, Teddy!'

I do as she asks, I close the kitchen door, then I go to the bathroom, stand in front of the mirror and look for him.

ADA

Singing and Shadows

Teddy's eyes run over me like bristles. I want to ask him to look away, but the words gum up my teeth and I cannot get them out. He is strange to me today, his features are sharper, he walks close, too close, so that every other step, our feet bang together.

'Here, let me take that.' He grabs the bag, little finger grazing my knuckles, leaving a vein of heat in my skin.

'It's only got lunch in. It's not heavy.'

He shrugs, smiles.

'Bean, don't go too far.'

Albie gallops over, throwing himself into our bodies. The bag smacks to the ground and three oranges are tossed from the lip. Teddy kneels, gathers them up, holding the last one to his nose. His eyes come to me, and he breathes in. Deep. As if it is *me* he is breathing down, and not half-bad fruit.

'Mummy! That hurts!'

I jump, see five marks in the meat of Albie's palm. 'Oh! I'm sorry, bean.'

He grumbles, rubs the marks away. When I look back at Teddy, his eyes are on a piece of loose thread in his cuff. He picks it free, throws it to the ground. Then he smiles at me. And I breathe.

'You OK?' he asks.

I nod, pat myself down, as if checking I am all here. 'Yeah. Fine.'

He ruffles Albie's hair, walks with him ahead. They are talking, their faces light, carefree. I watch the back of Teddy's head, recall a conversation I overheard earlier. Two townspeople walked past my window, the men with oily chins and sweaters tied neat round their shoulders.

'I saw Teddy in there yesterday, inside the shop,' said the first.

'Well, he does work there.'

'He looked ... different.'

'How so?'

'I don't know. Just different.' The first man paused, picking at a large spot on his chin. I was close enough to see crusts drop into his collar.

'What was he doing?' asked the second.

'He was singing.'

'Singing? Can't imagine anyone singing in a place like that.'

'That's what I heard. Came right through the open window. A nursery rhyme, I think.'

'Odd.'

'Never seen Vincent look so rattled.'

'In that case, I hope he keeps singing. I hope he sings day and night, and he shakes the bones from that man's body. Only what he deserves.'

Teddy turns, and I glimpse his smile, wide, full of teeth. His hand is gentle round Albie's, as if he is made of glass and not bone and blood.

'Where's your mum, fella?' Teddy pauses, waits for me to catch up. He is looking at me again, but not like before. 'Albie found a one-legged pigeon.'

'Hmm.'

I shake the shadows from my mind. Teddy is just Teddy.

ADA

Mother and Father

'How did your mother die?'

Teddy picks at the skin round his nails and tiny beads of blood emerge. 'It was a stroke.' He winces and sucks his finger. I regret asking the question.

'I'm sorry. I can be tactless.'

'No. Don't be. She died of a stroke when I was seventeen. It happened so fast and … quietly. I was sitting with her at the time.'

I take his hand. 'You were with her. It would have given her comfort.'

His eyes snap up to my own. 'I – I hadn't thought about that.'

'You're not a mum. Believe me, it would have helped.'

'She'd suffered for so long I liked to think she could finally rest.'

'Was she ill?'

'No. No. I didn't mean that. She could never be still. She was always moving, always talking. Toward the end, she didn't know what she was saying, her mind wasn't as strong as it used to be.'

'Did you live with your father after she died?'

His faces twitches, and I wonder what I have said wrong. 'No, no. I didn't. He was dead.'

'You said he wasn't a good person? What did you mean?'

'He hurt people.'

I glance at the scar on his temple, like an apple seed. 'He was abusive?'

He shakes his head. 'Not to me. I don't remember him.'

'At all?'

'At all. What I know of him, I learnt from my mother. Before she died, it all flooded out.'

'What did?'

'Everything he had done,' he says, as if it should already be plain to me. 'My mother carried it all like it was her burden. It killed her in the end. He killed her – in his way. She was only young when she died. She didn't look young though.'

'What was your father a collector of?'

'What?'

'Not long ago you told me he collected things.'

'He didn't collect "things",' Teddy says.

'Insects? Animals? Did he study them?'

'No.' He is looking at something to the right of me, intently, as if it is something he has never seen before. I touch the side of my head, my ear, my mole. My mole?

'You don't want to tell me, do you?'

'I don't like to talk about him.'

'Oh. I'm sorry.'

We stop. We continue.

'People,' he says, finally.

TEDDY

Venom and Vice

Mr Vincent is upstairs, tapping, writing his notes, but I am not the man he knew before. Now I do not stay for him, to understand him, my relevance in his shop. I stay for her. I cannot leave her. We are the same.

It strikes me he knows her far better than me. He is a collector, he will know her rhythms, her routines. He will have a clearer picture than I can hope to gain in a matter of months. When he appears at the bottom of the stairs sometime later, I tap the counter with my hand. 'Come here.'

He does as I ask.

'Tell me everything?'

Silence.

I run my fingers over the bowl of rings, inset with brown and yellow incisors, nudge it off the shelf. It shatters, a wave of tooth and shard across the floor. I feel the crunch under my boot. His body jolts, as if he has been struck. His mouth opens, closes, and his eyes widen into large black buttons.

'It's been two years, you'll be an expert on her by now. So come on, tell me, I want to know.'

I slam my hand into the shelf. Glass and pot and porcelain crash to the floor. A keening sound erupts from his mouth, sharp and animal.

'Tell me!'

His body shakes, finger to toe. I grab him. His gasps, short, desperate sounds, like a child. I hear the thump of his panicked little heart. Feel it in my skin like there are two now, not one.

'Tell me.'

I lean close, closer, rest my ear against his lips. Finally he speaks.

I wait for him to finish, then say, 'Stop following her round the shop, stop touching her, dipping your clammy little fingers into her pockets and taking her things – yes, I've seen. I've seen it all.'

He is looking at me from under the wiry white roofs of his brows. He moves away, puts the counter between our bodies.

'She doesn't know what you're really like. You're always careful, aren't you?' I say.

Mr Vincent opens his mouth to speak, pale tongue like gristle. 'Why her?'

'What?' I demand.

'Why her?'

This is just another crumb for him to pour over. Another piece for his collection.

'She is important to me.'

There is thunder between our chests. I can almost hear it. He smiles that smile. I pick up a safety pin, twist it between my fingers. His lips would be warm, soft as butter.

'She'd be so frightened. If you told her who you are. Who you've got inside you,' Mr Vincent says.

'You leave her and the boy be.'

He nods. Looks at me, searching for something, like fingers burrowing deep into the earth. My chest tightens. I know what for. My mother looked for it too.

He's not there, I think. But the words drop from my lips as well.

'He *is* there,' he says as he moves by me. 'She's brought him out of you.'

I laugh. I laugh even after he has gone. He's wrong. He's so wrong. I am not my father I am me. Me.

I go to a rusted old mirror, wipe the dust with my sleeve. I look. That is not his face, it is mine. Those eyes, that chin. They are mine. That smile, twitching in the corner, like a bug under my skin. It is mine too.

I close my eyes. Breathe. I open them, pat the corner of my mouth with my finger. Make it still.

TEDDY

Perfume and Possession

I could be the boy's father. I could swaddle him, run a cold cloth over his skin when he is ill. I could cook for him, nag him to clean up his toys. I could love him like he is my son. I could read him stories like my mother did for me. What would she think if she saw me? My mother? She would be proud.

She would say, 'Teddy Bear, you're such a good father. I'm proud of you, darling.' She would laugh, like she used to, we would laugh together.

'Thanks, Mum.'

'I love you, Ted.'

'I love you too, Mum.'

🍎

Ada has gone home and the closed sign has been turned, but still I smell the perfume she regularly pats onto her wrists. Spices, ginger, it is warming and I breathe it in. But there is something else too. Oil, her unwashed skin. The salt of it. I lick my lips.

Mr Vincent watches me. Finally, I say, 'Why did you kill him? Your father?'

Silence.

'I hated him.'

'Why?'

Silence again.

'I could tell her who you really are.' He throws out his stomach, chin thrown into the air. A flash of courage, of fire.

'And I could tell them about what *you* did. You've lived here for fifty years. You've built your collection here, you've built a life here. What did you do before this? Where did you live?'

He sinks his teeth into his lip.

'Rye is ripe for rumours. Do you really think you could stay here if they knew?' I laugh. 'They'd run you out of the town. They've wanted you gone for five decades. And if I can find proof, so can they,' I say.

'Stop.'

'They'll discover what you did to Gilly.'

'Enough.'

'Why risk what you've built here?'

He nods, looks me in the eyes, and I know he won't speak.

The smell of her hangs in the air. I follow it, holding everything she held. The books, the bell jars, the cotton and lace. I hold them to my banging heart, breathe her in, until my lungs are full and she is deep in my skin.

TEDDY

Good and Evil

'Perhaps we are all monsters, really,' Ada says.

'Why do you say that? Where has this come from?' I ask.

From the corner of my eye, I see Ada shrug. She is small today, her skin clammy, her hair mussed into feathers, poking out from her head. Like a bird. My bird. I want to stroke it down, unpick the knots. Tidy her up.

'Perhaps we all have a darkness inside of us that we hold down like a scream. Even as children.' She looks at Albie, playing a game of chicken with the tireless waves. He squeals, stamps his feet into the sand, fists pumping the air with weapons only he and sea can see.

'We all have good and bad inside us, Ada.' I take her hand. Her fingernails are bitten, ragged, and I rip at the tiny arrows. She winces. Yanks it away.

'What you were saying before about that killer with a hunger in his belly. You think he had that as a boy, or he picked it up like an infection? Something life put inside him?' Her face is grey as slate. She is looking at me for an answer. I pull back her hand and tidy up her nails. She does not notice, her eyes are at once full and empty. 'Man passes on madness to man.'

'Where has this come from?'

She looks away, looks back, sighs deeply. She is coming back to herself. 'My aunt texted me yesterday and ... it churned a few things up. Things I've been trying to come to terms with.'

'What?'

'Jerry came to visit us just after you and I met. She told me about my mother's childhood,' Ada says.

I wrap my arm around her. I am listening but only half listening. There is a clot of blood on her lip, like a red bead. She licks it away, and I am disappointed because I wanted to.

'Her father abused her for many years. He turned her inside out. And I never knew any of this.'

'Why do you think he did that?'

She picks at her lip. 'Perhaps he couldn't hold down his darkness. Perhaps someone hurt *him* as a boy, and trauma is something we carry in our blood. It was bound to come out. Some men just like to hurt women. But women are not dolls, you cannot put our bodies back together once you have taken them apart. My mother did not fit back together. Not as she should have.'

This is what she has been holding back.

'But she got away eventually?'

She says, 'Yes. Dad helped her.' Tears drip into her open hands. She wipes them into the sand quickly as if they are bruising her.

'My grandfather. One of *those* men.' I see fire in her face and wonder if she will burn me. 'Women shouldn't have to be afraid. We shouldn't have to protect our bodies with alarms and sprays. Tell me, when you go out at night, what do you have in your pocket? Money? Yes. I have in mine a siren, a plastic voice I need because my own voice isn't loud enough. It calls for me, for help. I have it in case a man like my grandfather comes.' The words shoot from her crusty lips, a fire spitting ash. They are hot, I feel them on my cheek. I warm myself with her heat. She has such a lovely heat.

'Do you have it now?'

'Yes. My aunt gave it to me when I hit my teens. Still works. I'll give Albie one too when he's older. It doesn't matter that he's a boy before you say anything. Boys need sirens too.'

I think of those girls, my father's girls. Did they have alarms in their pockets? They can't have been loud enough.

'Wouldn't it be good if we could take the bad out of a body like we take out a heart or a lung?' She smiles sadly, then shakes herself like a dog, free of a flea. 'Eurgh. I've been so dreary today, haven't I?'

'Not at all. It must have been nice to see your aunt. Was it the first time she's visited you in Rye?'

'Yes. I hadn't seen her in two years. Not since I moved here. We talk on the phone occasionally but ... she's busy. Back-breaking job, husband, sons.'

'But she's gone now.'

'She's gone now.

'At least you'll always have me.'

She frowns. 'Pardon?'

'Nothing,' I say.

ADA

Nettles and Knives

'What are you doing?' I ask. Teddy's arm is around me again, fingers twitching at a knot in my hair. I push him away. 'Can you stop please?'

'Sorry,' he says, but his voice is sharp, full of nettles. He was doing that yesterday, as we spoke about my mother and grandfather, fiddling with my hair. It irritated me.

We walk in silence. I check his eyes. It has become a habit almost. I check when I want to know which Teddy I have with me. He is the second man today: elusive, persuasive, possessive.

'You … you seem different lately. You don't seem like yourself.'

His head cocks, his eyes are on me, wide and black. 'I am,' he says loudly, rushed. 'I am me. Who else would I be? Of course I'm me.' He laughs, high and strident. The sound tears into my ears.

I stop, stop him too. 'What's wrong? I'm worried about you.'

'No need to worry. I'm alright.'

'It was just little things at first, things I put out of my mind, but you are behaving oddly. *You are.*' He looks at me sadly, his face falling, dripping, like paint down a wall, and guilt nudges me. 'Here.' I take his hand. 'Let's walk together.'

He smiles then. The left corner of his mouth twitches, as if there is a bug under his skin, a moth fidgeting to be out. I want to stamp it down with my finger. I do not like the look of it.

'How is work?'

'Very good.'

'Hmm.'

'I'm going to dress the window on Sunday.'

'Really? I thought only Mr Vincent did that?'

'I'm going to dress the window on Sunday.' He says again, grins. 'I can't wait for you to see it.'

'Um ... me too.'

'I want to be there when you see it,' Teddy says.

'If you like.'

There is something touching my ear. I turn around and it is him.

'What are you doing back there?'

'You have a mole.'

'I know. Is it bothering you?' I tap his hand away.

'It's soft.'

His hand is back. I shift, put some space between us but it does not feel enough.

Albie comes to us, and Teddy lifts him up, runs with him in his arms, as if he is an arrow flying from a bow. 'Spread your arms, fella. You're flying. We're flying together!'

Their laughter roils through the air, a ribbon blown and stretched in the wind. I want to laugh too. But I can't. The laughter in the wind stops at me, drops like rags. Because that rock is in my belly again. I have swallowed something cold and hard, and now it sickens me.

'Higher! Faster!' Albie screams. Teddy obliges, playing with my son as if he is his son too. 'Alright, alright. You're a big boy though, you know. You're heavy.'

'Be careful,' I say.

'OK, Mummy.'

Albie wriggles, coiling himself round Teddy. I want to part them, put my body between theirs. I bite my lip, rip a shard of dried skin away. Blood becomes a river over my tongue. I wince, cup my mouth, and suddenly Teddy is here, touching a tissue to my lip. The blood soaks into the white. And Teddy strokes my face.

'You can stop now.'

He snaps his teeth together, and it is the *snick* of a knife through an apple. 'But I don't want to.'

TEDDY

Photographs and Fallen Birds

He has photographs of her, Ada. Crusted with a veneer of dropped food and oily finger-marks, tied with a ratty piece of string. The bottom step of the staircase lifts up, and I found him on his knees there yesterday, rubbing his hands along the collection: everything he has ever taken from her body – bracelets, rings, even a hangnail, pinned into a velvet cushion. Strands of hair, tissues, notes. Photographs.

I wanted to break his head upon the stair then. I closed my eyes, threw the greased ball of it down, and it cracked. I could smell the stink of him in my nostrils. Blood. But then I opened my eyes and he was still there, a tick, thick and full and greedy.

I collected it all up later, of course, left him an empty space under the stair. I thought he'd learnt his place. I thought I'd pinched that fire in him. I thought he knew Ada was mine, and not his. He will learn it now. I will make it clear.

🍎

He is upstairs, typing. I pull a stool into the centre of the floor, run my hand along the bellies of all his birds. I wonder if he gives them names. If one of them is called Ada. They are soft, like silk. Gilly'd thought a flock had flown through the window. She'd wanted them to be free. They will be free now.

I cut the first bird's string, and it falls, empty of blood and of grace. Thunder across the ground as more follow. Their eyes blink at me, large and questioning. I cut, cut. And the birds are alive again, flying again. Until they fall, and then they are puddles of feathered things on the floor.

Is this Ada?

Is this?

This bird?

It is not Ada anymore. I laugh. I throw down the scissors, rip the creatures from their strings. Free, free now.

'Are you Ada? What about you?'

I wheel my hands through the air, beaks cut into my palms but I don't feel them. Blood drips into my cuffs. I do not feel that either. The typing has stopped. Is he listening? I hope he is listening.

Hear this one? And this one?

The floor is a dark pool, glistening like oil. I hear them in my mind, their voices. They thank me. They lift their dead eyes and look at me, shuffle their wings and praise me like I am their God.

They are finally free. And so is Ada.

I leave him to his fallen birds.

🍎

Ada comes into the shop and he stitches himself to her side, greasy fingers trailing down her back. She does not notice, her attention is on the boy. He is doing it to hurt me, to wound me. It is payback for the cut birds. His fingers say, *Mine*, his eyes say, *Do you see?*

Albie runs further into the shop. Ada follows. Mr Vincent takes a step, I make him take it back. We look at one another and there is fire inside our chests. We'll burn her. We'll burn them both. I lift the scissors, and before he can react, I lunge, cut a crooked shape into his earlobe. He stumbles, hands to his head. A red river running. I offer him a tissue from my pocket. He mops his skin, takes step back. He looks at me. Takes another.

He thinks it is the shop. He thinks it has turned on him. But it hasn't.

When he is distracted, I turn the dolls, face them away, as if now they cannot bear to look at him. I move the birds and foxes closer to the door, as if they are moving through the shop at night on soft, silent paws, trying to get out. I shred the buttery wings of his butterflies, silk confetti under my nails, which I pick out later with my teeth. I set wheels spinning, china rattling, I throw shadows he can never follow back to me. I unstitch and unscrew. I put life into still bodies, make them move. Moving away from him.

There are hundreds of clocks in the shop. Some as bright as gold, others dull, forgotten, rust in their gears. I go about the shop, set them all for midnight and when they go off, calling, screaming to him in his bed, I watch outside as the lights come on and his strange, stiff body stumbles about, afraid. He runs one way, then he runs another. He does not know which way to go. He cannot find them. I have moved them.

He thinks it is the shop. He thinks it has turned on him. But it hasn't.

The clocks stop, he returns to bed. Upstairs, he looks out of the window, quickly turns away from me. Was he shaking?

He was shaking.

ADA

Hearts and Blood

The shop window is robed in red, the red of hearts and of blood. Brocade curtains fall gracefully, tucked in at the middle like a woman's waist. In the centre is a bed of velvet, stippled with gold: rings and pocket watches, books with gold-tipped edges, dried flowers, bright and amber, butterflies, with their bronze-dipped wings.

'Oh my...'

But I am not looking at them.

I'm looking at the three wax dolls standing in the middle. A boy, a man, a woman, matching in green suits. The boy wears a cap, pulled low, the strange crushed shell of his ear poking out. The woman's mouth is painted red, bright and bloody. The man's chin is sharp as a blade, his arms are round the boy and woman, matchstick fingers digging into their bodies.

'Mummy! It's me. It's me!'

These little wax people look at me, as if they really see me, as if they wonder at my face as I wonder at theirs. My legs are shaking, banging against Albie's back. I want to push my hand through the glass, crunch them into balls. And I want to run. I want to run until I have worn my feet through.

The figures are different, but somehow look the same, as if they are the same person spread into three. Teddy. Ada. Albie.

'Woah! You love it that much?' Teddy catches me, and I reel away, dragging my son with me.

Albie is tugging on my fingers, confusion in his face. Words collect on my tongue, but they do not come out. People in the street move around us, a river of them, and I wish they would take me up like a rock, move me away.

'Ada? You've gone very pale. Are you alright?'

'That's ... that's ... Why did you do this?'

Teddy's face is puzzled, drawing in. 'I thought it would be a surprise. A little something to make you smile. Albie likes it. Look...'

Albie does. He is giggling, pointing a chubby finger at the boy. The boy with his ears, his mouth, his nose.

'They're us.'

'Of course they are. Who else would they be?' Teddy laughs. 'They're made of wax. It didn't take much effort really. A bit of paint, a bit of paring with a knife. You like them, don't you? I knew you would.'

Their eyes are black. Why are they black? Albie and I have brown eyes. I look at Teddy, the rock in my belly big as a moon.

He's given us his eyes.

ADA

Scratches and Kisses

They've got their eyes on me. The small people he made. They watch from their shelf, nesting in a bed the size of a shoe box. The boy between the bodies of the man and woman. As if he is their son, sleeping away a nightmare.

I made Teddy take them down yesterday. I made my shivering body still, forced him into the shop and demanded he remove them. Mr Vincent helped him, careful not to get too close to me, as if I might burn his cuffs.

Teddy asked why I was upset, eyes low and troubled, and I wondered if I was unjustified. Albie enjoyed it. He clapped and begged to hold his miniature. I would not let him.

'I thought you'd like them. I worked hard on them,' Teddy had said.

'I don't. I don't like them. Please don't put them in the window again.' I looked out then, at the townspeople moving through the street. They'd only seen dolls, children's playthings. They had not seen *us*.

We left, quickly.

Teddy came to our house yesterday evening to apologise again. I forgave him. I told myself I had overreacted, that the guilt in the shape of his mouth and wrinkle in his brow was honest. He had made a bad joke.

Now, standing in the shop, seeing them again, I feel unbalanced, as if the shop has moved, changed around me, and I must learn its new shape.

'Ada. Come here. You've got something on your face.'

He hooks a seed from the corner of my mouth. Looks into my eyes. 'Are you alright?'

'Yes.'

'I thought it would make you laugh. I *am* really sorry. It was wrong of me. I was just being stupid. Stupid!'

He scratches his neck, nails ripping through the skin. I pull his hand down, more out of habit than anything else.

'It's ... fine.'

A wind chime hangs above the counter, made from animal bones, yellowed and brittle. When a breeze snags open the door, the bones sing their strange clicking song. I feel like that wind chime now. Its bones are my bones.

Rattling.

'Are you sure you're alright?'

'Mmm.'

Mr Vincent does not look at me. Why won't he look at me?

'Shall we go and get some lunch?' Teddy again. He smiles, and I look into his face, inside his eyes, between his lips. He is just Teddy. He's being truthful. He's sorry. It is all in my head.

My bones still, and so do the bones above our heads. The clicking song finishes, and I breathe. 'OK.'

As we leave the shop, Teddy brings Albie's hand to his mouth, kisses the back of it. I see it. Mr Vincent sees it. I drive them apart, body between theirs, take my son's hand from him.

ADA

Sharp Hearts and Blunt Words

'He's such a good fella,' Teddy says.

'He is.'

'Our good little boy.'

'What did you say?'

He shakes his head. 'Nothing.'

Panic is stuck in my throat. I pinch my wrist, make it go down. Then I look at Teddy, look and look.

'The shop *is* different.' I say eventually. 'Mr Vincent is different too.' I say it, so I can see what else is in his face. But I just see Teddy. These past few days, he has been better. Like his old self. We neither of us have mentioned what happened with the dolls, or how he kissed Albie's hand.

'Yes. I think I've finally settled there.'

'Hmm.' *But you hated it*? I think. *You were afraid of it.*

'Where is Albie's father?'

The question is sudden, blunt. I must close my mouth, taste and try the words before I speak. How to explain and keep some semblance of dignity?

'He ... I ... He's not ... He doesn't know. I don't ... he's not around.'

'Do they look similar?'

'You're very curious today.' He watches Albie like a bird watching a mouse. But then he blinks, looks at me and his eyes are his own again.

'No. They don't. From what I remember, he had blonde hair, blue eyes ... and he smelt a bit.'

'So he looks more like us.'

'Me,' I say.

'What?'

'Me. He looks like me.'

'Yeah. Of course. He has your nose, your chin. He's the spitting image of you,' Teddy says.

I pause. 'You really want kids, don't you?' Or has he already had a child? Has he lost a son or a daughter? Has he just not told me about them? Is that what I see in the lines in his face? Grief? Is this the reason for his odd behaviour?

He is watching Albie again, and despite it all, I want to tell him to stop.

Teddy calls him over, props him on his knee. 'Hey, fella. Would you like a cookie?'

'Yeah!'

'Only one though, OK? Let's save the rest for dessert.'

My heart jumps, as if it has been tugged by string. How can I tell him to stop? To remind him that one day he will have a family, a son, but not my son.

'Hold still.'

Teddy licks his finger, dabs the sugar from my bottom lip, sticks it between his teeth and sucks. I rise, cringing, walk to the bin, throw away our rubbish. When I return, Teddy is holding Albie tight to his chest.

'Who loves you?'

'Mummy does.'

'Who else?'

'...You do?'

'How much?'

'This much?' Albie throws out his arms.

'That's not enough. I love you more than that.'

'This much?'

'That's better.'

I lift Albie into my arms, 'What are you doing?'

Teddy rises, shrugs. 'Just playing.' His lips are pinched into a grim line.

'You're ... you're angry with *me*?'

'No of course not. It's just we ... we were having a good time together.'

'Why were you saying those things to him, Teddy?'

'I should get back to the shop.' He kisses Albie on the ear, slips past. I watch him go.

'Mummy?'

'Yes.'

'When's Teddy coming back?'

'I don't know. Bean, what else did he say to you?' My heart is rapping through my bones. Albie stares at Teddy's retreating back, a fold of longing in his brow. I touch it with my finger, tap and it goes as he laughs.

'He said I'm a good boy. He said he loves us, Mummy. Do we love him?'

TEDDY

Father and Son

Ada's hand is around the Albie's. His face is open, light, freckles like brown crumbs. The sun punches its way through the clouds and turns the ground into a chess board, and we are the pieces, moving between shadowed squares. Ada is talking about the shop, about Mr Vincent, his behaviour.

'Is something bothering him? He seems very jumpy.'

'He's fine.'

'You really think so? It's like he's scared in his own shop.' Her eyes are sharp, there is darkness where darkness shouldn't be.

'He's fine.'

'Hmm.' A wrinkle between her brows. I reach out, touch it, and it flattens. She gasps. 'What are you doing?'

'Getting a bug. Wrinkly little thing.'

She breathes and smiles. 'Oh. Thanks.'

'You seem a bit on edge?'

'I am.'

'Why?'

She looks at me, looks into me. For something. What something? 'I'm not really sure. Just a weird feeling at the minute.'

'Odd.'

She is looking all over my face now, for a way to get in. 'Odd,' she agrees.

The park is full, bursting with mud-freckled children and bug-eyed parents. Cries of delight are long and low in my ear, an interminable noise that wraps round my head. Albie does not make such a racket, his voice is clear and sweet. But then I suppose all parents are biased in that way.

Albie and I sit together on the ground, twisting grass between our fingers. I cup my mouth to my hands and make a blade whistle. His eyes widen, lashes grazing his cheeks like bits of soft cotton. Ada has gone to retrieve his hat from by the swings. I smile, draw him close.

'Albie, can you say "Daddy"?'

He nods. 'Yes.'

'Say it. Say Daddy.'

He laughs, shakes he head. 'You're not my daddy.'

'Are you sure?'

He frowns. He has that wrinkle between his brows like his mother. 'But...'

'Say it. Now, please.'

'Daddy.'

'Yes, son?'

ADA

Rust and Resin

Something *has* changed inside Berry & Vincent. It is not the window display, cotton-and-lace gloves hanging amid orbs of old pocket watches, like a constellation of strange stars. It is not the sign, nothing that tips or has slipped and become askew. There is something. I tell myself there is nothing but, yes, there *is* something.

Teddy welcomes us, says, 'I'm on my break now. Would you like to go to the park again?'

'Can we get some bread? For the ducks?' Albie says.

'Of course we can, bean,' Teddy replies.

That word, it is a box to the ears. 'What did you just call h—'

He puts a hand on my back, and I feel as if it might go right through me, he might tear me into an unfamiliar shape. 'Darling, are you OK? You look a bit peaky.'

'I ... I'm fine. I just need some air.' *I have not imagined it all. I have not.*

Mr Vincent shrinks away from Teddy, and I wonder, has he always been such a small man? Then I see it, the rusted dynamic, and I wonder who now is the proprietor and who is the assistant. We leave the shop.

I thought it must be grief, the anniversary of his mother's death, the absence of a child, a wife, a family of his own, a trigger that had jolted him, unbalanced him. Now I see that it is not.

There is a smile on his face, and it frightens me.

'So I was thinking tonight I could come over and read Albie, here, a bedtime story? Huh? Would that be fun?' Teddy leans in, brushes his lips against my cheek. 'And then maybe we could have some "us" time?'

My heart thrums. The townspeople will hear it. They must hear it. I remind myself to be calm, for Albie's sake. Calm, calm, calm.

'Teddy, tell me what's happened?'

'What do you mean?' He laughs. 'You're a sweet thing. You're good to worry about me. To take care of me.'

'What's wrong with you? I thought I was imagining it all, the things you said. Then I thought you were grieving, going through something, and I wanted to be there for you. You're my friend. But now you're frightening me.'

'I think we should encourage Alb to make some friends. You know, try and get him ready for school next year,' Teddy says.

'I already do.'

'When he goes to school, we'll have some more time for ourselves. We could even have a trip away? How about that? You and me? Some grown-up time. I could take you back to my old house, where I grew up. I wish you could have met my mother. She would have loved you.'

'Stop!'

Albie jumps, skids to a halt, and I kiss him on the head, whisper, 'Bean, you go on ahead and play. I think Teddy and I should have a little chat.'

'What the fuck is going on with you?' I stumble back, and he dives forward, a strange, archaic dance. Teddy grabs my hands, holds them to his lips.

'Let go. Let go of me!'

He steps back, hurt in his eyes. 'I ... I love you, Ada. You know that.'

'You need fucking help.'

'Ada—'

'Enough! I mean it, Teddy.' I call to Albie, swing him into my arms, leave. Before I round the bend, I glance over my shoulder.

Teddy is waving. And then my son waves back to him.

TEDDY

Him and Her

The door opens and I think it is her. It isn't.

I think of the newspaper cuttings and pictures upstairs, all shredded, dirty confetti on the floor. I panicked when she left me like that. I couldn't help myself. I tore through it all, mechanisms and springs and reels from his typewriter strewn about. I have one of its keys in my pocket. A keepsake.

The pulse in my wrists drums like wings. Everything moves too quickly: my breath, my thoughts, my hands as they fasten round my neck. Blood soaks my nails, these cuffs. Fresh cuts over old. It burns. A fire over skin.

Mr Vincent watches from the corner, twirling a peacock feather between his fingers. It looks like an eye. Like all things in this place, it has its eye on me. Blood patters on the counter. I must stop, my mother would say: *You'll get scars scratching like that, Ted.*

Mr Vincent comes to me. He moves with madness, this man. Then he drags the feather across my knuckles. 'She is pulling away from you because you frightened her.'

'She isn't she isn't she isn't.' The words burble from my mouth, a torrent – I will drown us. 'She isn't she isn't.'

'She is afraid of you. What have you done?' he says.

'I'll bring her back to me. I will.'

'How?'

The feather tickles my neck. It is wet now, runs red now.

'She will never come back.' Mr Vincent nudges me in the ribs, nudging my panic, higher, higher. 'You have frightened her. And we have lost her because of you.'

'I'll bring her back.'

'We have lost Ada,' he says again.

'We...' I look at him, wipe my fingers on his jacket. 'We?'

He steps back, hands up, between us. As if they could stop me. 'I'll bring her back. She wants this family. She wants it too.'

My pulse is a death rattle now. I snap the feather, throw it down. We have a birdcage, tall as any man, elegant bars made of iron. It is old, rusted with its own history. But its door opens and its lock closes.

I look at Mr Vincent, gesture to it.

Panic sluices like water over his face, into his hands. They shake and shake and shake. 'Please...'

I force him inside, close the door on this mad bird. 'I'm going to bring her back.'

ADA

Good Men and Bad Men

I open my eyes and see him. I tell myself he isn't really there; this is a product of the sleeping pill and my wearied mind. He is just a shape, an outline like an illustration in a book. There is no substance, there is no pulse or breath or movement.

But then he smiles, and I coil my legs to my chest, make a grab for something, anything on my nightstand. There is nothing. My thoughts dart to Albie next door, and panic is wire round my throat, each breath an ache.

'I missed you, Ada.'

I could call the police, but by the time they arrive, what might he have done? I could barrel my way past him, push him down the stairs, but he could snap me if he got a good grip.

I open my mouth to speak, but the words are lodged between my teeth like seeds. 'How – how did you get in?'

'You've been so distant recently. You've started pulling away from me.'

Noise is rising in my throat, a scream, perhaps if it is loud enough, I could wake my neighbours, wake Rye, draw all its people to my door. To help us. No. I cannot. I mustn't wake Albie. He must stay in his room.

'What's happened to you? You weren't like this? Is it something I've done? Something I've said to you? I'm sorry, Teddy, if it is, but you must stop.'

'Nothing you say could ever hurt me. I love you, Ada. I love Albie. You must know that. You're my family.'

'Teddy, I understand you are lonely, but we are not your family.'

He laughs, and I think it will shake my heart from my chest.

'Is it your mum? You miss her, don't you? But you can't replace her. Not with me, not with—'

'I've been looking for so long, my darling.'

'For what?'

'A family. And now I've found one. Only you will do.'

A sob breaks from my mouth.

'Don't cry.' He moves closer, and then I see it. He holds something in his arms. It is large, curled round him. The shadows shift and slip and a shape forms.

It is a pack strapped to his chest. No. It isn't. Teddy opens his hand to me, an invitation. The thing he holds quivers, like a waking chil—

TEDDY

Teeth and Tendons

She stands by the sink, my mother, sleeves of soapy suds. She is stamping her feet across the tiles. Bang, bang. The tendons bulge beneath her skin. Then she begins to sway, faster with every word falling from her lips.

I cannot remember the last time I saw her remain still. In sleep, she is just as lively. Although to think that, she would have to be alive. And I'm not sure all of my mother is.

'Mum?'

She turns. I scratch the nape of my neck, digging with my nails. Then her eyes widen, impossibly large.

'He did that. Does that. Did that. I used to say his stresses went to his neck and he'd scratch and scratch. Until his skin was red. Flakes of it on his collar. I had to brush them off. But sometimes they wouldn't come off so I'd use tape. I asked him to stop. Said he'd hurt himself. But he didn't.' The words spew from her lips.

'He ... he did this?'

'You look like him. I didn't know him as a young man, but I've seen pictures. You could be John.'

Sickness rises in my throat. I stagger to her side. 'Mum – Mum please don't say that.'

There are tears in her eyes. They are in mine too.

'He'd get home and sit down, sucking at the air, as if he was struggling to breathe. He wasn't. He just liked the sound of the rattle. The tin noise through his teeth.' Her words are faster now, a stream I can't break.

'Mum. He's gone. He's gone...'

'He's still here.' She looks at me.

'He's gone. He's dead.'

'I begged him to stop making that noise. But he wouldn't. He'd rattle and whistle until I thought that noise would tear me clean through.'

'Mum, breathe. I promise you, he's gone.'

'Please, Teddy. Make him stop. He never stops.' A sob rips through her lips. I see her crumbling, turning to dust. And I worry because I cannot mend dust.

'All those little girls. They were so small. He took them, put them in his van with his boxes and packages, as if he was going to deliver them home. He didn't. He killed them. He killed them. Only one girl survived. Little Tina Clay. She escaped. They only found her after he died. She was so scared. She saw him kill the girls before her. She said he kissed them as they died, kissed their eyes. Little Tina killed herself when she was fifteen.'

I wrap my arms round her shoulders, tight as I can, to keep her together. 'Shhh. Mum, it's OK.'

'I should have known. I should have known. If I'd guessed earlier, she would never have been taken. Nor the sisters. Not any of them. She'd be alive. I killed her, Teddy. I killed little Tina Clay.'

'You didn't kill her. You didn't know. How could you?'

Her eyes fall on my hands. 'Before, before I ever thought it could be him, he used to come home with blood under his fingernails. I asked him about it, he said he kept getting paper cuts. Paper cuts! But, no, he was cutting someone else.' She taps each of my fingers, tears dripping off her nose. 'Wash your hands, John. There is blood under your nails. Wash your hands, John.'

'He's ... he's gone, Mum. There's no more blood.' I rest my head on her shoulder. I am too big now, I might break her. 'I love you, Mum.'

For the first time she looks me in the eye, and warmth spreads across her face and she looks like herself. But then the warmth is gone. 'Go and wash your hands.'

I let her go, and she returns to the pots and pans, still talking, but to me or to herself, I cannot be sure. I go to the bathroom, lather my hands, brush until my fingers are stained red, as if I have been ripping berries from a bush.

I brush and brush until I have washed all the girls away.

🍎

I don't have long. What will she need? Shirts, trousers. I throw them in the bag. Some are frayed. Perhaps I could buy her some more. We could argue over how expensive her clothes are in the shop. But I will give in, as I have seen so many husbands do before.

Next, I move through Albie's room, drop toys, clothes and books into the bag. I could read to him. She will do one voice, and I will do the other.

'Another, another!' he'll say, and we'll relent, because we are happy he is happy.

There is a picture on his bedside cabinet. Albie grins up at me from the arms of an unfamiliar man. He has a long face, like a horse, and greying hair. But he has her chin, Albie's ears.

I throw the basket of toy cars in the bag as well, slip out the door and return to the shop. Mr Vincent is waiting.

ADA

Fear and Fever

'Albie. Albie. Albie.'

My heart raps in my chest. I half expect the bed to be empty, just a creased sheet and impression in the pillow, but I recognise that familiar shape, the tightly curled S. He sits ups, smiles.

I take a breath, think, *He's here. He's here. He's here. He's here.*

It was just a dream. A drug-induced bad dream. Teddy was never here. We are safe. 'We are safe,' I say.

'Safe?' Albie asks.

'Safe,' I confirm.

🍎

'Where are we going?' he asks later, buttoning up his shirt.

'We're going for a walk, bean. Mummy needs to clear her head and have a good think.'

'Why?'

'Because I have to make some decisions.'

'About what?'

'About the future. Come on, get your coat on.' I funnel his arms through the sleeves, help him with his zipper. He tucks something in his pocket, and I debate reminding him that sand and saltwater will rust it if he isn't careful, but I keep my mouth shut.

'Is Teddy coming with us?'

The name jolts me up, makes my teeth clamp together.

'No ... no, bean. Just us. I think Teddy might be a bit unwell.'

'Does he have a cold? Does he need honey-and-lemon water?'

'No. It's not that but I think we need to stay away from Teddy for a little while.'

Lines mark his smooth forehead. 'Why? Because we might catch it?'

I rest my head on his. 'Yes, yes. We might catch it. And we don't want that, do we?'

'No,' he agrees.

🍎

The breeze is strong, the salt sticks to my hair and to my lips, and I lick it away, feel the coarse tang of it on my tongue. Albie runs ahead, foraging for dried seaweed and marooned fish because he says he is a wild boy. Teddy is forgotten. For the moment, at least.

We cannot stay here.

We'll return home, we'll throw everything into bin liners, call the estate agent, go to my aunt's. Albie will be confused, but even the most frightening scenarios can be disguised as adventures. We must leave Rye.

The walker ahead loops a lead round the dog's neck, moves back up the slipway. I want to call him back, ask him to stay. I thought coming to the beach would help clear my thoughts, provide some clarity, but I feel open, watched, an insect to a bird.

I pull out my mobile with shaky fingers, dial his number. 'Dad?'

'Ada, darling, I'm at work. Can I call you back later?'

'Wait. Dad, I need your help.'

'What's wrong?'

'Can you pick us up tomorrow, take us to my aunt's?'

His voice lowers an octave. 'Why? What's going on? Are you OK? Is Albie OK?'

'We're fine. We're fine. But we need to get out of Rye.'

A pause. 'I ... err, I'm not sure I can do tomorrow, darling. Your mum's home and she'll wonder where I've got to.'

There is a rock in my stomach and in my throat. I try to swallow but I can't. The words, when they come, are broken, chipped. 'D-dad pleas-please. I need y-you to do this for me.'

He sighs, and I want to scream at him. I almost do. A noise catches on my teeth, and Albie turns, tips his head. 'Mummy?'

'I'm OK, bean.'

He continues with his search.

'Ada, darling? Are you still there?'

'I'm here.'

'What time shall I come?'

'Two o'clock tomorrow. I need to pack and get everything ready.'

'What are you going to tell Albie?'

'I'll say we're having a special trip to see his cousins. He'll like that.'

'Please tell me what's going on.'

'I will tomorrow. I can't explain it all on the phone.'

I end the call, see my reflection in the screen. My face is as pale as the bleached driftwood. My eyes are sore, scratchy and even the sharp breeze can't paint some colour into my lips. I glance at Albie, see he is OK, continue.

But then I stop, turn, focus on the figure forty paces behind us. I think it is the dog walker, returned for his ball, but then I see the brown hair, the clumsy gait, the lines deep like matchsticks in his skin.

'ALBIE!'

Albie stumbles over the rocks, shoots into my arms. I look up but now Teddy is gone. And I wonder if he heard my conversation, I wonder if he was ever there. I search the rest of the beach. Albie squirms in my arms but I cannot let him go.

He is there again. In front of us this time. I rub my eyes, close them, open them, but he is still there. And I know I am not imagining it. I would recognise that walk anywhere.

What do you want?

He stops, turns half way, looks at us over his shoulder, as if we have fallen behind and he is simply waiting for us to catch up. We near the town, and I lose sight of him. My hands shake as I lead Albie through the street.

He tugs on my shirt, asks, 'Mummy, what's wrong?'

But I barely hear him. Because, now I see Teddy everywhere.

'Mummy?'

🍎

There is a knock at the door. I drop the bin liner full of Albie's clothes, pull the curtain back and look through the window.

I have never seen him leave the shop. Yet he stands on my doorstep now, and I want to press my thumb to his cheek, to check he is real, animate.

'Mr Vincent? What ... what are you doing here?'

He opens his mouth. Closes it, snaps his teeth.

'Come to the shop. This evening. Wait until you see him leave. He'll be gone for an hour.' A pause. 'To look for you.'

'But why? What's happened to him? You can see it, can't you? Is it something I've done? I don't understand.' The words barrel out my mouth, a relentless flow. 'It ... it's like he's lost his mind. Has something happened to him? Do you know anything about it?'

'Come to the shop. I'll explain.'

And then he is gone. And later, I know I will follow.

'Mummy?'

I close the door, check it is locked, turn to see Albie standing in the hall. His hand is balled around something.

'What is it, bean?'

'Is Teddy coming round again tonight, to read me another story?'

'What?'

'Is he coming again? He gave me this. He said I could have it.'

He holds his hand out, and I see what sits in his palm. It is no bigger than a fingernail, a black square with a single letter in the middle. A key. A typewriter key.

A.

Ada. Albie.

TEDDY

Bitter Fruit and Fallen Things

My mother is talking, as she always is. I lean in, close, closer, to listen. Prayers. My mother is not religious. I'm not sure she knows what the words mean.

'...thou art in heaven, hallowed be thy name.'

She rocks back and forth, back and forth, and it reminds me of the rocking horse she bought me as a child. It was an old thing. With a red felt nose and threadbare ears because I rubbed them. I loved how fast my mother could make it go.

'Thy kingdom come, on Earth as it is in Heaven.'

'"Have you even washed your hair, Teddy? It's a rats' nest. I bet I could find some droppings in here."' I smile. 'Do you remember saying that, Mum?'

She shakes her head.

'Do you remember reading me Jack and the Beanstalk *when I was little? You'd give all the giants squeaky voices to make me laugh?'*

'He ... he got you that book.' My heart plummets. 'He planned on reading it to you. He loved you but he never spent any time with you.'

'But you did. You read it to me all the time. You read me all the fairy tales.'

'I didn't understand, Teddy. Why did he do it? Why did he hurt them and not you?'

'I—'

'He liked the girls, I know that. Always the girls. "His girls." But he never laid a finger on you. What man could love his family like

*that? Then go and do what he did? I don't understand, Teddy.' She
wrings her hands, nails cutting into her skin. I gently pull them
apart. 'It must have been because he saw himself in your little face.
And he wouldn't have wanted to cut into himself would, he?'*

'I don't know, Mum. I don't know.'

*Her eyes dart round the room, and I wonder what she sees, if she
sees anything at all.*

*'He kept them where the apples grew. That's where he took them,
killed them, buried them, one atop the other.'*

'Do you mean the orchard? I know, Mum. The police found it.'

*'He'd come home smelling of apples. Sweet, sickening. A rot. It was
on his clothes, crushed into the soles of his shoes. I had to pick out the
pulp, the juice would be on my fingers.' She is moving faster now.*

'Mum?'

*'All those apples – I can hear them. Can you? Can you hear him
walk over the apples? It's loud, Teddy. Ever so loud.' Her voice rings,
soon the woman next door will bang on the wall, demand we be quiet.*

*'He carries the girls, crushing them with his boots. He buries them
beneath the apple trees. When the apples fall do you think the girls
hear them? Pop! Pop! Do you think they hear them below?'*

'Mum, you need to be quiet. Shh! Please. Try to be quiet.'

*'Pop! Pop! Their bodies helped the apples grow. I can smell them.
I can smell them on his boots.'*

🍎

She's here!

She's here, I tell the bats and beetles, in their glass jars and beds
of bottle green. She's here, I tell the wide-eyed dolls, their strange
bent-up faces. She's here, I tell it all.

Usually there is noise in the shop: the walls creaking, blustering
about their joints, the clocks, the pans and pots that meet.
Sometimes it feels as if the shop has a pulse, it breathes, it breathes
with me. But now it is reticent, reserved.

'Mr Vincent? Please, I don't know what's wrong with him. He was in my house in the night. I woke up and he was there! I was terrified. What's happened to him? What's changed him?'

I watch from behind a shelf of waxworks. She stands opposite Mr Vincent, her hands covering the boy's ears. There is a look of fear on her face, and I wonder why. She should be overjoyed. It's moving-in day. Doesn't she see the blinds are down? The lights are dimmed. The doors are pulled to, locked. Double-locked. The shop is closed for business.

It's closed so we can welcome her.

'Is he just lonely? He ... he's pretending we're his ... his family. He's frightening me, Mr Vincent. We're leaving tomorrow.'

I heard her on the beach, talking to her father. It should hurt me, but it doesn't. It's just a game; she's a playful thing.

'He's left me no other option. I thought about calling the police, but there's no way I can prove anything. I just need to get Albie away.'

'Mmm. Where will you go?'

'My aunt's. I won't bring us back to Rye. Not now.'

She does not know what she says.

She does not know what she says.

'We'd better go. I've packed up the house. Everything is ready. I hope you'll be alright with him, Mr Vincent. Be careful. Tell everyone to be careful ... if you can.' She takes a step toward the door. 'Goodbye.'

We move as if we are extensions of each other, mechanical and thoughtless. I reach for her, and he reaches for the boy. The shop is still holding its breath. The eyes on the shelves watch us. They used to frighten me, now they are my audience. They cheer me on.

She begins to scream. Albie screams. I scream, laugh and laugh, so if anyone hears, I can say it was nothing but a joke told between coffee and sandwiches. But no one will hear. These walls are thick, and the street is empty.

'Noooooo! 'ET 'EE 'OO!'

I clamp the cloth tighter. She wriggles and strikes, but then her breath slows, her eyes close.

'Mummy!'

'It's OK, fella. She's OK. She's just sleeping.'

I look at Mr Vincent, nod. He pushes the boy forward.

'Be careful,' I hiss. 'That's my son.'

And finally the shop breathes.

🍎

I pinch her cheeks, make them pink, remove her shoes, rub warmth into her chill feet. Something sweet, fruity scratches my nose. A perfume. I dip my head, sniff at her neck.

Apples.

The tang of it sits in my nostrils. I turn to Mr Vincent. 'Fetch a bowl of warm water, a cloth and some soap. Now.'

He drops Albie, and the boy scrambles to his mother, curling himself around her on the mattress, skin so puce and plump, he looks like a berry. 'Now, now, careful, bean. Mummy needs her sleep.'

He tries to speak, but his words twist.

'Shh, shh. She's alright. She's just very tired because I made her jump.'

He looks at me with two big bug eyes, and I smile. My little boy.

Mr Vincent appears, sets down the bowl and cloth, steps back, watches.

'Out.'

His left eye twitches. He leaves.

I run the cloth gently across her neck, chest and wrists. 'There now. Can't have you smelling like that.'

Mr Vincent is waiting outside. I step close, tap my finger, once, twice, against his wrinkled old temple. 'You do not go in there.'

No reaction. I pinch the skin at his hairline. 'You do not go in there.'

He cries out, arms swinging. But still he does not speak. I drive my fist into his gut, say, 'What do you do?'

Finally, 'I do not go in there.'

On the shop floor, I peel back the blind, unlock the door, turn the sign. The shop is open for business. I tidy the counter, file away lists and copies of receipts, blot crumbs from the cash register.

Mr Vincent scuttles to my side, eyes down. When the bell rings, I still half expect it to be Ada and Albie. It is a woman, a stranger, a tourist. I open my arms, polish my smile.

'Welcome to Berry & Vincent,' I say. 'How may I help you?'

ADA

Rising Voices and Moving Shadows

A bucket in the corner. From it rises the stink of piss; there is a stripe of it in the dirt. I glance at Albie. How long have I been asleep?

We lie on a mattress, lumpen and hard but for the silk sheets and downy pillows. Fanned round us like the face of a clock are books, and shoals of crayons and pencils and neat piles of paper.

I rise from the mattress, barefoot in the dirt. 'No! No-no-no-no-no.'

I shake the door handle, pull, but it will not be moved. 'Please, no. Please!'

'Mummy?'

I spin round. Albie is sat up, his eyes are wide. In a moment, he will cry, wail – I recognise that look.

'It's OK, bean. It's OK. I think Teddy and Mr Vincent have forgotten to unlock the door. I'm just going to call for them, OK? It's fine. We're going to be fine.'

'I couldn't wake you up, Mummy.' There they are. The tears riding along his cheeks. 'I tried and tried.'

I snap at the air, try to breathe, but I cannot.

'Mummy?'

I scramble forward, curl my arms around him. 'It's OK, bean. It's OK.' I rock us, back and forth, back and forth.

'What's wrong with Teddy?'

'I don't know.' I breathe, say, 'We are OK. We are OK.' But my heart smacks against his chest and tells him we are not.

'I'm alright, bean. I'm awake now. And we're going to be just fine.' I ease him back, rise, go to the door. 'Teddy! Teddy!'

I slam my palm against it, scream. There is no response, and I wonder if they can even hear. 'TEDDY! Let us out!'

A sob is rising up my throat, but it isn't, it's something else. My knees knock together and I collapse, retching into my hand. Albie begins to scream.

'MUMMY!'

I close my eyes, open them. I am still here and my son is still red-faced, bright as summer fruit.

I must think, find a way out, but my eyes are gritty and my thoughts are wool. The cellar is near empty. There is nothing I can use, no tool to pick or pry. There is just a single bulb hanging above us, and the shadows that reach and shiver with every flicker of its light.

TEDDY

Toil and Trouble

There is a man outside the shop. He has her chin, her ears. I think back to the picture in her house. Yes, this is him. Her father. I leave Mr Vincent behind the counter and go outside. There is a breeze today – it buffets my clothes, picks my hair with its cool fingers. The sky is grey as ash, heralds the forthcoming storm. I can feel the buzz of it snapping at my skin.

The man hears the shop bell. I put a smile on my lips. 'You look lost. Can I help you?'

Up close, he is older than I thought him to be. His eyes are red, sore, there is a smudge of dirt on his chin. He cuts a sad figure. 'I'm looking for my daughter. You might know her? Her name's Ada – Ada Belling. She has a young son called Albie.'

'Yes, I know Ada. I haven't seen her in a few days though.'

His shoulders slump. 'Oh. I'm trying to find her. We were supposed to meet on Tuesday. I was to take her to her aunt's. Do you have any idea where she might be? I've tried the house. Her things are inside packed up. I've tried the harbour and the café and that little inn. Can you think of anywhere else?'

'She's takes Albie to the park quite a bit. You could try there too?'

'I've already been there.'

'It's not like Ada. Just disappearing,' I say.

'You knew her well?'

'We were friends. I'm still new in the town, she was very welcoming.'

He nods. 'What's your name?'

I stick out my hand. 'Teddy. Nice to meet you…?'

'Henry.'

'Is there anything I can do to help? You've got me worried now.'

He smiles, but the smile is brief and his eyes are already darting across the street. 'I'll find her.'

'Do you have any ideas where she might have gone? Is she already at her aunt's?' I recall hooking my thumb round his daughter's chin last night, trying to cheer her up, rubbing the delicate shell of her ear until it cracked.

'No. She's not. I've already checked. I … I don't know. She's been gone three days. I should call the police.'

That word smacks me in the chest. This is not supposed to happen. She's had enough of him, always choosing his wife over her. She's had enough of this town with its shadowed streets and sour residents. She's left. This is what he is supposed to believe. He is not supposed to come here, to come this far. He is not supposed to love her enough to continue.

'She might have just gone away. A spontaneous holiday.'

He bites his lip. 'Maybe. Maybe I should give it a few more days.'

'Why don't I give you a call if I see her?'

As he writes his number on a piece of paper, I glance at the shop. Mr Vincent watches us from the window. His face is waxy and expressionless. Like a mask hung with string.

🍎

We've been a proper family for three days. In the mornings, I arrive at work with a smile, call a greeting to Mr Vincent, take my love and our son in my arms, kiss them, hold them until there are tears in their eyes. Then, when the day is done, I whisper a goodnight into the air before I go to bed, imagine my words bouncing down the cobbles like dropped pennies and meeting her ears without a single note of my love misplaced.

The boy is curled into his mother now. The most I have seen him move these three days is when I open the door and he runs from the bucket, pulling his trousers up and tripping as he goes, frightened like a hare of a fox.

Ada's face is pale, her hair knotted and dirty. I must bring her some more warm water and fresh towels. That's what a good partner would do. For now though, I kneel by Albie, run a finger over his temple.

'Don't touch him!'

She does not know what she says. She does not know what she says. It's a game, just a game she plays.

'Darling, come on. Hasn't this gone on long enough now? Talking to me like I'm dirt, not letting me touch my son. Trying to hurt me.'

Her eyes widen.

'I know living together is a big change. You're not used to it. You've been on your own for so long. But we're family now.'

She lunges, scrapes her nails across my hand. I wince, push her back, take Albie in my arms, like a babe freshly swaddled.

Ada stills.

'He's nice when he's like this.' I smile. He doesn't stir. 'Hard to believe we made him. He's so beautiful.'

'P—please. Give him to me.' She reaches out.

'No. Your hands are shaking. You're too emotional, you might drop him.'

'I won't, I won't. Please, give him to me.'

I stand, rock Albie back and forth. Ada leans, stomach to the floor, as if she is about to catch him should I lose my grip. She is still so pale. With one hand, I pinch her cheeks. Better.

ADA

Rage and Rosebuds

There is no means of telling the time; no clocks or natural light. By the dryness of my eyes, I think it must be night. Mr Vincent lowers himself to the floor, crosses his hands, crosses his legs. Shadows gather round him. And I am not sure what is his body and what is darkness. Perhaps it is the same.

'I ... I don't know why you're helping him. I don't know why you did what you did, but you must know this is wrong.' My voice is quiet, beseeching. 'Is he outside the door? In the shop? You can help us. You could distract him. That's all you'd have to do.'

No answer.

'Do you have a key? You could give it me. We could make it look like we escaped. It would be easy.' Would it? Do I even know?

I rise, inch closer, but something in his face tells me I must stop. I sit back down. 'Why did you do it? Did he tell you what to say? To get me to come to the shop?'

Again nothing.

'Does he have something over you? Is it blackmail? I can help. I will help you, but I need you to help me first. Please, Mr Vincent, speak to me. Has he told you not to?'

Albie begins to cry, so I cover his eyes with a hand. 'Don't look,' I whisper.

We sit in silence. His small hand grows tighter and tighter in my own. Mr Vincent has brought something in, carried it through the door, a fog that sits heavy on our chests, picks at the hair on our heads.

'You know me, you know my son. Please.'

I look at him, look away. I realise that no words from me will make him speak. His is a silence I cannot break. Not now.

🍎

I do not know how long we are like this. Time is relative. I cannot measure it, I can only guess. Albie eventually falls asleep. Mr Vincent does not move, he does not twitch or fidget or shift. Not even an inch. Tiredness blurs my vision, my eyes close, my head dips, and I come to with a jump. And he is there. Still.

'What do you want?'

Silence.

I keep myself awake by counting the dried pips scattered on the floor. Teddy brings us oranges, juggles them to make Albie laugh. But it's a laughter only he hears. When he leaves, we stuff the half-moons in our mouths, juice running down our chins, then spit the pips onto the floor. It's a game of sorts, to see how far they will fly. It's the only game we can bring ourselves to play.

'Look at that one, Albie. Look at it go!' My plastic voice is meant to keep his mind light, lifted.

'I want to go home.'

My voice will plummet then, so I pinch my arm, and the pain makes it high again. 'Look Albie. Did you see that one?' Really I am saying, *I know I know I know.*

'I want to go home.'

The breath leaves my body. I am emptied, and with this tin voice I say, 'We will, we will, we will soon.'

🍎

I know it is morning because the fug of Teddy's aftershave is fresh, sharp in my nostrils. My eyes are sore, dry. I have not slept. Albie is awake, preparing for what he must do.

'Good morning, my darlings. How are we today? Feeling fine? Glad to hear it. Glad to hear it. Have you had a good sleep? You look rested. Me? I'm good. Slept like a baby.'

As if I have spoken. As if I have even asked.

'Come on then, let's get ready for the day.'

Teddy carries a bowl of warm, soapy water, flannels draped over his arm like a waiter with a service towel. This is our routine now. He will bathe Albie, rub the warm flannel under his arms, dry him off, fasten his buttons. And I must sit, watch, bite my tongue, until he is done. The first time, when he tried to touch Albie, I struck him, my fist in his throat. He choked, globules of spit landing in the dirt. I smiled because it was a victory, albeit a small one.

But then he pinched Albie's skin, rosebuds of red and pink along his arms, and I knew the pain was meant for me.

'There we are, fella. All done. You're such a good boy. You've got to keep clean. Mummy and Daddy can't have a smelly Albie, can we? Tomorrow we'll wash your hair, shall we?' He runs his fingers across Albie's scalp. 'My, my. What a rat's nest. I bet if I dig around, I'll find some droppings in here.'

I cringe. He says it every day. I wish I could stretch his words, wrap them round his neck like noose, pull till he goes limp.

'How about I bring you down some toys from the shop? A little treat? For being a good boy. How about that?'

'Don't talk to him.'

Teddy sighs, the put-upon husband with the complaining wife. 'Come on, Ada, darling. Don't be like that? You know it upsets me. Why don't you just let go of whatever is bothering you?' He gestures around as if our feet rest on marble floors and that stink on our skin isn't fear. 'I know this has been a big change. But I think you need to at least try and get settled. This is our life now.'

He turns his attention back to Albie. 'So how about it? Huh, fella? Fancy some new toys? Your daddy has his own shop. I can bring you anything you like...'

'Let us go.'

'How about some more cars?'

'Let us go.'

'Or would you like some sweeties? Which ones do you like? I used to like lemon drops when I was your age. How about some of those?'

Albie ignores him, dives into my arms. I gently push him to the side. He remembers, folds the sheet across his head. I make sure he can't see, take a breath, take another. As Teddy gathers up the flannels, I lunge.

I throw my weight into him, press my thumb into his eye socket. He lands with a grunt, striking out at me with his free hand. My jaw cracks, I swallow a chip of tooth. I draw back, with all the strength I have I drive an elbow into his gut.

'ALBIE!'

He throws the sheet to the ground, runs to the door as I've taught him to. I follow, stumble on the first step, hit the floor. Pain shoots up my side.

'MUMMY!'

Teddy's hand is a manacle round my leg. There is a comma of blood on his chin. I aim for it. Nothing breaks but he slumps down, releases me. I sprint to the door, press my eyes to the keyhole. He's there. Mr Vincent. I see his wrinkled hands, the stains and tears in his jacket. 'Please,' I say. 'Please. We're here. Let us out. Please.'

Teddy groans behind us, drags himself into a sitting position. Albie begins to scream. I curl my arms round him, tuck his head into my shoulder so he cannot see. 'PLEASE!' My voice is high. 'Let us out! PLEASE! Open the door!'

The body through the keyhole shifts, lowers, and then I see his eye, so close to mine on the other side. 'Please,' I say.

But my plea falls at the foot of the door, and this door will not move because now the man on the other side is turning. And he is walking away.

TEDDY

Hearts and Hurts

There are pips on the floor, a smattering of them, their fleshy membranes still intact. I see marks, impressions of hands and feet, a map of their movements in the dirt. The stink of the bucket is a heady cloud. It has only been three days since it was emptied, and yet it surprises me, how much my son can shit.

They peer up at me, eyes blinking in the light. The boy winces, covers his face with the back of his hand. Ada wraps her body round his, their arms and legs are tangled. I do not know where my son starts and she begins. Sometimes I will go back out, close the door, open it, watch them de-tangle, then tangle up again. And I wish I was at the centre of that knot.

'Morning, fella. Ada, darling, if you hug him any tighter, he won't be able to breathe.'

Ada's eyes are granite.

'Ada, darling. I'm sorry I left you. I am. It was hard for me too.' There is a rock in my throat, pressing on my windpipe. 'I ... I missed you. They were agony, those three days. I wanted to know if you were OK – if Albie was OK – but I couldn't come. I was at the end of my tether. I had to find a way of showing you that you can't hurt me like that. You can't attack the people you love. It's cruel. Don't you see?' I am talking faster now, the sentences blurring together. 'I love you. I love our son. We have a new life together – we can be happy. You see that don't you?'

'Stop! Enough!'

I take her hand, she presses her nails into my palms. Red-and-white crescents. 'That! That is what I mean. You're always trying to hurt me. But I love you, and I won't give up on you.'

The boy is shaking. Why is he always shaking?

'We need some time for ourselves. Some time to reconnect.' I draw my phone from my pocket, scroll through my music, select a song. 'Would you like to dance?'

Her eyebrows ping into her hairline. Her lips part. I can see the pink, warm flesh of her mouth.

'Oh come on. For me?'

'You weren't like this. You weren't.' She shakes her head. 'Or perhaps you were. You came here didn't you? To Berry & Vincent. All of Rye, and you wanted to work in this place. They were right, the townspeople, about Mr Vincent. About it all. But we were all wrong about you.'

'What?'

'I used to listen to them. Molly and Charlotte and the rest of them. They'd talk about you. They said this place would end up hurting you. That it would put something bad in your belly and you wouldn't be able to take it out. But it was already there, wasn't it?'

'You don't know what you're saying. I don't have a bad bone in my body.'

She laughs. The boy jumps, I jump, because she does not sound like herself. 'I was so fucking lonely, I should have known. I can smell it on you now. Every time you come in here.'

'I think you should calm down.'

'You've got a nice face, and that's a terrible thing, because no one will ever think to look deeper than your skin,' she says.

'You're upsetting our son.' I poke his cheek, wriggle his nose. 'Albie, fella, would you like to have a little dance with Daddy?' The music is still playing. I reach for him but Ada flicks my arms, rises. I wrap my arm round her waist, breath in the oily musk of her hair, down deep until her breath is mine.

'There now. Isn't this nice?'

I lead her slowly around the cellar. She is a tense little doll. She just needs time, I tell myself, she just needs time. Albie watches us from the bed, legs tucked up tight to his chin.

'This was my mother's favourite song. I had them play it at her funeral.'

'I don't care. I don't care about your mother. We are not your family.' Her voice is sharp, clipping my ears.

'Don't say that.'

'"He doesn't know what it is he's found". That's what all of them kept saying. They tried to make you leave. They thought a nice man like you would get eaten up by it all. I wish you had. I wish you had never come to Rye.' There are lines in her forehead. I want to touch them, take them between my fingers.

'Come now, Ada. Let's stop this.'

'We don't love you. We don't belong to you.'

Her words. Their edges blur, crumple, like paper in the rain. I put them back together, in a neater order.

We ~~don't~~ belong to you. We ~~don't~~ love you.

'Shh. I know you do. I know.'

'What?'

I kiss her temple, run my mouth down her hairline, take her earlobe between my lips, tug it gently. A tremble rides down her body, so strong. I see her falling, cracking, my little china doll. But it's alright. I won't worry. I'll catch all her breaking pieces.

'Do you like this song?'

'No.'

'No one came to my mother's funeral. She didn't have any friends or family. It was just me, the priest and Nina, my social worker. The pews were empty, the impressions of past mourners crushed into the velvet. I remember wishing I could rip the pages from all the bibles, make paper men and women to sit and weep. They would pat me on the back, speak goodbyes with their inky lips. I cried. I was loud. Too loud. I couldn't help it.'

'See wood av ben ash aimed ov oo.'

I press my palm tighter over her mouth, smudging her words.

'The priest went through the motions, but I could see he didn't want to be there. He spat out the words, as if they hurt him. He blamed her. So many of them blamed her.'

Ada drags my hand away. 'Blamed her for what?'

'They all did. All the people who came. They looked like soldiers, standing stiff under their umbrellas. Waiting as we took my mother's coffin to the plot.'

'Mourners?'

'Of a kind.'

I see them again, their lips thinned to red lines, the bulges in their pockets. Rounded, hands rising, drawing back, and the curve of something pale arcing toward my mother's coffin. Eggs and tomatoes, anything that could make a mess. Even the children came with their pockets ready to empty.

'They shouted at me, at my mother. Called her a whore, a bitch, called her Satan's Mistress. They blamed us. All because of my father.'

'But ... who did he abuse? How many people did he hurt?'

I look at her. 'Nina stood with me as they lowered my mother into the ground. The cemetery workers kept them back, but I could still hear their voices. And I wonder if, wherever she was, my mother could hear them too.'

'Why did they blame your mother for your father's actions?'

'They said she was part of it. They were wrong though.'

The people, the family of all 'his little girls', they had to have someone to blame. My father first, then my mother. After my mother, came me. I can hear them now, calling at me, see the spit fly from their mouths.

'I hated that they blamed my mother. She didn't deserve it.'

'But ... why?'

Again, I rest my palm over her mouth. 'They let me throw soil onto her coffin. I thought burying her was the right thing to do.

I thought that's what she would have wanted. She was restless for so long, and I thought she might like to belong to one place, to finally be still.'

Ada is drawing away, centimetre by centimetre. I pull her back. 'As they shouted, the mourners, I imagined I could hear her heart in the dirt, beating. I imagined I could feel it in the soil, tapping against my soles. She died before she could watch the end.'

'The end of what?'

'Our show.'

'Who blamed her? And for what?' she asks.

'When I went back, the soil smelt of piss. Someone had tried to set fire to her headstone, someone else has tried to break it. The cemetery workers pitied me, helped me clean it. The next day, it was ruined again.'

'Why did they do that?'

'Don't you know?' I look at her. 'You still don't know me?'

'What are you talking about?'

'I thought you'd have realised by now.'

'Realised what?'

I release her, and she stumbles back. I have marked her arms. 'It doesn't matter,' I say, and I take her hand and kiss each of the pebble-shaped bruises.

'Mummy?'

She moves to his side. 'You're OK, bean.'

'I'm hungry. My tummy hurts.'

'I'll go and get you some food,' I say. 'What would you like?'

He shifts away; he is a mouse and I am a bird. But I am not a bird. I am his father.

I rub my thumb across his fingers, see them as they would have been when he was a babe. 'You know I remember when you were born, your hands were so tiny, nails no bigger than bread crumbs. And when you cried, you'd ball your fists so tight, they'd go red.'

Albie looks at his mother, a question in his face. She shakes her head, an answer in hers. I cannot stop. The words are sweet in my mouth. I lick my teeth, swallow.

'You were the most beautiful baby. Everyone said so. Mummy and I would take you out, and people would fall over themselves to get a look at you. "Look at him," they said. "Oh! Just look that that face. I've got quite a sweet tooth and I could eat this baby up. My God!" But only I could make you smile.'

There is a noise coming from Ada's throat.

'I taught you to ride your bike in the park, remember? Do you? I knew you'd have it cracked by the end of the day. You're such a clever boy.'

He is tugging on Ada's shirt, his head swivelling back and forth between us. 'But Mum … Mummy…'

'Mummy was waiting when we got home, wasn't she? She gave you a great big kiss. We were so proud of you.'

Confusion settles on his face. Ada is still, eyes on me, not even our son can move her.

'The next day we went back to the park, and you spent hours riding round. You went so fast, didn't you? You made me dizzy. You were the fastest boy in the park. All the other children were amazed. They clapped. Remember that? The whole park clapping for you.'

'But … but … but…'

'I was so proud of you, fella. How much we laughed.'

He is sobbing. The sound of it breaks Ada from her reverie. She blinks, once, twice, curls her arms round him, covers his ears.

I smile, rise. 'I'll go and get us some lunch, shall I?'

No response. But Ada is still watching me. I close the door, lock it, the sound of those stories in my ears. Like music.

They sound so good they could be real. Why can't they be real?

They have not moved by the time I return. I set the plates down, draw two oranges from my pocket, juggle. Is that a smile? That's a smile.

'See, fella. Look at Daddy go? Want me to teach you?'

He is smiling so much he cannot speak.

ADA

Blood Orange and Blood River

For three days, we lived in darkness. It was a punishment for my attacking him. They left us alone. For the first time in my life, the silence was welcome. But the absence of food was not. We drank stale water and sucked on leftover oranges, juice down our chins and on the sheets, pips flying through the darkness somewhere like tiny missiles. I made noises to make Albie laugh.

'Mummy?'

'Yes, bean?'

'I wish they'd turn the light on. I need the toilet.' His way of asking if I would help him find it.

'Come on. I need it too.' I didn't.

We stumbled through the darkness, feeling our route by the shape and cut of the flagstones. I wanted to scream, beg them to put the light on, but I bit my tongue, swallowed the blood and helped Albie squat over the bucket. When he was finished, I ripped off a scrap from the bed sheet, draped it over the top. It helped. But only a little.

'I don't like this, Mummy.'

'I know, bean. I don't either.'

'I can't see. It's ... it's black.'

'Close your eyes. We're OK. We're OK.'

He settled, went to sleep. I held my finger an inch from my face and I saw nothing.

🍎

Behind Teddy's ear, a vein throbs like a river, large and blue. I want to cut it, burst its banks. The thought is delicious. He is sat with Albie, tracing the lines in his palm, dripping poison into his ear again. Fiction that makes my teeth hurt. I wish he had left us in the darkness.

Four days ago he spoke of Albie's birth, of teaching him to ride a bike, and I thought my blood had hardened in my veins. I could not move. When he left, I wiped Albie's face with my shirt sleeve, held him until the tears on both our faces had dried, crusted, then I whispered the truth into his ear, trying to right his mind.

But even now, I wonder what words of Teddy's will remain. And I wonder how I can clear them.

My hand is wrapped around Albie's. When I see him doubting his memories, his own version of life, I tap his wrist, draw him back. I do not know whether Teddy believes it, and this is a higher rung to his madness, or he just likes the sound of it, these untruths, that they could become the truth if I let Albie believe it.

'And that's when Mummy got sick. She must have caught something on the plane. And I was worried about you catching it, so I booked another hotel room and we went for nice days out on our own, didn't we? Mummy didn't want to hold us back.'

Albie looks at me, a concerned, sympathetic glint to his eyes, and I quickly tap his wrist.

'That didn't happen. Albie and I have never been on holiday. The first time he went on a beach was when we moved to Rye.'

'You must have forgotten because you were so ill.' Teddy smacks his lips in annoyance, then pinches my cheeks. I want to rip his fingers off.

Then he says to Albie, 'When you were on the beach, fella, you started shouting "Shark! Shark!" pointing to the sea. Terrified everyone. A few kids started screaming, but it was just a dolphin. I got a few glares from the mums after that.' He laughs, and I marvel at the clarity in his eyes, the easy upturn of his lips, as if it was real, as if he remembers.

'There was no dolphin, Albie. There was no holiday.'

'There was, darling. You've just forgotten. But you remember, fella, don't you?'

Albie nods. Dear God. He nods...

'We are not your family. We are not your family.'

Teddy rolls his eyes. 'Don't be silly. Of course you are. Once Albie was asleep in the hotel room, I'd bring you some food, try and make you feel better. It must have been awful being stuck in that room all week.'

🍎

I should have taken more care, I shouldn't have trusted so easily. I should have kept us apart until I knew him, all of him. And Mr Vincent? He comes every night now. Crosses his hands, crosses his legs, the yellow light making his wrinkles look like dough. I should have listened to all those rumours, sharp as knives.

'Is Teddy coming back?'

'Yes, he will, bean, but you pretend to be asleep, OK? You mustn't listen to him. Nothing he says is true.'

'Why does he lie?'

I sigh. 'Because he's a very bad man.'

I still feel as if I am in a dream, choking, and in a minute I will wake up, and there will be nothing in my throat.

'I'm going to get us out of here.'

But how? The door is locked. I have no means of getting my hands on a key, or fashioning a key from something. I cannot knock it down. No one would hear even if I screamed from sunrise to sunset, the walls are too thick. Teddy and Mr Vincent have a system. One comes in, the other waits outside. They take turns, as if we are animals to pet and play with.

My only hope is to keep trying to tug at Mr Vincent, loosen his resolve. It is all I can do.

The light flashes overhead. I rise, hold a book either side of the bulb, slam them together. The glass crunches, falls into the sheet I have tied round it. I take a breath, untie it, return the books to their corner.

'It's alright. It's alright,' I keep whispering, for me, for Albie. I smooth my hand over the wall, stepping lightly in the darkness, until I come to the far-left corner. Here, I open the sack, the shards fall into the dust. Later, if my other attempt fails and Mr Vincent comes, perhaps he will cut himself. A patchwork on his skin. A small prize.

'What now?'

'Get back. Cover your head.'

🍎

I hear his footsteps, followed by Mr Vincent's. They are heavy, dragging. I know every piece of Teddy: the smack of his lips after he eats, the sound of his breath, the tin music of air between his teeth. I also know there are seven steps from the shop floor to the cellar, seven from the bed to the door.

'Quick! Be quiet and don't move unless I say.'

I make sure Albie's eyes are covered, then I kneel, brace.

The door opens and I feel the cool crush of fresh air on my cheeks. Teddy steps through.

'What's happe—'

I strike the back of his knee with my foot and he falls, meets the floor with a grunt. I turn, see Mr Vincent in the doorway. I jam my body between the opening. The wood smacks my chest and for a moment, I cannot breathe.

'Mummy! Are you OK?'

Fingers curl round my hair, tight. I scream, my arms wheeling through the air as I fall back. The door bangs shut. 'NO!' Teddy is on top of me, and I buck, and scramble in the dirt.

'Mummy!' Albie beats his fists against Teddy's arm. 'Stop it! Let her GO!' I hear the swift whistle as his hands ping back and forth through the air.

'Enough, boy!'

There is a gasp, a thump and I realise he has been thrown back. Teddy is breathing hard, I can taste his breath, feel the patter of blood on my neck. 'Albie? Albie!'

A noise, a scuffle. His fingers, touching my temple. He's alright. He's alright. He's alright.

'Please. We are not yours. We don't belong to you. Let us go. Please.'

The sounds of Teddy and I merge. We breathe as if we are part of each other. I close my eyes, kiss Albie's fingers. Strength seeps from my body. Into the dust into the dirt.

'Please. Let him go. I'll stay if you want.' I am sobbing, tasting the salt of his sweat and my tears. 'I'll stay with you. I will. But let him go.'

His answer is the soft press of his lips to my brow.

TEDDY

Violence and Vengeance

He writes about me still. I hear the scribbling of his pen, the low, animal sound of his breathing. I glimpse that familiar scrawl.

> *Teddy moves with a lilt on his left side, as if all the ill life he has lived is stitched into his shoulder. Is this where every sadness and anguish drips and pulls from? Did his father have a similar movement?*

Do I? Do I really? I look in one of the shop's besmirched mirrors. He is right. My left is significantly lower, my right shoulder hugs my ear. My body droops, like wax over a rim. He is right.

Vincent continues scribbling, looking up occasionally to view me, my body, the things I do. Perhaps he will read aloud, read me the story of myself:

'*How much of his mother is inside him? Is there more of his father? I would like to tie him up by his feet, put a cut into the side of his neck, bleed him and see what runs out. How much of Johnny Colne would come out?*

'*Is blood permanent? Is blood the law of life? Always to be one thing. Do we live by rules made by the thin rivers under our skin? Are we simply new shades of old colours? Can we purge ourselves fully of these ties? Or will these ties always bind us, tighter than knots?*'

Sweat beads along my scalp. The scribbling nests in my ears, like an itch. My blood runs hot, so hot I think it will burn through my skin.

'Stop it.'

I snatch the paper, tear it through, and it falls like motes to the floor. Vincent smiles – a smile that hurts my insides. He continues writing, scratching my name into the wood.

Teddy. Teddy. Teddy.

The noise is louder, filling the shop like a rattle. 'I said stop.'

Teddy. Teddy. Teddy.

My fingers are on my neck suddenly, digging, cutting. I am panting, nails wet and red. 'Stop it!'

His hand moves on its own now, it is so familiar with the shape of my name. He looks up at me, waiting, waiting ... he is trying to nudge something out of me. But I will not be moved. I will not.

This too, this behaviour of mine, will be written down later, catalogued, captured in red ink. He looks at my fingers, licks the air like he can taste something sweet there. Then he lifts his finger to the scar on my face, measuring it, looking, looking always at my edges for *him*.

'Stop it.'

Mr Vincent pinches the meat of my wrist, the skin over my knuckles, the folds over my elbows. He touches it all.

'Stop.'

I smell the dirt of his body so close to mine, full of iron, like rust. Now I smell like him too. His fingers are everywhere.

'*Johnny* touched this skin.'

The words make my feet water, I am moving back, away. But he throws himself forward, and the air leaves my lungs. The air leaves the shop. Mr Vincent neatens my collar, smooths my cuffs, licks his thumb and combs my brows. I smell stale spit. Then he turns on his heel and begins to cash up, as if nothing has happened at all.

I know he is trying to stir a memory. But what about his ghosts? What of Mr Vincent's little ghosts? There are more than mine in this shop.

'How old were you when you killed your father?'

He falters, looks at me once. The amusement that was on his face dips into something red.

'You were only a boy. Do you remember how you felt? Did you feel good? Good and free?'

I move toward him. 'Did he know it was you? A man murdered by his own boy, he would surely know.' Vincent wobbles, drops loose change.

'I made sure he knew.'

'What about your mother? Did she know? What must she have thought? Can you even imagine? Your poor, poor mother.'

He looks his age, Mr Vincent. He looks like an old man.

I smile, neaten his collar, smooth his cuffs, lick my thumb and comb his brows. 'You're a mess.'

His old hands are quivering. I pat them into his pockets. 'I'll clean the windows. They are filthy. It's my shop now, after all. Isn't it?'

When he doesn't respond, I jab his bony old ribs with my finger. He grunts, nods. 'Yours now.'

I gesture to the door. 'Why don't you clean that bell? It needs a good polish. Go on.' I nudge him away. 'Make it ring.'

ADA

Prayers and Omens

The door swings open and Teddy enters carrying a tray. Bread and cheese and oranges. I never want to taste another orange.

'Here we are. Some lunch. Eat up, fella, you need to keep your strength up.'

Albie glances at me, and I give a nod. He crams the food in his mouth. Teddy sits beside me, watches Albie. 'Good boy,' he says.

'Tell me about your father?' I say, 'What did he do? Why did no one go to your mother's funeral?'

The question has been cornering me, worrying away at my thoughts. Did he have more than one family? Was he a serial abuser?

Teddy shakes his head. 'He took my mother's peace. I don't think she ever really found it again.'

'Did she not meet anyone new? After your father?'

'No. She didn't trust anyone. She wasn't lonely though. We had each other.'

The words are thick in my mouth, and I struggle to speak. 'You loved your mother. She loved you. But what would she think, Teddy, of what you have done?'

He frowns, the lines in his face deepening. 'What have I done?'

His hand is tightening around mine. I hear my heart thumping in my ears and I tell myself to keep breathing . The skin around Teddy's mouth is taut, and his eyes are hard, like the black bead eyes of all the stuffed animals upstairs.

I no longer think of the shop as Mr Vincent's. It has exchanged hands. It is under new management. Albie and I are Teddy's possessions. One day, our bones will lose their movement and he will have to move them for us. I see him curling my fingers round a cup, raising my arm, higher, higher, until the cup reaches my mouth. He will help us to and from the bucket, he will clothe us, bathe us, and when our words dry and become brittle, he will speak for us, our voices from his mouth.

He is talking to Albie now. I inch closer, try to put myself between them.

'I see a lot of myself in you, fella. A lot of my mother, actually. Your grandmamma. She used to take me to feed the ducks when I was little. Every weekend, without fail. Have I told you this?'

Albie shakes his head.

'She'd buy me a whole loaf of bread, and we'd walk to the park, even if it was raining.' Teddy tucks a strand of hair behind Albie's ear. 'When you were younger, I did the same. You probably don't remember but the ducks followed us home once.'

Albie's eyes widen. 'They ... they did?'

'Yep. A long line of them, all the way. You loved them, gave them all names. You were so upset when they left.'

Albie is leaning forward, eyes bright. Panic jumps in my gut, and I try to catch his attention.

'We returned to the park the next day and they were all there. Billy and Olly and Suzy and Jonny and the rest.'

I think, *Albie has forgotten, he has forgotten again.*

Look at me, look at me.

But he is caught.

I reach out, tap the back of his hand. His eyes come to mine, he blinks, retreats into himself, as if he is disappointed it isn't true. Teddy doesn't seem to notice and continues.

A sob bursts from Albie's lips. The air is thick now, so thick I could nick it with my nail.

'Do you remember, fella? Do you remember all these times together?'

'You're not my daddy.'

The smile on Teddy's face runs, wet paint down a canvas. 'What?'

'You're not my daddy. You're not my daddy!'

Albie's words rise and tangle. Louder now. Teddy's lip twitches, it is an omen. An omen I have come to dread.

'Albie, be quiet. Albie, stop it,' I say. I try to draw him close but he will not be moved.

'You're not my daddy. You're NOT my daddy!'

'Stop!' I shout, and I try to cover my son's mouth. To stop these words.

'You're not my daddy. You're NOT my daddy!'

Teddy strikes him, so fast I do not see his hand move. Albie opens his eyes, wide, confused, as if he is unsure what has just happened. Then he teeters, falls into me. A red bud appears on his cheek, and he begins to scream.

Teddy's mouth pops open, his eyes bulge. 'You ... you shouldn't have been so rude to your father. It's ... it's naughty! We need to teach you some manners. You're a bad boy.'

'Touch my son again, and I swear to God, Teddy, I will kill you. I will fucking kill you.'

I look at him, with this humming, heaving mass in my arms, and I want to put my hand through his chest, take this heart, this cold and stony thing, break it, make it powder.

TEDDY

Killing Hands and Cutting Words

'John?' she says when she wakes. 'John?'

'No, Mum. It's me.'

There is relief in her eyes.

I run the damp cloth across her forehead, buds of sweat and oil soaking into the cotton. Her hair is a tangled mess, breadcrumbs and old spittle glued to the ends. I must wash it when she is better.

'Mum, you're burning up. I've got to cool you down.' I drag the blanket back, remove her socks and jumper, roll up her trousers and sleeves. 'Can you sit up and have some water?'

She nods her head, but her eyes are strange, far away, and I wonder from what distance she has heard me.

'Here you go.' I press the glass to her lips, cup the back of her head with my palm. 'Keep drinking. We need to get you better, OK?'

She pushes me away. 'I thought you were Johnny. You sound like him, you look like him.'

'I know, Mum.'

She reaches for the bedside cabinet, takes something in her hand. I grit my teeth. The beads are black as beetles. Her expression has changed: it was distant and blurred, now it is tight, the edges sharper, all her concerns returning, thickening her skin. If I press my finger to her chin, it will meet something unrelenting as wood.

The beads were a gift from Father. When he was convicted, she ripped them from her body, furious fingers snapping a cord so thick *it should have needed cutting. They scattered, she said, on the ground, under mucked rugs and tables, and into dusty skirting.*

She never told me she collected them up.

'Where did you find them? Were you going through your wardrobe yesterday?'

She looks back at me. 'What will you do, Teddy? What will you do when you are older? When you are lonely and the girls won't stick? And friends scarper? Because of your face. You have his face. You could be twins.'

Her eyes are red, sore, the skin will scab if I let it. 'You don't need to worry about that yet, Mum. I'm only seventeen.'

'He ate with his fingers, that front lip of his pulled up so high, I could see his gums. Pale. It used to make me sick. It was the one thing that I hated about him.'

'You sound like you've been swallowing razors. I'm going to get you some honey.'

She grips my arm. 'You do the same. You eat with your lip back and your gums out. How are you going to find a girl like that?'

The panic in her face makes my heart jabber. 'Mum, don't worry. I'll be fine. You don't need to worry about the future yet.'

'Who's going to love you? How are you going to have a family?' *Her voice is louder now. But there is no malice in it, only concern.*

'Mum, calm down.'

The beads rattle in her hand. I want to take them, crunch them with my boot. 'I'll be OK.'

'He was always a peculiar man. He'd starch his shirts, his collars and his cuffs, perfect, then go out with tomato seeds and syrup dried onto his trousers. He'd walk with his right shoulder raised a little higher than his left, as if he had a weight strapped to his side. At night, before he could sleep, he had to blow on his pillow. "Removes the dust," he said.'

'I'm going to get you some honey.'

When I return, she is calmer, her eyes half closed. I blot her forehead with a fresh cloth until she finally sleeps.

Then I take the beads from her balled hand, take them outside, bury them in the soil. But later, she wakes and cannot find them, and there is little peace to be had. I dig, plucking them from the soil until my nails are gummed with muck. I return them to her palm.

And there they begin their rattle.

🍎

They are cold to the touch, dulled from my mother's fingers. I will give them to Ada. Perhaps she will smile at me, thank me with a kiss, swift before Albie sees, but flushed with something hot. 'I love them. Thank you, Teddy. I love them so much.'

'I thought you might. They belonged to my mother.'

'Help me with the clasp. What do you think?'

'So pretty.'

🍎

The day is a fine one, clear and fresh, and white shirts and sheets hang like tufts of cotton wool in the gardens ahead. We had a handful of visitors to the shop yesterday. Mr Vincent stilled, as if he was a puppet with no puppeteer. He does not want people in the shop, he especially does not want them to touch its things with their sticky hands. But I like it. I like the wide-eyed stares as they enter, the curiosity and the fear at it all.

'Oh my Lord, look. Look!'

'I don't like it in here.'

'Is that a...?'

'Don't look. Let's go.'

The way they trip out the door because they can only bear to be inside for so long. I used to look like them.

I tuck the beads in my pocket, head to the shop. The town stirs with theories, wilder and wilder each day. But as yet, I have seen nothing and heard nothing of the police. Only yesterday a man claimed he'd seen Ada in Hastings: 'Bright as a button, with that little boy in tow.' Another man said he's seen her in the next village, 'doing a spot of shopping'. There are versions of her scattered about the county. Some even as far as London.

'You might ask Teddy. He works at Berry & Vincent. Only been here a little under a year now. But he seemed close to her.'

'In what way?'

'They were friends, I think. Often saw them together.'

'Don't bother with Teddy. Talk to Mr Vincent. He'll know something about it. Rye hasn't been the same since he arrived. The things he's done over the years.'

'Can you elaborate?'

'We came to you lot before about him once. You were useless.'

'I'm sorry to hear that. And Miss Belling, can you tell me more about her?'

My feet stick to the cobbles. I cannot move them. One of Rye's elderly couples stand in their doorway. I cannot see who they are speaking to. The man has his head down, nodding as he scribbles in a notebook.

'Yes, I agree with Bill. Go and talk to Mr Vincent. I wouldn't be surprised if he's done away with her. Always so quiet and watchful, you know what I mean? Ran poor Mr Berry out the town. Maybe he did the same to Ada.'

'And why would you suspect him?'

'Where are you from? You've obviously not been in Rye long if you've got to ask me that.'

'I'm sorry?'

'Get yourself to Berry & Vincent, Detective. All I'm saying.' It's not all she says because then, 'Mind yourself with that man.'

I back-step, crane my neck, catch a glimpse of a badge, a brief flash of silver. I run to the shop, close the blinds. Mr Vincent stands behind the counter. He looks at me, his lips move, and I think, *He's speaking, what's he saying?* But all I can hear is the rush of my own blood and the rattle of the beads as they settle in my pocket.

ADA

Screams and Whispers

Here the darkness is long. I work happy words round my mouth, speak them into the sickness of this air, to make my boy happy. But then they curdle, and I spit them out instead. I am careful.

I speak of the sun and not of the moon.

I speak of light, fire. But not of the darkness, not of the burn.

I speak of sweetness, honey on the tongue. Of sea salt on skin. Of footsteps through this door and back into the world.

He cries, yes, his face a red rumple of envy for these simple things. But then he smiles, ties himself like a knot across my stomach. He is too big, too heavy, and I cannot breathe. But I will not remove him, so I take small breaths, my head becoming light, my heart heavy as a rock.

'What's that, Mummy?'

'What's what?'

'That.'

I hear it then. A fingernail across wood. On the other side of the door.

'Mouse?'

'No,' I say. 'No mouse.'

I expect the air to give way, for Teddy to enter with all his madness. Albie and I cinch together, limbs like ropes wrapping round one another. But the door remains closed. Why is he doing this? Why does he not just come in?

'Teddy?'

No answer. At least not in words. A hum rises like a heat haze, blistering the air, running across our ears. It is deep, the sound, gravel. I want to clap my hands together. To break it.

Vincent.

It is as if this sound is driving us further into the earth. I feel further from the surface than I ever have. Albie is whimpering now. I think, *It can't hurt us, this voice.* But if a voice ever could, this one would. I know it.

'Mummy, come back.'

I knock on the door, once, with my finger, and he knocks back. Tap, tap. I am here.

Tap, tap. So am I.

What does Vincent want? Does Teddy know he is here?

Vincent's voice rises, into words, into such strange words. He is singing to us.

About a boy, a man, a traveling show. About girls who fly through the air like wingless birds, men so large they look like mountains next to their children. Families who come from the towns to watch the families from the show move and act and exist for them. Then he sings about a fire, a burning, of all that life. He sings about the death of the man, the freedom for the boy. Sings a song of murder like it is a lullaby.

I look through the keyhole. His is on the other side, one black eye peering into mine. He has been watching me this entire time. I fall back, the air rushing from my lungs. Blood ribbons along my wrist. Albie drags me back. I go with him.

We bury our heads in our hands, as if in prayer. And we wait for this song to end.

TEDDY

Fate and Fury

'My mother had more than her share of encounters with them, but she kept it all hidden from me. Before she died, her mind was weak, it wandered off, and she told me things, so many things. That's how I learnt about the women.'

'What women?'

Their smiles were gummy and red. Their hair, bleached to straw, was drawn back into tight pigtails, making their scalps pucker. They abandoned make-up for a guise of innocence and purity, but I always spotted the bits of eyeliner or lipstick leftover in the cracks of their skin.

'"Hello, hello, Teddy Bear," they said. "Aren't you going to invite me in? Come on, Teddy Bear. Don't be rude to me. I've come such a long way. Let me in".'

'What women? You aren't making sense,' Ada says.

'They came to me in school uniforms, scuffing their shoes against the doorframe. The first time, I assumed the woman had got lost, knocked on the wrong door. I assumed she was late for a slutty fancy dress party, or she was some stripper-gram, but then she spoke and with a twist of my gut, I knew.'

'I don't understand. Why did he have fans? Was he famous? What was his name?'

Ada is curled round Albie on the mattress, the black beads rattling in her palm. For a moment, I thought she might throw them at me, but then she looked at our son and slumped, the bones of her spine poking through her shirt like tree roots through soil.

'He was famous in a way.' I edge closer to Ada, rub my finger across the veins in her wrist. Mr Vincent is outside, he thinks I can't hear him snuffling at the door like a pig stuck in muck. I wonder, does he stand there for me or her?

'For what reason?'

'You really don't know?'

A stillness has come over her face, a look of concentration. She is so young. By the time he had killed his girls and been found bloodless in his cell, she would have still been an itch in her father's trousers. This face I swear was in every newspaper, on every bulletin on the television, but now it is just a picture in books and on forums, a memory buried in many minds.

'During his trial, women were attracted to him, some wanted to help him, nurture him. Some thought they could, claimed he was innocent despite the evidence. The blood they found on his skin, the pictures they found balled up in his socks.'

Her expression changes now, draws inward, brows down, lips pulled back, like a scrunched up piece of paper. The boy is awake, his face oddly vacant. And I wonder if he is listening. He should know about his grandad.

'What ... what did he do?'

'Of course, they also came for me when I was older. They looked for it inside me, all of them, for that rot.' I scratch my neck, sniff the blood on my fingers. 'I don't know how they found me. But they came, a stream of women dressed as good little girls, trying to tempt me. Red lips. Always such pretty red lips.'

'Tempt you to do what?'

'To hurt them. To fuck them. To let them save me.'

Ada gasps.

'Why do you think they dressed as his victims? I was his son. I was the next best thing.'

'Who was he? Who was your father? Tell me.'

'John Colne.'

She shakes her head.

'They weren't the worst. There were others. Women who came and pretended to be my mother, who called my real mum a whore, a cruel cunt, who believed my father deserved better than her. They cursed her, spat her name in my face. They were the worst. My mum didn't deserve that. She didn't deserve any of it.'

'What happened?'

'I called the police. Moved house. They found me again.'

'Who are you, Teddy?'

She is looking at me, the muscles bunching in her neck. I want to poke them, feel them move. I'm not worried about her knowing the truth now. She loves me. She won't leave me.

'You know I think it was fate. We were intended for each other.'

Her mouth pings open.

'I came to Rye for a reason. So did you. My mother used to worry I wouldn't find someone. I would never have a family. But look at us.' I sweep out my arm, gesture to the home we have made, humble but good enough for now; to the boy we have made, sweet and cherub-faced.

'I came to Rye for a fresh start. Away from my mother.' Her words are sharp.

'So did I. Your mother. My father. We are opposites but we match.'

She snaps her teeth.

'Before you came along, I didn't have much luck with women. My first relationship lasted the longest. Her name was Jane. She used to say I had a very familiar face, but when her sister discovered who I was, it ended.'

There is a crust of blood at my hairline, but I cannot stop picking.

'I've been on a grand total of five dates. I've slept with four women. I've not had a relationship that's lasted any longer than five months.'

'Why are you telling me this?'

'Because there must be no secrets between us. I want you to know everything. I want to share this with you.'

'Why now? After all this time.'

'Because I know for certain that you love me, that you won't leave me. That my mother was wrong to worry.'

'What happened to your girlfriends?' Ada asks.

'I remember one of them seemed different from the rest. She seemed sweet, kind. I thought she liked me. I took her home, then the next morning, she was gone. I found a post on her social media saying she'd slept with Teddy Colne, the son of the killer. She was going to start a blog about it, her experience with me.'

The skin is raw now, but if there is pain, I cannot feel it. Ada is watching me, the drip-drip of blood on the floor. In the dirt.

'That made life hard for a while. It always is when someone recognises me. I've moved more times than I can count. I've tried cities, hoping to blend, to hide. I've tried the country, the isolation. I've kept things, mementos from the places I've gone. A collection of sorts.'

'Did you do anything to the girls?'

I look at her. 'What?'

'Did you hurt them?'

I shake my head. 'But they might say I had.'

Ada doesn't respond. She can't. Because have I ever hurt her?

I smile, but it feels bitter even to me. 'True-crime addicts, they always found me like vultures to a body. Biographers, psychologists, cultists, journalists, Satanists, copycats. Men who claimed to be murderers, who wanted to meet me, to honour my father. I've had preachers rattle off their beliefs, telling me they can absolve me, purify my blood, ensure me a seat in Heaven.'

'Why don't I recognise you? Like they did?'

'My father was before your time. He was murdered in prison. My mother died of a stroke, retribution was served. Our name and face faded.'

There are tears in her eyes. They make trails in the dust on her cheeks.

'All those girls who found you, wanted you. Why do this to me? Why us?' Her voice rips, I want to take it, stitch it up. Give me a needle and thread.

'Ada, darling, we are the same. I saw you walk past that window every day. You looked so lonely. I used to wait to catch a glimpse of you, prayed for you to come into the shop. We needed each other. We were brought to each other.'

'That didn't mean I belonged to you.'

I sigh. 'We belong to each other.'

'Is anyone looking for us? Anyone from the town? My father?'

'You are not lost. You are not missing.' They don't seem to realise this.

A sob breaks from her lips. Albie fidgets, puts his hands to his ears. She quickly pushes them down, holds them still.

'Don't cry, darling. I know it's stressful, but you'll settle eventually.' I touch my hand to her wrist, tap my fingers along her skin.

'Stop it.'

'My father used to do this.' I follow the green veins, play my fingers against them. 'Mother said he was so gentle, afraid of breaking her. It was like he was playing the piano. China keys, his fingers like hammers. She said, "How can a man be so good and so bad? Such an angel and such a devil?"'

'I don't want to hear.'

Ada moves away. I pull her back. 'I've not finished.' The words are coming fast now, a ribbon of them, making my jaw ache.

'"He loved me, Teddy Bear, he did. He never hurt me. I was not like one of his girls. Those poor little girls."'

'Stop it, I used to say. Stop!'

'"He had such nice hands. Soft. Small. They were delicate. You wouldn't think they could hurt a thing."'

Ada is shaking, her eyes glassy and still.

'Stop it, Mum. He's gone. He's gone.'

'"Look at your hands, Teddy Bear, like his. Johnny Colne's. Go and wash them. Soap, don't forget the soap. Wash them away. Watch the girls go down the sink."'

'I won't be lonely, Mum. I'll be OK. You don't need to worry.'

'"You'll frighten them away. You have your father's face. They'll all run like rabbits. Like little rabbits they'll run."'

'I found someone, Mum. I found a girl called Ada. We have a son called Albie.' I close my eyes, speak to the air. 'I found a girl called Ada. We have a son called Albie.'

TEDDY

Love and Madness

Her name was Tilly.

She was my second girlfriend. She chewed the corner of her mouth so that there was always a mark, a red moon, and when I kissed her I felt her blood coat my teeth. She was small. So much smaller than me. She had a child's hands, pale and soft. She would also pick at the skin round her nails. Holes in her mouth, holes in her fingers. I tied a rubber band round, round so she couldn't move them. But then she stopped feeling anything at all.

It was a hot day, the day she left. Men and women lolled on the grass, parched and panting like dogs. The park was full, the sun burnt sweat from hair, blistered the air, made all bodies sore, aching. We had found a quiet place. I watched her chew the corner of her mouth, a habit I was disgusted by as soon as I met her. I looked at the restless chug of her lips, the sweat on her brow like countless clear bells. Her lank hair, the oil on her nose.

We had not been together long, but I remember the sickness I felt looking at her. It hurt my gut. 'Ted,' she said, catching my eye, 'Why are you looking at me like that?'

I shook my head, and she went back to chewing. 'Stop doing that. It's disgusting.'

'Why does it bother you so much?'

Tears welled in her eyes, dripped onto her wet, wet face. I thought, I should kiss you, I should say I am sorry, but all I wanted was to take each tooth from her mouth, leaving her like a gummy child.

I snatched up her bag, mopped her face with a tissue, my own getting slick and hot.

'What are you doing now?' She shouts this, and the people around us turn and look.

There is that furious energy in my fingers, like fire. Nothing can get it out. Not even the rain. They are not gentle, as they beat into her small face, soaking up all that wet, leaving small buds of pink across her cheeks. She is crying quietly. No one can hear, they have gone back to their own quiet worlds.

I take the red lipstick from her bag then, run a stripe of it across her mouth. 'What are you doing?'

'I'm making you pretty.'

🍎

There was another woman after – Sarah. She was quiet. She always had grit under her nails, behind her ears. She chewed gum, but she never brushed her teeth. She washed her clothes but never her own body. In the summer, the stench made my nose ache. I couldn't tidy her up. I really tried, perhaps a little too hard, because she left me, feet kicking up thick tresses of dirt as she ran.

She might have said I tried to drown her in that river.

But I was only trying to clean her.

🍎

Then there was Sybil. I touched madness with Sybil. But in the end, she thought she'd touched madness with me.

Where Tilly was small, Sybil was large, two heads taller than me, with hands wide as trunks, and hips to match. Her face was like wood – you'd have to hack at it to find a smile. We met in a coffee shop. She seemed normal at first, but then don't so many people?

But madness spilled from her seams like filling from a child's toy. And chaos manifested, ran through our short time together like water and rot. If I refused or rejected or denied her, like a child, she would fasten her lips together, a slice of white in a red face, fist her hands and hold her breath until my will gave. And it was always my will that gave in the end. It had to. Otherwise, her face would blister, red, red, and then a frightening shade of purple. Her eyes would roll back in her head and she would lose consciousness.

'Sybil!' I would scream. 'Stop this. You're behaving like a child. Stop this now. Sybil!'

In the beginning, I always thought she would gulp one enormous breath before the end, wheeze and topple into my body, apologise for this madness.

'I'm sorry, Teddy. I'm sorry. I don't know why I did that. It was stupid. Forgive me. Please.'

I lived on sharp rocks to please her. I mollified her, stroked her ballooning cheeks, persuaded her to breathe, breathe, when she had these quiet rages. She'd open her eyes after, veins like rivers thumping under her skin, I would clean her up, tease her face and body into perfection.

'Enough, Teddy,' she'd say, and swat me away.

I liked her hair. It was long, a rope, tresses of brown silk I'd comb every evening. It soothed me, making her better, making her neat and making her shine. But then she hid the brush, and when I forced her to sit, be still, used my fingers, my fingers were not gentle.

She was loud, Sybil. Her voice boomed. It could bleed through walls, bleed ears too. Every word, even one shared over a pillow, were blasts of hot breath.

'You're shouting again.'

'I'm not shouting. Stop being so fucking possessive, Teddy. I'm tired of it.'

In the night, I'd make my thoughts sweet with how I'd put a cork inside her throat. Her imperfections grated on me, more and more, until my resolve weakened entirely.

Our final argument made my ears ring. I'd had that fire in my fingertips for a while, and when she fastened those lips, dug her nails into her thick thighs, I watched her face swell and grow red, I did not try to stop her.

No 'Sybil please. You must stop this. You will hurt yourself. Please. Stop this. You're frightening me.' No pleading. No settling or calming.

It surprised her. I could see in her eyes. I only sat there, smiling. She started to teeter on her seat, her eyes to flicker under her lashes. I stood then, slowly, wrapped my hands round her throat and forced the little air there was left right out of her body.

'If you don't want to breathe, then don't breathe,' I whispered.

I'd never seen Sybil afraid. She threw her hands against my chest, shoots of red bursting her irises. She convulsed, a messy, thump across the floor, then her head went limp. I released her. Left her, blacked out, in a soil of her piss and sweat. I packed my things, walked out the door. I didn't see Sybil again.

🍎

One with a paste of sweat thick and stale across her body, always. Always with a red moon of blood on her mouth.

One with a breath sour as milk left too long in the heat. And with a heat in her throat so loud, it made your ears red.

One with a still voice, and a scum of dirt on her ankles. She walked barefoot, and so, when she returned home, she looked like a grub taken from the dry, dry earth.

Not one of them was who I was looking for. They were imperfect, and despite my best efforts, filing them into a better shape, they couldn't be what I wanted.

But Ada.

Ada is perfect.

ADA

Small Bodies and Still Hearts

There is a hole torn in our pillow. Its insides bulge, white and soft, like cream. It smells just as sweet, the wool damp and slightly cloying. I think soon it will be time for Teddy to come again, and I pull tufts of it from the hole, ball it up, gently stuff it into Albie's ear. His hair, a few inches longer now, disguises my efforts.

'Mummy, it itches.'

I withdraw the balls of wool, roll them in the layer of butter slicked to our plates, return them to Albie's ear.

'Better?'

He nods. We resume our positions. We wait.

There was always something about Teddy. A familiarity to his face that I could not isolate, I could not pin-point.

Johnny Appletree, I knew his father as.

But how did I forget?

I was young when I first heard his father's name. Fourteen, perhaps. The name held no interest for me, it bore no weight on my life. Not like it had those girls who died. It was a conversation between my parents, halting, and with enough pauses to seem suitably sympathetic:

'All those girls. They reckon there were more. They just haven't found their remains.'

'Why did he do it?'

'Some people said he thought he was helping them, preserving them, before their youth vanished and they lost their purity. Other people said he just liked the buzz of it, like a hunger that needed sating.'

'Why just little girls though?' Mother asked.

My father shrugged. 'Maybe he just liked pretty things.'

'What was his name?'

'John Coin or something. Killer Coin. Odd name.'

'Odd man.'

'Johnny Appletree, that was his other name.'

There was a picture on my father's phone, a headshot of Teddy's father. I glanced at it, saw a scruffy man, looked away.

'To do such things. What a beast.'

'What happened to him?' Mother asked.

'He was killed. In prison. Quite gruesome, it was.'

'I didn't realise you were there.'

A sigh.

'No need for sarcasm. Says here he was a delivery man. A white-van driver no less. Typical that.' A smirk. My father continued, reading from the online article, but I cannot remember what he said.

'Does it say what he was like? Was he a loner?' My mother, scrupulously flicking bits of imagined dirt off her skirt.

'No. He had a wife.'

But I did not know he had a son.

I did not know he had a son.

I didn't care to watch the documentaries and series my friends applauded. Perhaps if I had, there wouldn't be butter on my fingers, the false memories in my son's mind I try with all my might to take away.

What did my father say? I close my eyes, draw his face, hear his voice. How did he take them? What did he do to them?

Albie shifts and his trousers, clean, crackle like paper. Brown paper.

Paper packages.

That was what he did. He packed the girls into his van, slotted them between his parcels and packages.

'The only girl to survive gave an interview, to make the public understand,' my father said. 'He cared for them, fed them, cleaned them – it was almost as if he loved them. He always killed them, although that wasn't his favourite part.' His favourite part was something else. What was it?

The context is different, but the men are the same. Like father, like son.

I should have known. When he told me about his father that day in the park, I should have guessed there was more he kept back. His life connects now, I can see the trajectory of it. His happy upbringing, his years in care, the lonely life that followed, hounded by fanatics and lunatics.

I think of that day on the beach, when we spoke of impulse, and trauma carried in blood, and I want to laugh. Then I want to scream.

Why did it have to be us? Why not the other women who hunted Teddy down?

I wonder if he had not sensed the loneliness in me, perhaps things would have been different.

'Mummy?'

'Yes?'

'What's wrong?'

Albie is sat up, his woollen earplugs in his palms, looking at me. I did not even feel him move away.

'Nothing, bean. Nothing. I'm alright.' I'm shaking. 'Come on. Come here.' I open my arms, and he slips into them. We take up our positions again. Prepared.

'Are you cold?' Albie asks.

'No. I'm not cold.'

He tucks the blanket round me anyway.

'Thanks, bean.'

I was awake all of last night. My limbs are heavy and dumb. A thickness coats my teeth, and I lick it away. I wipe my fingers along my skin, feel it there too. Fear. It is all over me. He is due soon

I've tried everything I can think of. I've plotted and kept my patience, the little I have of it. I've tried to escape. I've hurt him, my son and myself in the process, but have I really got close to escaping?

There is one thing I haven't tried. And I must.

All this time, I've thought Teddy would simply keep us here, like frightened mice in a filthy cage. But what if those little girls' fates become our own? Death and soil. They have in most ways. How long until we are bones in the earth?

※

Teddy comes with a smile. How did I ever think it a fair one? Albie is curled onto his side now, feigning sleep, wool stuffed in his ears.

'Hello, darling. Did you have a good sleep? I'm sorry I couldn't come this morning. We've had a change-around in the shop. I was busy with Mr Vincent.'

The beads he gave me are in my hand. Rattle, rattle. I gather my courage, send them scuttling across the floor. One bounces off his leather shoe, he steps back, stands on another. It crunches, becomes powder.

'Oh!'

He kneels, rubs his fingers through it. Then he looks at me, and for a moment, I regret what I have done. He rises, fury filling the air, his arm draws back—

'Tell me about him?' The words come out as squeaks.

He pauses. Then:

'That belonged to my mother!'

'But before that it belonged to him,' I say.

He is caught off guard. His hand lowers, rises, lowers, as if he can't decide what he wants to do. I want him to hit me. Just not yet.

'Tell me about your father, Teddy.'

'What?'

'I remember. I remember hearing about him. Seeing a picture of him. You look the same. You could be brothers.'

'I've already told you about him.'

'Not everything. Why did he take them? The girls?'

'What—?'

'What did he do to them? He didn't rape them or torture them. Did he just like watching them? Did he like talking to them? Did he play with them like they were his dolls? Did he do what you do with us?'

Sadness wraps round his face. His hand lowers to his side. 'My father was a bad person. I'm not. I love you. I take care of you, provide for you. We're not lonely anymore.'

I rise, move closer. I feel his breath on my skin. Can he hear my heart banging? Can Albie? Can Rye? It's all I hear.

'He pulled them into his van, didn't he? Drugged them, drove them to that place. I can see them all stacked up, the little bodies, like boxes and paper packages, like gifts. Pretty things for him to unwrap.'

His brow sinks over his eyes, his lips curve down. This isn't the reaction I want.

'Why are you behaving like this?'

'What did he do then? Killing wasn't his favourite part was it? What was?'

He shuffles, tries to take my hand. I push him back.

Then he says: 'My father liked to dress them, neat and nice, my mother said. He liked to collect them up. He buried them, all of them close together, so they wouldn't be lonely.'

'Why?'

He looks at me, smacks his lips together, and it is a crack of thunder inside my head. 'Why not?'

The breath catches in my throat. 'That rot is there. It's quiet but present. You are what everyone always expected you to be.'

Still there is no anger. Just boredom and irritation.

I think about the girls, their bodies under the earth, heaped together. Bones to bones. I think about his father, the man who lives in Teddy's face. He is there. It is his voice, his touch.

'You're his son. Your blood is dirty.'

Nothing. I have this wrong. I take a step forward, feel his mother's necklace break under my foot. The black beads. It has always been her. His father is just an empty figure. I laugh.

'Your mother would be ashamed of you.'

It catches me off guard. His hand is at his side and then it is on my face, sharp, throwing me back. I land on my side, fingers at the lump on my lip.

'I'm sorry. I'm so sorry, Ada. You made me do it. You ... you get me so confused and frustrated sometimes. You twist me up. I ... I just lose my head. It's ... it's not my fault really. I can't help it. You ... you mess with my head, don't you? You do. And you really shouldn't.' He is beside me, drawing me to my feet. 'I'm sorry. Are you alright?'

It is not guilt on his face. More a softening of his resolve. I breathe, move my jaw. 'You hurt me.'

'You shouldn't have said what you said. It was cruel. You hurt me first.'

He sounds like a child, meek, squabbling over nothing.

'You can make it up to me. I think I landed funny. Let me stretch my legs. Take me upstairs. Let me walk round,' I say.

He shakes his head.

'Albie needs the exercise anyway. Didn't you when you were a boy? Didn't your mother nag you to get fresh air and exercise?' I bring her into this conversation now because I know it will soften his resolve. Make him pliable.

'My mother...? She ... she used to say my legs would turn to jelly.' He pauses, looks at Albie with a smile that makes me sick. Nods. 'OK.'

I have been holding my breath, finally I release it. My heart jumps to a kinder rhythm. I pray, firing the words off between clenched teeth. Please, please. I am about to turn, feverish with hope, to wake Albie, when I feel Teddy's hand tighten round my wrist.

The smile is gone, his face is slack.

'Let me go, Teddy.'

His eyes are on my mouth, the blood oozing from the cut. The air thickens and I feel I might choke on it.

Slowly, he runs a finger along my lip, smudging the blood. His voice, when it comes, is empty and strange, and I wonder what is going through his mind.

'Let's put some colour into those lips.'

🍎

Upstairs, I am lightheaded, drunken. The air is thin, clear, and I gulp it down. The space beckons me and repulses me all at once. The shop is just as strange as it has always been, but now it feels like a cavern, me a mouse stuck inside. It could swallow me. It already has.

Mr Vincent stands by the door – I see its key poking from his fingers. His expression is vacant, I want to cut some expression into it. Teddy keeps a firm hand on my shoulder, humming, his strange turn forgotten.

'Is it nice to stretch your legs, fella? We don't want them to turn to jelly, do we?' A laugh. 'Hold my hand. Let's walk together.'

'No.'

Another laugh. 'Alright. Alright. You be a big boy.'

The blinds are down, the streetlights picking at the edges like yellowed fingers. The shop is tense, its breath held in tight. Albie stares about, wide-eyed, as if he had forgotten the image of all these things. Bears and dull-eyed dolls and glass jars of buttons and birds and rings and plastic cars and leathery faces and waxy bodies and things I cannot name. So many eyes all on us.

'How does that feel, fella? Nice to stretch your legs?'

'Yes.'

'Love you, fella. Tell Daddy you love him too.'

'No.'

Laughter. 'I love you anyway.'

We are walked round the shop, pets on a leash. I'm not going to attempt an escape. Better to wait, to plan. I've been a good girl – he'll bring me up here again. As we round the bend, walk back to the stairs, my reflection catches my eye. A mirror, tarnished and dull hangs to my left. My feet clump to a stop.

I see myself, the blood dried to a crust on my lips, and I remember what my father said:

'His favourite part. Dressing them up. Red lipstick on their lips and cheeks, like dolls. Perfect, pretty little things.'

Albie is tugging me, but my legs won't move. Teddy taps me on the shoulder, and finally we continue, descend. The door closes behind us. The shadows welcome us back as if we are two of their own.

'Mummy? Your ... your lips.'

He's made me look like his father's dead girls.

TEDDY

Smoke and Mirrors

The bell rings. Mr Vincent and I move, draw together, it is instant, an instinctual response. We stand, shoulder to shoulder, behind the counter, push smiles onto our lips. The silence is taut, thick, I could bite it through with my teeth.

The men enter with their collars drawn up against the chill. They bring with them the acid tang of coffee and cigarette smoke. It's a heady blend, and it makes my eyes water. Mr Vincent moves from foot to foot. I nudge him. He stills.

There is no need to be nervous. We are prepared. We are ready for this. 'You must speak,' I reminded him, moments ago when I saw them coming up the hill. 'You have no room to make errors. Understand?'

He knows what he is and isn't allowed to say. I've schooled him on his responses, his actions, so he can appear to possess some semblance of normalcy. We are just two collectors in a shop. Nothing more.

'Good afternoon, gentlemen. May we have a moment of your time?'

The taller of the two men gazes round the shop, takes an immediate step back, as most visitors do. He has bold eyebrows and full, pillowy lips. He looks better suited to a magazine cover than a police investigation. His companion is small, fair, with wheat-coloured hair and lines in his face.

Bold recovers, offers a polite smile. He pulls out a notebook, licks his pencil, regrets it. Wipes his tongue on his cuff. Fair meets my gaze, nods.

'I'm Detective Inspector Purcell. This is PC Miller. As I'm sure you're aware, a local mother and her young son have recently been reported missing. Do you know them – Ada and Albie Belling?'

The question is rhetorical. They know the answer. They've had it confirmed by the townspeople.

I speak first, lay my hands flat on the counter. It's an open gesture, a confident and honest gesture. 'Yes, we do. I haven't seen her for a long time, though. Did her father call you? Mr Belling? He's been around Rye looking for her.'

'Her father has expressed his concerns, yes. We have been going door to door, asking for any sightings of Miss Belling and her son. We believe her to have gone missing around the twenty-third of March. Can you recall the last time you saw her? Any unusual behaviours? How did she seem, emotionally?'

Bold is scribbling in his notebook, his writing such a chaotic mess, I wonder how he will decipher it later. Fair is watching me, little bug eyes running over my features. He knows, he knows this face.

'She was kind, sweet. When I came to Rye, she made me feel welcome. It's difficult in a new place. I ... I think she might have been a bit lonely herself. She walked around the village a lot, round and round. That's what first struck me.'

'And more recently?'

'We became friends. We'd go to the park, have lunch together occasionally.'

'And did Miss Belling mention any concerns; for example, was she receiving any unwanted attention? Was anything bothering her?'

'No. No. But I do think she seemed ... off. Sort of nervous.'

'Any guesses why?'

'No. I'm afraid not. She didn't mention anything.'

Those eyes, scouring my face. This must be Bold's first time meeting a serial killer's spawn.

'During the course of our enquiries it's been noted that Miss Belling was more than a "little nervous". According to witnesses, she came across as agitated, anxious, in the days leading up to her disappearance. Can you remember how her son, Albie, seemed in the lead up?'

'He was absolutely fine. He was well, healthy, so I don't think she could have been worried about him. I assumed she'd gone on holiday. Or she was staying with her parents. Then I saw Mr Belling, and he told me she'd disappeared. I hope she's OK.'

The scratch, scratch of Bold's little pencil. Mr Vincent takes a breath. Finally, he speaks. His voice is scraggy but passable.

'Has she ever taken off before – Ada? She'd only lived in Rye two years but nothing like this has ever happened.'

I glance at him. There is a knot of concern on his brow, something I taught him to fasten there. His words are mine, carefully practised, to the slightest cadence. I brushed his hair this morning, smartening him up just in case, stuck a finger into his gut when he grumbled. He could be normal now. Could be.

'I'm not at liberty to say, but we will do our best to find Miss Belling and her son. May we have a look round?'

Mr Vincent nods, spreads his hands. 'Of course.'

They move into the aisle, their backs to us, poking things with their pencil stubs. Mr Vincent looks at me. I smile.

Perhaps now it will seem to Bold and Fair just a simple case of bad apples. Small towns can sour over time, turn against each other. Berry & Vincent is just the brunt of a few terse arguments. Mr Vincent is no more rotten than Molly or Charlotte.

At least until you cut into him.

We watch from the counter. I've hidden the stranger items in the shop's collection, covered them over. The door to the cellar is concealed by a shelf so stuffed with books and jars and toys and trinkets, I wonder how it still stands, how it does not bow and crack like a log in a fireplace. Still, we hold our breath when they pass it. We cannot help it.

'Are you able to tell us what Miss Belling and her son were wearing the last time you saw them? Also, we'd like to see any CCTV footage you have? It would be helpful to get a clear picture of the two of them.'

Mr Vincent bites his lip. 'We don't keep anything like that in here. I'm sorry.'

'Right. And Mr Colne, can you remember what she was wearing the last time you saw her?'

He's slipped up. He didn't ask my name, and I didn't offer it.

'No, I'm afraid I can't. It was a while ago now.'

Blue torn jeans, black boots and a shaggy grey cardigan. She had a red band in her hair. It's in my pocket now.

'Alright. Thank you for your help, gentlemen. If you remember anything or hear anything, please contact us.' Fair slides a card into my hand.

They leave. I watch them through the window, wonder if they will glance back. They do not.

We turn to each other, Mr Vincent and I, and smile.

ADA

Live and Die

There is a piece of black thread loose in his black shoe. He dresses sharp now. He could cut us all to ribbons. His jacket is buffed to a reluctant shine; his hair is ruched into a slick wave. I wonder, does he think himself more than a proprietor of an old antiques shop? I wonder, will he ever feel remorse, say, 'I finally see what we have done'?

I list their behaviours in my mind, the father's and the son's:

Johnny Colne made his victims fat with sweet meats and cheeses, fine food that was found in their stomachs later. *I see Teddy opening the door, arriving with food, oranges tucked deep into his pockets.*

Johnny Colne painted their faces, and when they were found, these rows of little girls in the soil, their lips were still red. *I touch my fingers to my mouth, recall the taste of blood.*

Johnny Colne bathed them, dressed them in fresh cotton shirts and woollen jumpers because where he took them was cold. *The clothes I wear now, slightly fusty from spending so long on the shop floor, scratch my skin. I want to burn them. Give me a match and I would.*

🍎

I wake to his face above mine, a large and pale moon. I scream, Albie screams. Mr Vincent only watches me, a smile like a sickness on his lips. I tell him to get out, to GET OUT! But he remains standing there in the shadow.

'Mummy...'

'What do you want?' I demand.

Mr Vincent flicks a switch, and yellow light pierces my eyes. I cover my face. When I look up, I see what he has done.

I see what he has done for us.

Across the walls are countless photographs, portraits, black and white and peppered with damp spores, dust, stains of ink, blood. Some are crusted, peeling, others are torn right through. And in all of them, their faces no bigger than my thumb, children.

So many children

I cover Albie's eyes.

Mr Vincent rocks on his heels, hands tucked behind his back like a proud man. A proud madman. He is still smiling, and if I could scratch away a smile, I would do.

'Mummy? What is it?'

'Nothing. It's nothing.' The breath lodges in my throat like a rock.

He has decorated our walls with dead children.

And he thinks he has done a good thing. He thinks this is a kindness.

He touches my cheek as he leaves, grazing it with his thumbnail. I wipe his touch away, and when the door closes, I tear every photograph from every brick, dig a hole in the soft ground with a spoon and give these children a burial.

Albie is shaking. And so I lick the dirt from my lips, begin my chorus of good words to bring him back to himself.

I speak of birds and of wings, of movement, a storm of it; I speak of music, so loud and chaotic, it is like a fever; I speak of the freedom of water, rivers, able to drift you to a new place. I speak of so many things to quieten the scream wobbling in his throat and to bring fresh dreams.

Tonight, if I sleep, I will dream of children in the earth.

TEDDY

Tragedy and Trauma

I drag my thumb across her face, the nose and chin smudging, stretching into a strange shape. The ink stains my skin. There is a woman stood next to me, reading the cover, her eyes flickering to Ada and Albie's faces. She sighs, says, 'Poor girl,' more to herself than to anyone else.

Doubt is a barb in my chest. Have I done wrong? Should I have left her be? No. No. She was lonely. She wanted a family. She wanted to be my family.

In my mind, I tap the woman on the shoulder, say, 'She's happy now. They are happy now. We're not lonely anymore.'

And the woman smiles, goes on her way. Ada and Albie peer up at me, countless faces from countless front pages. The same picture, printed again and again. In it, they wear simple smiles, curled round each other on a picnic blanket, their hair turned golden by the sun. I wonder who took it. Her father perhaps?

Now his photograph is everywhere. And the headlines:

'Mother and Son Missing From Rye'
'Ada and Albie Belling Missing. Police Appeal for Information'
'Local Woman and Child Disappear.
Residents of Rye Aiding the search'
'Where Are Ada and Albie?'
'Have Ada and Albie been Taken?'

The regional papers flesh the story out, but in the nationals they appear as little more than names, a three-sentence description and a plea for sightings, information. There is a brief statement from DI Fair himself. I turn the page, begin to read.

'Ada and Albie Belling were last seen on Monday, 23rd February in their hometown of Rye, Sussex. Ms Belling is described as five foot, with a slight build and long dark hair, and was last seen wearing jeans and a grey jacket. Her four-year-old son is described as having short brown hair, brown eyes and an ear deformity on his left side.

Specialist officers are searching the area for Ms Belling and her son. We are concerned for the two of them and their safety and ask that anyone with fresh information on their whereabouts come forward.'

Online, they have been sensationalised. On Twitter and Facebook, their names are trending, #AdaAndAlbie. Strangers post their thoughts and theories on their whereabouts, sending their respects and sad emojis into the void. And the void eats them up, makes room for more.

None can resist the excitement, the drama of a mother and young son disappearing. There is something delicious about it, you swallow it down. Where could they be? What might have happened to them?

I pull out my mobile, scroll through the new posts on Twitter.

@JJenson: My thoughts are with #AdaAndAlbie's family. I can't imagine what they must be going through. Sending love and light to them in this worrying time.

> **@VonnyVon:** @JJenson Wha a lil bitch. Wha kin o person doz tis? Runs ov wi er ow kid? Provably ded in a ditch. Kin o sorri 4 the kid tho.

>> **@EmMitty:** @VonnyVon Oh I just can't bear the thought of it.

That poor, poor girl. And her little boy. What she must be going through. I hope she's safe somewhere.

@VonnyVon: @EmMitty Na. Runs ov wi er ow kid? Nasti bitch, ya ask me. Mabe she killed im. Lucks ike a nutter. She's too smilee on at piccy. Na ones tha appy.

There have been sightings across the country. One woman spotted Ada and Albie as far away as Scotland, in a little town called Peebles. Another claims they are in Cornwall. One man says he saw Albie playing with his daughter outside his house but there was no woman. No mother. Perhaps Ada abandoned him. Perhaps he ran away.

They are everywhere.

The media attention settles on Rye like a malevolent eye. The townspeople preen and spruce themselves up for the walk to buy milk. Journalists and photographers arrive with their cameras and shined shoes and sharpened pencils and slick smiles. When they visit Berry & Vincent, their eyes wide coins, I take cover in the back. Better my anonymity be preserved. For how long though, I cannot be sure.

There is life and movement, but underneath it all, Rye is tense like a flexed muscle. No one can hold a conversation, speak a word, without that word being 'Ada' or 'Albie'.

'Where's she gone, do you think – Ada?'

'Swanned off somewhere sunny, I bet. No thought given to the boy's stability and welfare. The young don't take responsibility these days. Especially not Ada Belling.'

'Didn't realise you knew her so well?'

'I didn't.'

'Hmm.'

'Did you?'

'No.'

'Hmm. I know what her lot are like. Causing a fuss for the attention.'

'Obsessed with attention, the young.'

'Despicable.'

'It is.'

A breath.

'One of the journos took my picture earlier. Interviewed me. Think I might be in the papers tomorrow.' A bloated belly thrust to the heavens.

🍎

Bold and Fair went door to door yesterday, calling on Berry & Vincent once more.

'Were there any newcomers in Rye round the time of their disappearance? Anyone you suspect might have been involved with her?'

'No. No one. Why?'

'We have to cover all bases, Mr Colne. Did Miss Belling ever mention any ... sour exes? The boy's father perhaps? Do you know his name?'

'I don't know his name. You think it could be him. Albie's dad?'

'As I said, we are covering all bases.'

It was easier this time. We were calmer. And their questions were shorter, revealing their desperation. The main reason I've even come to the town shop today is for them to see me, a normal man fetching a paper and milk for his afternoon flagons of tea. I am no one. I am like all the other men in Rye. Speak to me and I will tell you everything.

At least all that I am willing to share.

ADA

Death and Deathless

When Albie wakes in the night, his heart is loud as a bell in a church, his hands pawing at his head, as if he is trying to take something away. I settle his sweaty body in the curl of my arm, tap my fingers to his chest. Make a new rhythm, trick his poor restless heart into calm.

'Mummy! MUMMY!' He will scream.

'I'm here.'

'Where is he? Where is Teddy?'

'Teddy's gone. He's gone.'

'Are you sure?'

'Yes.' I kiss him, tap, tap, tap, until he sleeps again. 'It's alright. You're alright. We are alright.'

But it is not just him. Some nights I rush to the bucket, watch pieces of bread and fruit dapple its bottom. I try the trick on myself, but the tapping becomes too hard, puts bruises into my skin. My body is too small, my bones are too weak to crack these walls.

Calm down, calm down, I tell myself. I remain by the bucket, empty except for the knot in my stomach. I wrap my arms round myself, pinched together, watching Albie in bed.

I don't know how much time has passed since our interval on the shop floor. It might be days. It might be longer. The knot in my gut tells me it is the latter. I recall the blood on my lips like a slathering of warm fat, it makes me sicken.

I must get onto the shop floor again. I try to recall all its curiosities. 'It must be small, the thing I take, either sharp or heavy, easy enough to slip under my shirt.'

'What are you saying?' Albie asks.

'Mr Vincent will no doubt be watching.'

'What?'

'Sorry, bean. Thinking out loud.'

Perhaps Albie could distract Teddy. Pretend to want a toy or plastic car. They never enter together. One man I might be able to overpower, two I cannot. It will have to happen down here.

🍎

My vision blurs. When it clears, I see Albie looking at the door. He is pointing. What is he saying?

What is he saying?

'He's coming. He's coming. Teddy, Mummy!'

I listen but no one is coming. It is the mind playing tricks on him. Mine's played them on me too.

I must think of their weaknesses. I must. Mr Vincent: his age, his shop. Teddy: his knees, his mother. His knees. I'll go for his knees. They're swollen like melons, stretching the seams of his trousers. They must be painful. I wonder how he bears to walk. Something heavy or something sharp. The shop. I must get to the shop floor.

Albie's voice fades into the background.

Mr Vincent. He's just an old man. Weak, his bones brittle. I could crack him, undo him. I pull myself up. Albie is rocking himself, face screwed up so tight, he looks like an apple, gone old and soft in the bowl.

I go to him, pull him to his feet. He is crying still, a low keening sound coming from his lips. I kneel, ask him to look at me. Look at me!

He goes silent. I place my hand on his chest, feel the restless brag of his heart.

'This,' I say, 'this is yours.'

My other hand, I move to his temple, feel the damp warmth of his skin beneath mine. 'This,' I say, 'is yours.'

I press his hands together. 'These too.'

I touch his lips, his ears. These are yours I tell him. These do not belong to them. He nods, wipes his eyes. We do not belong to them, I tell him.

'We do not belong to them,' he says.

We repeat it to each other until our lips are numb with the words.

TEDDY

Arrival and Departure

I once thought this shop a collection, private, personal, dressed in the cords of an antique shop, an illusion fine as mist. I thought the items were not for sale, that each and every one carried a discreet barb, to deter curious fingers and full purses. But I see that I was wrong. Some things are for sale, and Mr Vincent is something of a salesmen.

A woman walks in, a tourist, big-eyed and sunburnt round the edges of her face. Vincent ruffles his collar, barks out that strange voice of his, 'Welcome, miss, to Berry & Vincent. Are you looking for anything in particular?'

'Erm ... no, no thanks. Just looking.'

He wafts an arm round her waist. 'Then please ... allow me to give you tour.'

He guides her deep into the shop, dusting as he goes, revealing stuffed things, dead things, things which look like they have a little too much life. There is a flush of courage in his face, like a blush on the skin.

'And this, see this, miss. You can touch history with this.' It is an old crusted pipe he is trying to sell her, the musk of tobacco still engrained in its pouch.

She does not want that, I want to scream. Or those. He has forced a clutch of death portraits into her fingers. When she glimpses those of the children, her fingers shake, like pale leaves.

'I ... I ... What are these? Oh my God. Oh! That little boy...'

I throw out my hand, drag Vincent back. 'Get behind the counter. Now.'

'No.' His teeth bared like a feral creature. I dig my fingernails into the warm soak of his skin, deeper into that soft place under his arm. He twitches, tries to vault away. My fingers keep biting, further and further. They bite to blood. I can feel it coat my nails.

He whimpers, lowers his head. 'I'm behind the counter.'

I release him, take his place, take the portraits from the girl. 'You don't want to look at those. You want to look at pretty things.' I gather to me jewels, glass beads, shells so bright they look like silk – rolls of silk, I rinse her in wonders. And when she leaves, her purse is light and her arms heavy.

I tap the bell above the door. Listen to it ring. 'You live behind there now.'

🍎

Bold and Fair are aware of my identity but seem to have kept it to themselves. But how long until Rye knows? And the world? Customers would flood the shop then, faces flushed as they glimpse its prime piece on display. Me.

'It's as if I'm looking at Johnny Colne himself!'

'Look at his eyes. His eyes, Alice. Look!'

'Jesus...'

I would be propped inside a glass case, eyes open and staring, limbs lumpen with stuffing. I would not be able to move, but I would be able to listen.

'He's horrible.'

'Are you scared?'

'No.'

'Open the case, touch him. I dare you.'

'I can't do that.'

'Why not? You think he's going to bite you?'

'He might...'

I would.

'That face. Such an awful face.' New customers could arrive, wipe dirty fingers across my glass. 'Jeb, I don't like it. I want to leave.'

'Wait, I'm getting a picture with him.'

'Why?'

'Just because...'

Pictures, pictures. Pictures with a serial killer's son. Headlines that read: 'Are You Brave Enough To Stand Beside the Killer's Boy?' 'Johnny Colne's Very Own Flesh and Blood'. 'Come Inside Berry & Vincent and Meet Teddy for Yourself!'

The case has garnered an online frenzy. The newspapers serve up more and more fantastical headlines, pages so full, I think the text will begin to run, paragraphs of it drying into my fingers and cuffs. The news channels broadcast live from Rye, drawing fresh faces and townspeople alike. Even the reporters, usually dull-eyed and stiff, flick their notepads, eyes thirsty for juice.

No one can resist the lure of this story.

Mr Vincent and I watch it all from the sanctum of the shop, shoulder to shoulder, behind the dirty glass. We do not get many customers – they keep their distance, and I am grateful. The café, on the other hand is crowded with bodies.

I open a window, ever so slightly, and the voices come through:

'What do you reckon has happened to them?'

'My friends say she's probably, like, "faked" her disappearance for the attention. She'll be chilling somewhere enjoying the fuss, watching this all play out. But I reckon she's been taken, like, kidnapped, you know? Could be a new killer, got a thing for young mums.'

'Interesting.'

'Good theory, I've got, I reckon.'

'Wonder why her, though? Plenty of young mums about.'

A shrug. 'Lonely. Isolated. Easy prey, wasn't she?'

'I wonder if someone else will disappear soon. And where from.'

'Wherever it is, that's where I'm headed,' says the girl.

'Do you think the police look, I don't know, anxious? Sort of nervous?'

'You mean those detectives? Yeah. Maybe they have someone. Or maybe they've found them. Dead...'

The woman says, 'I heard that she was trying to get out of Rye, the day before she disappeared, Ada. That she sounded scared. Like she was running from something.'

The girl's eyes widen. 'What? Where did you hear that?'

'I have my sources. Apparently she called her dad all in a panic. Probably why the police are so het up about all this. Proof, isn't it? That something was going on with her.'

The girl rolls her eyes. 'That could just be speculation. Might never have happened.'

'No, no. It's real. I'm sure someone's done away with her. And you know it's always someone close. I bet you a tenner it's someone here. In Rye.'

'Nah. I think it will be someone further afield. Why go hunting so close to your own home? Better off with a bit of distance.'

The woman nods, impressed. 'I'd not thought of that.'

'My friends think I'm good at this sort of stuff. Think I could figure out what's happened.' An arrogant grin slick on her lips. 'You?'

'I like the buzz. Feels like you're part of something. I like puzzles too. Thought I'd come and see it for myself.'

'I met a woman the other day, Bess or Ness something, she's, like, proper into serial killers. Thinks they'll find someone soon, wanted to be here when they do.'

'Hmm.'

'Probably be a woman. Everyone always assumes it's a man, but I think outside the box.' The girl smirks.

'Have you spoken to the townspeople?'

'Yeah. They seemed to think she was a lonely little thing.'

'Places like this, they're so tight knit, but when push comes to shove, they'll out a mouse, say it's a rat, just for the sake of it. Did they mention any rats here?'

The girl shrugs. She turns, and Mr Vincent and I dodge out of the way. 'Lot of them said the guy in there probably has something to do with it, but I've been in. It's just some old dude. Doubt he can do much more than unzip his trousers for a piss.'

'Hmm.'

ADA

Salt Tears and Sore Wounds

Mr Vincent stands by the door, knuckles poking through his pockets. He must have his fingers wrapped round the key; I would break every one to have it. I wonder then, would he even react? Has he ever cried? As a boy with muddied knees? Or was he always this strange little creature, so stiff and cool, nothing able to make him speak?

The blinds are down again. The shop is quiet but for the crackle of the radio. A white noise that scratches my ears, makes my already jumpy heart leap a little higher. Teddy walks behind us, watching. I thought he would say no, tell me later, another time, but the mention of his mother again seemed to do the trick. She is the key to him. She softens his edges, she makes it easier to manipulate him.

'Albie needs the exercise, Teddy. It's not good for children to be sat still all day. Why don't we have another walk round the shop floor? It will be good for us.'

'Hmm.'

'Did your mother nag you to stop playing games and go outside? I bet she did.'

'Yes. You're right.'

A pause, so heavy it made it hard to breathe. 'What is it?' I asked.

'She would never let me go alone though. Not even to play in the park.'

'Why not?'

'Wasn't safe.'

He picked at his neck; I hate him picking at his neck.

'Because of your father?'

'I didn't understand why. I did when I was older.'

'To protect you?'

'Yes. When people recognised us, started to shout, she would talk over the noise. Distract me. Always such silly things she used to say.'

'Like what?'

'"I need some ice cream in my belly, Teddy. Strawberry. Hmmmmm. What about you? Do you want some ice cream in your belly, Teddy?" "Chocolate," I would squeal. And the men would shout louder and she'd talk faster. "Do you know what almost rhymes with Teddy? Jelly. We'll have ice cream and jelly for Teddy. Let's run. Why don't we? We're running for that jelly."'

'The men came after you?'

'Yes. But my mother could move like a fox when she needed to. She'd pick me up, and my legs would dangle, and sometimes she would trip over my feet. but she made herself smile so I couldn't know it wasn't a new game and the people we were running from weren't playing too.'

'You weren't afraid? At all?'

'Running, running, but she never ran out of breath. And she did it all smiling, so I smiled too. I was a child. I thought nothing bad could happen if my mother was smiling.'

Would she have smiled if she'd known what she was running with?

Albie is tense, holding my hand tight. He looks at me. Not yet, I think, not yet. I try to appear calm, but I am scanning the shelves, the tables, the boxes and chests, searching. Moulded puzzles, bits of rope and driftwood, books and magazines, and mixed into it all, the stranger things: a skeleton, heavy with two leering skulls; voodoo dolls of hessian, stuffed with wool and rice; a pig's face, with fine, fair hairs, hung in a large bowl; dolls' faces, animal faces, skeletal faces, so many faces, I hope to never see a face again.

But these things are of no use. What else is there? Rocks, paperweights, brass bells. No. Heat stirs my hairline. I tell myself to calm down, to focus, but every step brings us back to the cellar. Not yet, not yet. The radio is louder now, clearer, and I want to throw it across the floor.

'Mummy?'

I am about to shake my head, tell him no, but then I see it. A sliver of silver on the shelf: a letter opener. Not as sharp as a knife but it can do more than enough damage. I tap Albie's hand twice, instantly he drops to the ground, begins rummaging through a box.

'Mummy, look.'

'That looks fun. Ask Teddy and Mr Vincent if you can have it.'

They aren't looking me. They're looking at Albie. I back up, feel the shelf against my waist, the soft clink of jars. I'm about to reach for it when the radio tunes in and two voices replace the white noise. They fill the shop. but it's only me listening.

'And how did Ada seem to you, Mrs Belling, in the weeks before her disappearance? We've sources who claim she was distressed, anxious. What are your thoughts?'

'Unfortunately, I was away at conferences. and I did not get to see my daughter during this time. My husband says she did seem anxious about something. Although she didn't mention what.'

'You must be missing Ada and Albie so very much.'

'I am. I can hardly breathe when I wake up in the morning. I just want my daughter back. And my beautiful grandson. That's all I want,' my father says.

They know. They know. They know.

They're looking for us!

But they will have already looked here. They will have already searched Rye. And they did not find us. Have they been in the shop? Have they questioned Teddy? Do they know who he is? They must.

'And Ada rang you, Mr Belling, didn't she, the day before she disappeared? What did she say exactly? Can you tell us?'

I hear my father. The soft rumble of his breath near the mic. Before he can speak, my mother's voice rises. 'She said she had to leave Rye. She begged her father to come and fetch her. She sounded distraught. That's what he said when he told me about the call.'

'OK ... And, Mr Belling, what did you think was the problem, what do you think was bothering Ada?'

'We're really not sure. It could have been anything. As far as we knew, she was content. We hope she is OK. We hope they will be returned to us soon.'

'Has there been any progress with the investigation? You have any updates you can give our listeners?'

'I'm afraid not. We ask that if you hear anything or see anything, or if you have any knowledge of Ada's whereabouts, you please come forward. We don't know where our daughter and grandson are and we need to know they are safe. Please.'

'The investigation has received so much support from the public, is there anything you'd like to say, Mr Belling, to the men and women who are supporting the efforts to find Ada and Albie?'

'We would like to thank you all, of course. Your support has meant more than I can put into words. And I know wherever Ada is, she would be just as grateful.'

'Thank you, Mr Belling. And thank you both for coming here today. You and your family are in our thoughts, and we hope Ada and Albie are found soon.'

The show moves on to the weather. Something lands on my cheek. I swat it away. A bug, a fly. It's a tear.

Something is poking into my back. I realise it is Teddy. He's pushing me forward. Albie is up, walking ahead with his hands round a book. My breath sticks in my throat, the shop is swinging, like a pendulum. Or is it me. It's me, I think.

'Well, this was lovely. I enjoy our little family walks. How about you, fella? Did you enjoy that?'

A nod.

'Good. Do you want to hold my hand?'

'No.'

'Still too old for that, are you, fella?'

'Yes.'

The letter opener. I didn't get the letter opener. We are being pushed forward, back toward the door. Albie is looking at me, a question in his face.

In the cellar, Teddy dips his head. 'Come give Daddy a night kiss.'

Albie wheels back. 'I'm too old for kisses.'

And I think, *My God, he is learning. He is learning how to manage Teddy.*

'Please? Just a little one?'

'No.'

Teddy laughs, ruffles his hair, leaves, and the door once more swings shut. Just before it does, I hear the radio, the faraway voice of the weatherman predicting a flood.

🍎

Albie wakes in the night. There is sweat on his brow. I wet a corner of the sheet, blot, blot. He is crying, he is always crying in the night. I rest my hand on his chest, tap a slow rhythm for his heart to follow.

The police are looking for us. The public is looking for us. But, if they know who Teddy is, why haven't they found us already? Because there is no evidence against him, I realise. How can the police condemn a man for his father's crimes?

How long will they keep looking? They know something changed in Rye. They know I tried to leave. What happens when the public tires of our story? When our names are just names in a list, two of many who are missing. Our faces will leave the papers, we will be forgotten.

If only they knew we were under their feet.

'Mummy!' Albie is looking round for them, Teddy or Mr Vincent.

'I'm here. Did you have a bad dream?'

'Teddy.'

I sigh, draw him up. 'Listen, bean. We're going to get out, OK. People are looking for us. Grandad and the police. We're going to be just fine.'

'Did you get it?'

'No ... no, I didn't. Not this time. But I will. I promise.' He didn't hear my mother's voice. 'I will next time. OK. Will you help me again? Next time we're in the shop, you distract Teddy and Mr Vincent?'

He nods. I kiss his forehead. 'Good boy. I love you. I promise I'll get it next time, OK. It's going to help us get out.'

'How?'

'It just will.' I'll cover his eyes. I'll tell him to cover his ears.

He rubs his eyes. 'I hate Teddy.'

'I do too.'

'I want to go. I don't like it here.' His bottom lip wobbles, and I pat it soft with my finger.

'Close your eyes.'

He shakes his head, a sob humming from his mouth.

'Close your eyes.'

He relents.

'Good. Now where are you?'

'What?'

'Where are you? Where do you go when you close your eyes? What are you imagining?'

Something like a smile presses against his lips. 'The park.'

'What are you looking at?'

'The ducks. I'm throwing them bread. They like it.'

'Is it sunny? Is it rainy? Who else is there with you?'

'You're here, Mummy. And it's sunny.' The smile dissolves. 'Is Teddy coming?'

'No. Teddy can't come here.'

'Is Mr Vincent coming? I don't want them to come. Don't let them come, please.'

'This place belongs to you. And only you get to decide who comes and goes. Understand? Teddy is not welcome, nor Mr Vincent.'

He nods.

'Do you see them anywhere?'

'No.'

'Exactly. You're safe there. We both are.'

'But ... but...' The words stick to his throat. 'Teddy's here when I open my eyes.'

'He is, bean. But he's not when you close them. So close them.'

TEDDY

Rise and Fall

They know. They stand at the window, soldiers in ranks, only instead of rifles there are bulging handbags at their hips and greasy fish-and-chip papers. Their voices. They are so loud, rising and falling in perfect unison. I consider blocking my ears, but I will not buckle.

'I knew it. I knew I recognised him.'

'Teddy Colne. Colne!'

'Never forget a name like that.'

'Sickens me. Just sickens me knowing he's in Rye.'

It didn't take so long after all. I wonder who it was that started the rumour. No matter now. Their figures move and ripple behind the blinds, as if they are the limbs of a single beast, snapping at the door to get in.

Mr Vincent appears, comes to a stop by my side, his eyes widening in his little head. His clothes haven't changed from yesterday, but there is a new stain on his lapel: jam.

'They know,' I say. 'Open the blinds,' I say.

He looks at me, eyes wide. 'But...'

'Do as I say.'

He nods, draws them back, and suddenly, the beast stills, countless faces pressed against the glass, between streamers of egg whites. I will clean the windows later, wipe away the paint and egg and oily-nose marks. 'Carry on as usual,' I tell Mr Vincent. 'But keep the door locked. We're closed until further notice.'

We begin our morning routine, Mr Vincent does the books, stabbing the calculator, fast as if he is cracking the backs of fleas. I set to work cleaning; an old shop like this, there is a fresh layer of dust every day. Meanwhile, the voices rise higher as more join the beast.

'I knew all along it was him.'

'Arrogant arse. You had no clue.'

'And I s'pose you did?'

'I didn't say that. The rotten ones are tricky. They pretend to be like the rest of us.'

'Tricky? He's an evil bastard. He's got his father's blood in him. Sins of the father become the sins of the son.'

A new voice: 'I knew the very moment he arrived in Rye. I saw him, I did. Standing in the street, staring all funny at Berry & Vincent. Just stood there like he couldn't look away. Fuckin' weird.'

'I saw that too. I said to my wife he was a strange one. Rotten. Not surprised he wanted to work there. It's like for like, isn't it?'

'Well, I just can't fathom it. Johnny Colne's son in Rye all this time...'

'And now look what he's done. Gone and taken one of our own. Poor Ada, poor Albie. They were good people. Kind. Always there to give you a smile.'

'You called her a slut the other day.'

'I did not!'

'Don't matter now. She's probably dead. The kiddie too. Where've you put them, you nasty fucker?'

I didn't take them. I found them, I want to say. They were lonely. You made them lonely. Now they're not.

There is a buzzing noise. I see a scraggly youth moving in front of the window. Red letters appear:

Murderer

I've seen it before. Usually, I pack my things on the spot. The next town and home wherever my finger lands on a map. But I will not be run out of Rye. I've set up a life here now. I have a business, a family. And we will not be pulled away.

Still, I must do more to nudge away their gaze. I look at Mr Vincent. 'I'm going out. Keep the door locked. I'll be back soon.'

'Yes.' He bows his head. I must admit to enjoying it.

I take the back door and make for the town shop. The woman behind the counter jumps when I enter, a frightened rabbit in a field. Her eyes flick to the door, she calculates the distance, the timing. Just as she is about to set off, I grab a loaf of bread from the shelf.

She pauses, as if she can't fathom what she is seeing. I pick up a block of cheese, a tub of butter, smile at her from the counter.

'Just these, please.'

Curiosity killed the cat. But not this cat.

'How are you today? It's busy out there. Loud too. Have you ever seen Rye so full? I just hope all the commotion helps find them.'

'Y-yes.' She gives me my change.

'Thanks. Bye.'

I glance over my shoulder. and she is still stood there, a frown on her face, confusion, because I didn't try to hurt her. Kill her. Even though I have shopped in there countless times, and she has shown me pictures of her troll grandchildren.

I return to the shop. There, I slice and slather butter and cheese between bookends of bread. The beast has settled now, grown still.

'What's he doing? What's he doing?'

'He's eating, moron.'

'But...'

'But ... how can he be...?'

From the corner of my eye, I see heads turn, noses and breasts unstick from the window, bodies shuffling, eyebrows rising. How can a guilty man be sat so innocently eating a cheese sandwich with his fingers?

ADA

Burn and Blister

I expect to hear piss hitting the bucket, the scuffle of small feet through the dirt. I expect a sigh or a grunt of some sort, before the flop of an arm round my waist, a leg trapping mine. But there is nothing.

'Albie?' I say. 'Are you OK? Do you need help?'

I draw myself into a sitting position, wonder if he's had an accident. But there is no fresh tang of piss. Still, I say, 'Is it that zip again? Has it got stuck? Bean?'

I brush crumbs of sleep from my eyes, look for a figure, a thickening of the darkness. 'Albie? Are you finished?' I feel my way across the floor. I've used the pips to make a trail from the bed to the bucket, for when Albie wakes in the night and needs to go.

'Bean?'

The silence nudges my heart into a frantic tattoo. I quickly rise to my feet, throw my hands out. 'Albie?!' My foot knocks the bucket and it upends, spilling our filth onto the floor. The stink of it stings my nostrils.

He's asleep. He must be asleep. I go back to the bed, drive my hands into the tangle of sheets.

'He's not here,' I say. I scramble back and forth, searching corners with my hands. 'He's not here.'

I find my way to the door, and I am screaming. 'Albie! ALBIE!'

Teddy's taken him. He's taken him. I see all those girls, buried one atop the other, the red, red lips all the colour there is left in their faces. What if soon their congregation will have an addition? A little boy taken to where all the little girls rest.

'Albie!'

He strangled them. That's what he did. He killed them and dressed them up. It was his favourite part. I see Teddy doing the same. Making Albie perfect, taking him to the orchard.

'Teddy! Bring him back. Bring him back! I will kill you. I will fucking KILL YOU!'

There is spit on my chin. I drag it away with my sleeve. What if he's already gone? Even if he is upstairs, he won't hear me. These walls are thick, too strong for my weak voice to breach.

How long was I asleep? How long has he been gone? He could already be dead. I should have woken up. Why didn't he wake me up? I stumble away from the door, blood blisters freckling my hands. I should have woken up. I slump to the floor, curl into myself.

'Albie. Albie. Albie.' As if this chant will draw him back.

He cannot hear me. None of them can. Not Teddy nor Mr Vincent. If only Rye knew I was under its feet. It is night or day? It could be either, but my senses tell me it is night still.

'Please,' I say to nothing. 'Please bring him back. Bring him back.'

I curl my fingers round my throat, scream until I have used all my breath.

🍎

'Mummy?'

I open my eyes. The light is on now and I see Albie standing over me, his fingers round the belly of a soft toy. I am up in an instant. There are tears in my eyes again, on my cheeks, rivers of them. He taps my shoulder, tries to pull away. But I will not let go.

'Mummy?'

I look for cuts and bruises, for damage in his eyes that is not always as clear. For the first time, I notice Teddy, stood in the doorway with a grin on his face. 'I didn't want to wake you, darling. You were fast asleep. But I thought Albie should get some exercise. We had a good time, didn't we, bean? We had some snacks and a nice rummage through the shop.'

'Don't you ever fucking take my son again!'

'Don't talk to me like that, Ada. He is not just your son.'

'I mean it, Teddy. You do not touch him. You do not take him ever again.'

'I'm his father.'

'You are NOT his father!'

His face sags, as if I have hurt him. Then it shifts, becomes grave, and I am the frightened one. He takes a step, and my arms cinch round Albie, but then he stops, smacks his lips.

As the door closes, I hear the words, 'I am,' slipping back through. Teddy leaves the light on, and for this I am grateful. I look at my son, every inch of him.

'What happened? Bean, did Teddy hurt you? Why didn't you wake me? Tell me, did they do anything to you?'

He shakes his head, his lip wobbling. 'No.'

'Are you sure? You can tell me?'

'No.'

I carry him to the bed. 'What happened?'

'I walked round the shop. We had some jelly and ice cream. Teddy let me pick a toy.'

'What did he say to you? Where was Mr Vincent?'

'He was cleaning the ... the ... where the money is.'

'The counter?'

A nod. 'Teddy said I could have a toy if I was a good boy.'

'Bean, I need you to tell me why you didn't wake me, why you went with Teddy. On your own? You don't like soft toys.' I try to keep my voice light, but it is raw and he knows it.

'I wanted to help.' He pushes the toy to the side, opens his hand. A key, old and red with rust. Some of it has rubbed onto his skin. I lift the key, already I know it will not fit the lock. I cry and kiss him at once.

'We can go home now,' he says.

'Bean ... bean, I ... I don't think this is the right key. I'm sorry but it's ... it's too small.'

'N-no. It will. An-and we can go then.'

'It's too small.'

He shakes his head, stumbles to the door, as if I am wrong and he will prove it. But the key is useless, it turns nothing but air. He swivels round, and there are tears on his cheeks. 'It ... it doesn't work!'

I pat the bed. 'I know. I know. You were very brave, getting the key, but you must promise that you won't go anywhere with Teddy or Mr Vincent without me again? OK?'

A bubble of snot bursts on his finger. I wipe it away, curl my arms round him. 'I love you, bean. I love you so much.'

He is sobbing, a hum, like bees buzzing. If only the key had been the right one. Did Teddy see him take it? Did he even notice? And Mr Vincent, he didn't bother to guard the shop door, like a wrinkled dog. They believed there to be no risk with Albie on his own. Why would they think he could escape? He's a child.

But what if he could?

What if he managed it? What if Mr Vincent didn't bother to take the key from the front door and Albie was able to escape? I rummage round the bed, flatten a piece of paper over my leg, in felt-tip write:

My name is Albie Belling. I am four years old. My mother and I were kidnapped by Edward Colne of Berry & Vincent, number fifteen, Main Street, Rye. I have escaped. Please contact the police.

I tear a strip from the sheet, fold the note inside it, tie it round

Albie's ankle. Our time here might be brief, or it might stretch on and our names will be finger-shaped smudges on some newspapers somewhere. Our identities will become nothing more than two words on a list: *Still Missing*.

'Don't ever take this off. OK? Don't read it, don't let Teddy or Mr Vincent see it.'

He nods, yawning. They won't come back now. I kiss his head, and we lie down. But before we go to sleep, I take the sheet, wrap it once, twice, round our bodies; a drawing together, a binding. Tight, so I feel Albie's heart beat inside my skin.

TEDDY

Sharp Objects and Suspicious Minds

'They've come again.'

'I knew they would.' Bold and Fair. 'Let them in.'

'What do I say?' Vincent asks.

'Stick to what I've told you.'

Their eyes meet mine through the glass. There are scabs at my hairline now, thick as bread crusts, blood in the threads of my collar. I rub salves on the sores at night, but they are thick, and I feel as if I lay in a bed of butter. I must stop scratching. But how can I when Bold and Fair have their eyes on me and my shop?

Mr Vincent opens the door, comes and stands by the counter, leaning back, as I have instructed. His arms are folded, as I have instructed. People assume it's an admittance of guilt, of secrecy, but who doesn't think about their guilt and sins when they stand in front of the police? Like this, he looks normal.

They close the door behind them, lock it, and the voices outside become a dull roar in my ears.

'Hello gentlemen,' Fair says. 'We'd like to ask you a few more questions, if that's alright?'

'That's fine, Detectives.'

Bold gestures to the people outside, like predators to prey. 'You keep the blinds open?'

'They'll just get worse if I close them. Think I'm hiding something, wonder what I'm doing ... I'm hoping they'll bore of watching us dust and do the accounts. Is ... is there anything you can do? To ease them off?'

Fair shrugs. 'We'll have a word when we leave, but as this is a public street they can stand there as long as they like.'

I nod. 'Are you closer to finding Ada and Albie? Am I allowed to ask that?'

'We're exploring new avenues currently, but we are hopeful we'll find them soon.'

Why? What do they know? His answers are cold, abrupt, make my heart nag in my chest. No one saw Ada and Albie come to the shop that evening; the curtain twitchers had retired, the street was empty. We will be OK.

'You know who I am. Have you come to arrest me? Because of my dad and my friendship with Ada?'

Mr Vincent shifts, his flabby buttocks crushed against the counter.

Fair shakes his head. 'No, Mr Colne. We aren't here to arrest you. We simply want to ask you a few more questions about Ada and her son. Were you aware of anyone she was involved with? A romantic relationship perhaps? Anyone in town she'd didn't get on with, or had a disagreement with?'

I sigh. 'She used to say she was finding it difficult living in Rye because the townspeople were ... er ... a bit off with single mothers. She said they were old-fashioned, prejudiced.'

'I have multiple sources who claim she walked round the town, trying to get people to speak to her. Is that true?'

'It is. She was lonely. She found their ... behaviour challenging but she didn't have anyone else to talk to. She was caught between a rock and a hard place, if you see what I mean. When I first moved to Rye, I saw her go back and forth outside the window with Albie. It was ... sad. I felt for her.'

Their eyebrows rise. 'How did your friendship begin?'

'She came into the shop. She'd buy Albie some treats. Toy cars. We'd talk a bit. Then gradually we got to know each other. We'd walk to the park. Albie liked the ducks.'

'You were close to her?'

I nod. 'We were able to talk on a level, you know?'

'She knew about your ... history?'

'Yes.'

'How did she react? Did it affect your relationship?'

I glare at them. 'I'm not my father.'

'Of course. I'm just trying to get an accurate picture of her mental state.'

My shoulders sag. 'She was unnerved, I think, at first, but Ada was kind. She's not as quick to judge as everyone else is.' I gesture to the faces outside.

'The reason I ask is not because of your family ties, Mr Colne, but because you were closest to Miss Belling in the lead-up to her disappearance. Anything you can tell us could be valuable. The smallest detail, something you might have overlooked?'

'I ... I don't recall anything.'

'And how about Albie's father? Can you give us a name?'

Ah, I think. *Now we're getting to it.*

'Ada didn't speak about him. Have you asked Mr Belling?'

'We have. We have found no records for Albie's father, and naturally, we would like to cover all bases.'

'You think it could be him?'

'I don't want to speculate, Mr Colne.'

'But it could be?'

A sigh. 'To be clear, what do you know about him?'

'Nothing much. He was a one-night stand. Had blonde hair, I think she said.'

'That's all?'

'Yes.'

He repeats questions from their last visit, and I give the same answers. They are looking for discrepancies, subtle changes in my story, even if it's a different flavour of crisps. But I keep my story intact. I know their behaviour. I know how to sound honest.

'Wait. She ... she might ... she might have mentioned his name was Luke,' I say.

The notebooks reappear. 'Luke?'

'Yes. Yes, I'm certain it was Luke. Does that help, at all?' I ask. 'It does.'

'Can we do anything else to help you find Ada and Albie?' Mr Vincent chirrups into the conversation. I've told him what to say. I've shown him how to behave. I've painted his face, put a voice in his throat. He does well. He does not want to displease me.

Bold tucks his notebook inside his pocket. His wrists are soft and fat and I wonder how one might check the pulse of a man like that. You could lose your fingers.

'Thank you, gentlemen, for your help. We'll be in touch with good news soon, I hope.'

I stop them. 'Is ... is there anything I can do?' I gesture to the window with a wearied look. 'To stop them. To put an end to this? Can you suggest anything? I've had this before, and I've just upped and left. But I don't want to leave Rye. I've felt settled here.'

Fair shrugs, presses one of his cards into my hand. 'Keep your head down. They'll bore eventually. Don't give any interviews. Call me if you remember anything else.'

They leave, pausing on the way out to shuffle the hundreds of feet back. Then they are gone. Looking for a man named Luke. And before the cameras can see, Mr Vincent turns, looks at me. I nod. He did well.

🍎

The shop front is in the papers now. A full-page photo. The smudged ink distorts it, makes our figures behind the glass look foreign, inhuman. And the headlines are bolder than they were when I was a boy.

'Johnny Colne's Son Found in Berry & Vincent, Rye'
'What Is the Killer's Boy Doing in Rye?'
'Teddy Colne Discovered in British Town
Where Mother and Child Disappeared'
'Like Father Like Son. Has Teddy Killed Ada and Albie?'

There are more journalists and reporters, some from as far away as Europe, come to sample the madness of Rye. The disappearance of a young mother and child. The reappearance of Johnny Colne's only son. It's delicious and everyone wants a lick of it.

ADA

Help and Harm

Last night a hand circled mine. I jumped and bit through my tongue. Blood filled my mouth. I spat in the direction of the hand. A noise followed, a grunt, a cry. This morning, when they turned on the light, I saw the blood dried crisp to Albie's left eyebrow.

Only now, hours later, does he let me hold him, tight to me as if my heart has come from my chest. I want to press it back in its place. I explain I thought he was Teddy. I explain that, like him, I have nightmares. I rub the blood from his brow, covering his cheeks in kisses until he laughs and wriggles like a fish.

'What did you want, bean? In the night when Mummy got confused?'

He goes bright, points to the stripe on the floor. 'I needed the toilet. I had an accident.'

'It doesn't matter. We'll clean it up. Don't worry.'

He pauses, severe, puts his hands together like someone in prayer. 'Are we going to be here ... for ever?'

I don't know how to respond. I cannot tell him that I fear we will die here. Since Teddy told me about his father, there's been a knot, a forewarning in my belly that nudges me awake at night.

I simply say, 'No, of course not, bean.'

'Are we going to die?' As if my thoughts are his own.

I make him look at me. 'No. We are not going to die here, Albie.' *We might.*

He takes the old key from his pocket, turns it over in his hands.

The morning after it failed to turn the lock, he was silent. I could not make him speak. He sat on the bed, holding it so tight, its imprint was pinched into his skin.

'I have to get to the shop floor. Do you think you could help Mummy again? Distract them?' I am repeating myself, again and again, focusing his thoughts on the positive. What else is there to do?

He nods, his face brightening. 'What?'

'I've told you, it's something that might help us get home.'

'OK. And I can have some ice cream? And feed the birds? And go to the bookshop?' The words are rushing out now, water from a burst pipe. 'And we can go and see Grandad? And we can go to the beach and make sandcastles?'

I nod, smile, sit on my hands because they are shaking. 'Yes. We can do all of that. What do you want to do first?'

He purses his lips. 'Ice cream!'

'Ice cream it is.'

He giggles. Says, 'Chocolate?'

'Chocolate.'

'With jelly?'

'Why jelly?'

'Teddy,' he says simply.

And I think, *God,* please *let us get out*.

If we manage it, get what we need, I will cover his eyes, tell him to be still. He cannot see what I will do.

And should I miss? Fail? Will my gut have been right? Will it be me instead of Teddy? I've felt his temper flare, burning the tips of our fingers. What then will happen to Albie? The risk of it is almost enough to change my mind. But I must continue. I must.

Albie is growing tired. He wobbles, slumps to the bed, cheek squashed up. I look at him, my heart stamping. If we are lucky – we escape, we live – who will he be when he is older?

A muscle man, with legs and arms big as loaves, fast, fast enough to think he can outrun his past? A weak man, a frightened man who hides because hiding is all that is safe to him? Or someone else? Someone with a rot in his chest, which looks an awful lot like Teddy's?

TEDDY

Skin and Feathers

She stands with her back to me, chunky, box-like camera held to her eye, this woman, this stranger. The blinds are still down, but already the crowd is building, growing, becoming the beast that nudges its nose against the door. She must have broken in before light, before anyone walked the street.

I hold my breath, keep the fire in my belly from rising. I hear a soft *pop!* as she smacks her lips. The lock is broken but the blinds are still down and the door is still closed.

'Oh!' She is looking at the bird in the bell jar, removing the glass, running her finger along its wing. I see a smear of spit and jam across its feathers.

Don't touch it! I want to say.

'Aren't you a pretty little thing?'

In my mind, I scream at her and the heat from my throat burns her hair, her clothes. In my mind, I crush her, bug under a boot. That crack – her back breaking. In my mind, I lunge, and her pulse is a tap, tap on my thumb. She staggers, drops at my feet. Her skirt is twisted up, revealing thighs that wobble. I see it all as if it is real.

'T-Teddy! Pl-please...' she would say.

I press each syllable from her throat, blot them out. Then her heart. Make her quiet. Make her still. And she is better for it.

I rise and rub her sticky prints from the glass. It shines once more.

But I don't. I do none of this. I hold the heat in my throat, make it small, shake the images from my head, draw the thick card from my pocket, dial Fair's number.

🍎

Bold and Fair arrive within minutes. They tap on the glass, and Mr Vincent lets them in. He came down himself only moments ago, wearing the same clothes, the same stains. He should have heard. He should have known someone was in the shop.

I straighten my back, gesture to the woman. She has not left my side since the moment she saw me. 'I called you straight away,' I say, addressing Fair. 'I arrived this morning, found her taking pictures of the shop. Mr Vincent hadn't come down yet. I think she broke the lock.'

Fair sighs. 'Alright, miss. You'll be taken to the station where we'd like to ask you a few questions, and we'd appreciate your cooperation.'

She doesn't not speak. She does not look at them. She only looks at me.

I roll my shoulders, slump against the counter. *I'm exhausted with all of this, can you, see?*

'Was anything damaged?'

'No. Everything's fine.'

'Good. Miss, can you give me your name?'

No answer. 'They're like rats, these people, picking over my father's past,' I say.

'Will you be pressing charges, Mr Colne?'

I am about to reply when she pings up. 'Teddy, I love you! I've loved you since I was a little girl. I saw your picture in my mum's paper. You looked so handsome. I cut your picture out. My mum slapped my knees, made me go without dinner, but it was worth it. I used to look at it for hours, hoping one day I'd find you, and I did. I used to think we could be a family. We could marry and have children together. Your daddy would have liked that.'

Spit wobbles on her chin. I wince, push her away. *See this, see me defending myself?* Bold and Fair cuff her.

'Teddy, I love you! I just wanted to see you. Can I have a picture? Would you smile for a picture?' She is crying. 'Please. I've loved you for years. You could love me too if you tried. I know you could. We are the same. Your mum and dad would want us to be together.'

'Get her out!'

Bold pulls her out the door, and she screams. The cameras start their flashing. Tomorrow, the papers will say I attacked her.

The door closes after them. 'What's wrong with people?' I ask.

Fair shrugs. 'Just the way they are.'

'Are you going to arrest her?'

'Depends if you want to press charges.' He is looking at me, looking for cracks. I show him none.

'No. No. But can you ... keep her away? Keep her from coming back?'

'We can't. She has as much right to be in Rye as you do.'

'Are you any closer to finding Ada?'

You won't, I think. *I will keep her safe.*

'We're investigating a number of leads. Bear in mind, Mr Colne, you asked this only a few days ago. It takes time.'

I nod. They leave, their bodies merging with the tide outside. Voices rise:

'Teddy! Can you give us a smile? Teddy, what's it like being Killer Colne's son? Where is she, Teddy? Give us five minutes. We want to tell your story. Where've you been all these years? Come on, a few words! Do you plan on staying in Rye? Did you kill Ada and Albie? Where are they? Like father, like son. Like father, like son.'

I lock the door, look at Mr Vincent. There is panic in his eyes.

'You should have heard her. Why didn't you hear her? She could have found them!' The fire is rising again, filling me up.

'I was upstairs.'

'You do not leave the shop floor again. You sleep down here. You do not leave unless I am present.' It's in my palms, the heat. I close the space between us, wrap my hand round his neck. It's sticky.

'Do you understand how close that little cunt was to finding them?' My heart is drilling into my bones. 'Then they would have to go back to their old life? They'll lose me. The police won't understand. They will separate us. Lock me up. Throw away the key. You stay on the shop floor from now on.'

His grits his rat teeth, says, 'No.'

I swing and swing, until something gives. He screams, an animal noise. I cover his mouth, trap the noise between his teeth. Then I clean the bell jar with my cuff.

'There, that's sorted.'

Mr Vincent whimpers. He has not moved. I draw him up, walk him behind the counter, position him on the stool, fold his arms, his legs, press his features into something more pleasing. Then I open the blinds.

And we continue business.

ADA

Misplaced Heart and Incurable Blood

'My mother used to say, "My, oh my, Ted, all those apple seeds you're swallowing, a tree will grow in your belly. Spit them out." I looked and looked in the mirror, every night after that for an apple tree rising up my throat.

'This was before I knew. Before I knew where my father took the girls, why some people called him Johnny Appletree.'

'But your mother knew?' I ask.

'Yes, my mother knew,' Teddy says.

'It must have bothered her.'

'It did. All the ways I am like my father. My heart on my right side, my rare condition, my face, my walk, my mannerisms. These things must have hurt her.'

'Your heart...?'

'I've told you that when I was older, her mind wandered. Pieces of her were scrambled. The weight of all that my father had done stripped her, ruined her, like water over wet paint. But there is more.

'I was cleaning out her room one day and I found an old pair of slippers shoved to the back of the wardrobe. They were threadbare and full of holes. I stuck my finger straight through the middle, wagged it at my mother. She did not laugh, she did not see, she did not see much of anything.'

'Didn't you ever think you should call someone? Get her proper care?' I ask.

He looks at me with needle eyes. I bite my lip.

'I did care for her. She was better with me. She was safe. I loved her. Other people wouldn't have understood. They wouldn't have known to put three spoons of sugar in her tea, or that she liked to spritz her pillow with lemon water, or that she hated biscuits that didn't have chocolate on. "Bland as a cardboard box, Ted. Who wants that, I ask you?"'

'Alright. Alright. I'm sorry.'

He nods. 'It's OK. I forgive you.'

'You do that a lot. You quote her. Is that what she sounded like?'

'Yes. She occasionally had moments of lucidity. I loved those.'

He picks the flayed skin at his hairline. I want to bind his hands together, get my lips close to his ear and scream with all the breath in my lungs, *Stop! You're making me sick!*

'There was something inside her slippers. A roll of papers. She must have hidden them, forgotten they were there.'

I do not think I have ever seen his face so full of clouds. 'What were they?'

'Newspaper cuttings.'

'About your father?'

'About me,' Teddy says.

'I'm confused. How old were you?'

'Three. A year after my father was imprisoned, killed in his cell, the newspapers tried to revive the story. They wrote about me. About what I was, what I would become. Because every son is like his father.'

'Why did your mum keep those cuttings?'

'Suspicion. What she must have thought every time I took something, pins and bits of thread and keys. Collecting things, like my father collected girls. What she must have thought when I spoke and his voice came out of my mouth.'

'You think she was always looking out for bits of him in you?'

'How could she not? Wouldn't you?'

I stroke Albie's ear. 'Yes.'

'I tried to speak to her about it. But she couldn't understand me. I felt betrayed in a way. That she kept these things, hid them away. These suspicions about me.'

'What did the articles say?'

'That blood is incurable. What he had, I would have too. A rot, a rust, ran in my veins. Can't be cleaned or cleared or cured. Three years old and already ruined,' Teddy says.

'We don't get to decide what we inherit from our parents.'

'I have it all. I am full up. My mother wondered why he left me alone, when he hurt so many others. If perhaps it was because he saw so many similarities between us. "What man ever wants to harm himself?" That's what she said.'

'And if you'd been a girl not a boy?'

He shrugs. 'Perhaps I'd be where the apples are, and those girls he killed would be my sisters.'

Sickness roils in my belly. I turn my head away, look at Albie, waking up, rising. What would I have done in his mother's position? I would have always been looking, smoothing down his strange edges. I would keep him close to me, looking, looking.

'That's why she used to pretend it was the house "making mischief". She was trying to take him out of you, wasn't she?' I say.

He nods. 'She loved me.'

'What was her name?' I ask.

'Betty.'

'Poor Betty.'

'Come here, fella.' Teddy draws Albie onto his lap, kisses his head. 'Do you think Mummy is a little pale?'

Albie looks at Teddy, looks at me, nods. Then he rises and, with his small, chill fingers, pinches the red into my cheeks.

'Pretty,' my son says, and smiles.

TEDDY

Guilty and Damned

'Look at that boy's eyes, Marie. Black blots, like peppercorns. Turns my stomach. Can you see them?'

'I can. Strange little things, aren't they?'

'Gets them from his dad. I've seen pictures.'

'Gets everything from his dad. Can you see any of his mother in him?'

'No. Not a bit.'

This is what they say about me now. And more besides. I stand before one of the shop's many gilded mirrors. Silver-and-golden birds, open-beaked, open-winged along the edges. They look at me. I wish they would not.

Peppercorns, they chirp. Peppercorns. Peppercorns. I draw new, blue irises on the glass with a marker. Well, they arc not peppercorns anymore.

ADA

Cut and Cripple

It is time. I nudge Albie with my finger, and instantly he rises, leaps off the bed, stretches his back into an arc. Teddy is watching, grinning at the boy he calls our son.

He is not your son, I think. I tell it to his hand still tight round my own – too tight. I tell it to the crown of spit on my hand, where I can still feel his kiss.

Albie yawns, and I say, 'His back was hurting last night. I was worried. I think he needs more exercise.' I pause, my breath stuck like a ball of paper in my throat. 'Shall we take him for a walk round the shop?' *We.* Did you hear it?

He nods, looks at me. 'OK. That should be fine.' His words confuse me, unsettle me.

'Hey, fella. You fancy a little walk round the shop? I think we might have another box of toys you've yet to rummage through.'

Albie nods, takes Teddy's hand. Teddy knocks twice on the door. I note the swift, light rhythm that emulates it. Mr Vincent unlocks the door, and the four of us move up the stairs and into the yellowed light of the shop.

The window display has gone. All the toys and masks and pocket watches and rolls of ribbon, it's all gone. The window is empty, polished and free of its skin of dust. But why? So they have a better view outside? Or so curious eyes have a better view in? Do they have customers?

'Look at this, fella.' Teddy releases me, kneels, plucks a

contraption from the shelf. It is a toy car, old-fashioned and sculpted from copper.

'Wow. Look at that, Albie.'

Teddy glances at me, proud, as if I have made him happy, as if I am a good girl and all my odd behaviour, my attempts to leave, were just naughtiness, a game.

'What is it?' I ask.

'A music box. Turn that little wheel there. It will play.'

I do as he says, and it does. It's a tinkling sound and if fills the shop, makes my skin feel as if it is coming away.

Albie takes it, tucks it under his arm to keep. Teddy laughs. Mr Vincent grimaces. We move on. Please don't let it have moved. Please. I fire off prayers, tuck my hands under my arms so they do not shake. But it's there. It's there...

I pick at a loose bit of cotton on Albie's collar, and he drops once more to the box on the floor, as I have asked, as I have taught him. He throws out squares of lace and tulle, plastic toys and beads and dolls, throwing them higher and higher. Teddy is laughing, and Mr Vincent's face is darkening.

'Whoah! Steady on, fella,' Teddy says.

My heart is a sharp point, pressing on my front. *Now*, I tell myself. *Now!* I check they are not looking, lean my back against the shelf, and with shaking fingers lift the letter opener, slip it into the waistband of my trousers.

We move, on and on, and already I am thinking about what comes next.

TEDDY

Evidence and Accusation

The days are growing warmer, and it's the kind of warmth that slicks your underarms, makes you pant as you walk. I look outside and see countless bald heads, red and crusted, and I think steam will rise from them soon. The cameras have stopped flashing, if only for people to break, sip from bottles and snack on treats from the bakery. More have arrived since news of the break-in.

I hold my hand before my eyes, nudge my thumb to the side, and all the people are rubbed away.

'I'm going out. I'll be back later. Keep to the routine. Don't diverge from it. You don't speak to anyone. You don't let anyone in. You don't go into the basement. You keep to the shop floor. Understand?'

He is glaring at me. I flick his eyelid, and he winces. 'Understand?'

He nods. 'Where are you going?'

'A town a few hours away. I need to get something. For the family.'

'What?'

I do not tell him. He will see soon enough.

'What about the detectives?' he asks.

'See them coming, and you go upstairs. Don't let them in. Don't speak to them without me.'

'And them?' He gestures to the rows of eyes pressed against the glass. They are always watching.

'Stick to the routine.'

He gives a stiff nod, licks his lips. I do not trust him, but it is the only way of getting what I need. What *she* will need. I leave through the back door, and I hear voices rising, my name called out, rumours, accusations thrown into the air.

'TEDDY! If your dad was around what would you say to him?'

'What's it like being the son of a killer, Teddy?'

'Teddy! Tell us, what made you take them. What makes them so special?'

'Take me, Teddy. Me! She can't love you like I can.'

It is a manhunt now. And only time will slow the pace of it. I have done nothing wrong. These voices will quieten, the bodies will disperse, and Rye will be Rye again. We need only wait.

I pause, hear a new voice, heavier, bolder:

'The missus has had to flee. Can you even believe it? We've lived in this town all our lives, and now she's been forced out. She's taken the kids, bolted. Bolted! I'm staying behind to keep an eye on the house. Can't trust a man like Teddy Colne. He could burn the entire town to the ground if he wanted to. No. I'm staying, going to keep my eye on things. Pamela is scared out of her wits. She's taken the kids to a B&B until he's been locked up. We're going to be out of pocket now. Think Teddy should reimburse us.' A laugh.

'I agree. I'm taking my kids away too. We're leaving today. I'm not taking the risk. Imagine he takes a fancy to little Jessie or my Peter. Peter! He's into boys, isn't he? Not like his dad.'

'What I heard. You know, I used to see him sitting on his own at the park, just sitting there. I wonder now if he was there to watch the kiddies play.'

'Sickening. He should be locked up. We none of us are safe here anymore.'

Says the woman who asked me to keep an eye on her children while she paid for their dripping ice creams.

'They're the worst kind. Kiddie fiddlers. Makes my skin crawl just thinking about it. It's a good thing Pamela has gone.'

'The police are as good as useless. Haven't got any evidence against him. Well, I think it's a bit bloody obvious he's done it.'

'I agree. I wonder what he's done with them. The bodies.'

Says the man who spent an hour moaning about his family over a pint, slapped me on the back, told me I was 'a good 'un'.

'Probably in the ground somewhere. That poor little boy.' A sigh. 'I'd better get going, love. I've got to pack. I'll see you when I see you.'

I move on, nails biting into my skin. I jump in my car, squeeze the steering wheel. I lick my cuff, rub a curl of blood onto the leather. It will pass, it will pass, I tell myself.

I start the engine, drive, leave Rye and its rumours – so damning, if they don't choke a man, they will sit in his lungs, set in a rot and kill him later. If they knew we were happy, we were a family, they would understand. They are too small-minded, too plump and puffed with their own false stories and judgements. But they will calm. The rumours will ease, become dust. And all dust must settle.

🍎

I see a girl with ringlets so tight, I can scarcely fit my fingers between them, but she laughs when I try, pushes me away, then pulls me back for a kiss. I see a boy with a dimple in his chin – it makes him look strange, off-balance, but when he is older, he will be handsome. I see them as babes, small loaves, wrapped tight, their foreheads and cheeks wrinkled. I see them in my lap, her wrist to his toe, still pink from birth, their eyes closed. You, I say, to the girl, and you, I say to the boy. I love you.

And their names? What will their names be?

Ada is ready, I think now. It's as I had hoped. She's found her rhythm in this new life of ours. Settled into our home, our new family. I knew it would take time and patience. When I touch her now, she embraces me, smiles for me. She is the Ada I love. And I know she will want this as much as do. Later, when I ask Mr Vincent to take Albie from the basement, she will draw me to her, chest to mine, mouth to mine, and together, we will grow our family.

I take a fourth test, drop it into the basket with a grin. I look at the stick, the blue bars on the box, wonder which of my children will come first. The boy or the girl.

ADA

Crime and Punishment

Mr Vincent is where he always is. Though tonight there is something different about him. Albie is awake, he notes it too. Usually Albie sleeps by me, curved like a walnut, his nose pressed against my chest, so bent it is as if it has been folded in half. Now, he fiddles with the key, turning it this way and that, looking at Mr Vincent, looking at me, working away at the question that sits stubborn between his lips.

It's alright, I say, Sleep. But the words do not come out. I try again, and they are useless things, strange and half formed. Something sits at the back of my throat, I recognise the shape of it, the smoothness of its skin. Panic.

What's happening?

I am shaking and I want to be still, to keep my emotions to myself. But my blood and heart know what my mind does not. Something has changed with him. There is an arrogance, an intention, a danger that blisters the air. It walked in with him, it sits with him now, sits with *us* now.

'Mummy?'

I keep my eyes on Mr Vincent, but I feel Albie move. He is looking at me, for answers.

'It's alright, bean. Everything is going to be OK.'

'What's ... what's...?'

I dip my head, say, 'I promise. Everything is going to be OK.'

I have the letter opener tucked at my side. I planned to use it earlier, but Teddy didn't come. I waited and waited. I kept Albie close to the wall, safe. I practised, like a fool. I stretched and prepared, the blood thick in my veins. But he did not come. Why did he not come? Has he realised I've been playing with him? Does someone suspect him? Is it just Mr Vincent now? Is Teddy even outside, ready to unlock the door? Is he even in the shop?

'Where is he?'

Mr Vincent is silent, something of a smile on his lips.

'Where is Teddy? He's not here, is he?'

Perhaps the thought should bring me comfort, but it does not. I do not want to be alone with Mr Vincent.

'Tell me where he is.'

Nothing. My hands are shaking. I've spent so long planning for this, the thoughts are smooth from my mind working them over. I can manage one. He is an old man, a cripple. I could kill him. It would be easy. I've been preparing myself all day. It will just be a different man.

'He's not outside, is he? I don't think he's upstairs. Or in the shop at all.' My heart is banging. Is the key in Mr Vincent's pocket? Does he have it? He must.

Albie lifts his head. 'Mummy, what's wrong?'

My body is tense, coiled. Mr Vincent rises, about to leave, but then he pauses, comes to me. The downy hairs on my arms rise, stiff, and a voice, my voice, says, 'Brace. Brace.'

He comes, and I move with a swiftness, a thoughtlessness, as if my bones are not bones and there is no blood in my veins that can run out. I swing my body round, drive Albie back. He cries out. Calls for me.

I am low enough to swing out, drive the blade across Vincent's kneecaps. To punch it into the soft, flat skin at the back. Mr Vincent kneels with a click of his legs, presses his cold body to mine. Albie is screaming, and I throw back my hand, rest it on his chest to keep him where he is, Be calm, be calm.

'Mummy!'

Mr Vincent's fingers are at his belt, his zip. Albie moves, wriggles, tries to reach me, but I keep my hand firm, keep him down, feel his pulse stamping.

'Mummmmy!'

Vincent strikes me, sudden, hard, his rings gouging notches into my cheek. He drags me by the legs, until I am on my back, with more strength than I knew he possessed.

'MUMMY!'

'Stay there!' He is crying, and I scream, 'Don't move!'

He picks at my zip, his tongue between his teeth, pale as a fish. I lift the blade, slow, press it to his side. Between his first and second rib, where his old heart moves. I push, feel cloth and skin pucker but then I stop because I see the door is open.

I see Teddy, standing where the light and dark meet.

TEDDY

Life and Death

He sees me, and a noise comes from his mouth, the half-strangled yelp of an animal. He trips, over his feet, Ada's feet, over nothing. His legs are shaking, but I cannot move mine. My lungs are cotton wool. I cannot breathe. All that moves is my heart, and even this is sluggish, stilted, as if it has lost its ability to beat.

He is watching me, eyes wide. He says, 'Teddy.' The first time he has said my name. Fury nips at my neck, spots my vision. I throw out a hand for purchase, for balance.

'Teddy,' he says again. And I move. My fingers dive into the meaty folds of his neck. He screams, lands with a thump, begins to buck. Albie is crying, and Ada is soothing him. I cannot see them. There is a new noise now. A scream, a howl, curled into one. I look at him. But it is not him. It is me.

'Ted-Tedd—'

'How long?'

He whimpers, tries to turn onto his stomach. I drag him back. He splutters, eyes bulging.

'How long have you been coming down here? Tell me!'

'Mon-months.'

All this time I have thought him weak, used him like a puppet, but these bones are not wood, they move on their own. He has laughed at me, mocked me. And Ada? My son? He has sullied them, put his filth in their skin.

'Pl-please, Teddy...'

I drop to my knees. The heat is in my palms. He calls for help, for Ada. But before he can take another breath, I lift his head, this strange little head, break it once, twice, upon the ground. Blood sinks into his collar, cotton heavy with it. Then it sinks into the dirt, into the dust.

ADA

Bracken and Bone

I think he will collapse on his own and it will be one less man I'll have to break. But he doesn't. Mr Vincent looks over his shoulder, a throw-away glance, then his eyes widen as if they might fall from his head, land in my lap. He is clumsy, rising, wheeling backward.

Teddy drives into Mr Vincent with a force that rings out. Body against body. His teeth are bared, there is a flame in his face, red and burning. Albie screams, curls into me.

'It's OK. It's OK. It's OK.'

'How long?'

What?

'How long have you been coming down here? Tell me!' Teddy screams.

Teddy did not know. He did not know. I cry, my hand to my mouth. He did not wait outside, he did not share us. We were only ever his. All this time, has he had the key? Mr Vincent. Has it been tucked into his breast pocket all these nights he's sat with us? Might we have escaped?

I look at the door, then. It is open, the light from the shop floor meeting the flagstones. I try to move, but it is as if the tendons in my legs have been cut.

Move!

I must move. MOVE! I swing Albie round, force him to his feet. 'Go!' He pauses, looks back at me, and all of a sudden I am screaming. 'Go. Go! Albie, RUN!'

There are tears on my cheeks, in my mouth. There is blood too. I turn, see Mr Vincent splayed on the floor, Teddy above him, his hands round his head. I stumble back, away, away.

Mr Vincent's expression pales, empties, of all thoughts of me, of Teddy, of all of us, then he is just another dead thing on the floor.

He is gone. He is gone. He is gone.

I hold my hand to my mouth, fingers against a scream.

'Mummy!'

I turn, see Albie at the top of the stairs. Move. Move! I scramble from the floor, climb the stairs, feet slapping across the stone.

'Mummy!'

A hand curls round my leg, and I am falling to my front. Pain explodes across my body.

'Ada!'

He is there. Teddy, at the bottom. He scratches shapes into my skin – fronds of blood. 'Don't leave...'

He drags me back, and my ribs smack, smack against the steps. I press my fingers to my bones. They are loose, undone. I scream. I scream.

Down. Down another.

Two more.

Down. Down again.

'Ada, don't leave. Don't be scared. He's gone. It'll be just us three now. Come back. Come down. Let me fix you up.'

'Let go of me.'

'Ada, we're family. Let me help you. Don't run. Don't run from me!' His teeth flash, restless, animal. He will not stop. He will always want me. He will always want my son.

He will always want my son.

I kick out, and he releases, recoils. Shock on his face. I rise, stumble up a step, stop. I can leave. I could make it now. I could leave, but I don't. As he reaches for me again, I drive my foot into his kneecap, the strange swollen bulb of it.

I look at him. I take the blade, keep it low so Albie will not see, drive it into his chest, his heart. Not the left, the right. Feel it meet a cold thing. A strange rotten thing.

Then finally I leave.

TEDDY

Copper and Salt

She is gone. She is gone. She is gone.

Rising, step by step. Her hair, stringed with blood and dust, swings across her back, and I think how later, I will wash it for her, run the water through it.

It is all cold: the flagstones, her back to me, my heart.

At the top, she pauses, says something, but the air takes it. Words fall from my lips, hard and useless. Instead, I reach out, tap the stone floor. To make her see me, to stop this game. My Ada, always playing.

Blood gloves my fingers, runs as rivers down my chest. It numbs the wounds in my chest, not the bloody one, the other one: my heart. She will come. She will come. Soon this game will dull, and she will draw me up, bind me, clean and soothed in her arms.

I hear from above, the break of glass, four feet across the ground, four hands reaching for purchase, then two voices taken by the distance.

She is really gone, I think. She is gone she is gone she is gone.

I lay my head down, the cool press of stone against my cheek, but there is warmth from my eyes now. Blood and water. Copper and salt. It runs and it runs and it runs me out.

ADA

Berry & Vincent

ONE YEAR LATER

Here, we live so close to the edge, if we step through the door without care, we might fall into the water. It is the northern-most point of Scotland, a tiny smudge of an island that is rugged, wild, it will snap the fingers of any who tries to tame it. Albie says with a smile that we will fall off the edge of the world. It is a thought that he enjoys turning over, fiddling with, like a plaything taken from a box.

'Do you like it?' I asked him when we arrived.

'It's quiet.'

Simply this. And I knew he did.

🍎

We lived with noise in our ears; from the detectives, one fair, one bold, who had more questions, questions, even after they promised the last; from the reporters, who stuffed our faces with their microphones and notepads, greedy and red with ambition; from the public, who were restless, wanting to speak to us, to touch us, to be able to say they did; from the women, lovers of the father and of the son, who wanted to meet us, to scrape up what little there was left on our skin of them.

And always the voices:

'Ada, Ada! How do you feel? Do you miss him? What was it like?'

'Ada, a few words? How did you escape? What happened down there?'

'She's not right in the head now. You can see it. Look at her. Looks half mad. Gotta feel sorry for the kid. What's he gonna grow up like now?'

'Yeah, she's lost it. Someone should take that kid, care for him until she's better. Look at her eyes. Look! She's not right anymore. Understandable though, really.'

🍎

They tried. Even my aunt, who cared for us in her home, suggested we have space from one another, to heal, to process. I kept him tight to me then, tighter sometimes than I had held him in the shop. They would have needed to pick us apart, like pages of a book stuck together, close enough for you to mistake them for one.

For three weeks, I did not let him go, nor he me. We were always touching, arms hooked, a lock, unpickable.

We lived in a strange unbalance, the dizzying first step after spinning in circles. My father, when the time came, the courts had done with us and things at least on paper were laid to rest, was ready, hand steadying mine. One evening, Albie was asleep across my chest. Three ribs were broken, and I knew I should move him, but I did not. I did not want to. I looked at my father.

He nodded. He had been waiting. And now I was ready.

The following day, we left. On my way out of the door, I paused beside my mother, offered my hand.

She looked at it, her mouth open.

She would not be moved. So I moved for her. I took her hand, held it for ten minutes, and then I let go.

'I love you.' I said it over the rock in my throat, and the one in my chest. It was worn smooth then by the times I had turned it over.

'Ada,' she said. 'Don't forget your coat. It's cold in Scotland.'

I thought of my mother's sharp edges, the times I had cut my fingers on them. They did not hurt as they did before. I did not think they would again. I thought of the grief I'd contained over the years. That heat, that burn. I wished I could take it out, to look at it, to turn it round and consider it. To put it out.

Like a fire, between my thumbs.

I remembered the accumulation of hours in bathrooms, toilet roll mopping up tears and the oily red patch of a face in the mirror. I remembered grief like a cut, sharp and fresh.

Now, I could breathe, and those breaths were easy. I could stand, straighten my back, and I wondered at the clear air from that height.

Albie tugged on my fingers, and we closed the door behind us. 'Is it time?'

'It's time.'

I looked at the man and woman watching us through the window. They were smiling. Both. I kissed my fingers. And we walked away.

🍎

'Do you like it,' I asked him when we arrived.

'It's quiet.'

We both did.

🍎

Here, we were allowed to do as we pleased. Some days, we were loud, and the cottage, little bigger than a hut, rang with our voices. We laughed because we were laughing, we laughed at everything and nothing. We laughed because if we did not, we would burst.

Other days, we were silent, we could not be persuaded to talk, to do much more than sit with each other, rested and restless all at once. We waited for these days to be over, and when they were, we laughed at this too.

Here, I went from room to room, worrying away at the freedom, dizzy with the realisation that I could move without being led, that my steps were no longer restricted to seven. Eight and my heart would stick, clunky and panicked. My shirt would adhere to my armpits and I would struggle to breathe, wheeling back.

'Mummy?' Albie would say, and he would nudge my foot with his and we would move, take the eighth step together.

Here, the bed was too high, the bedroom too big, so I pulled the mattress to the floor, pushed it to the corner, a silken sheet tied round our bodies, bound up so we could not be taken apart. Only when we were together, on the floor, did we sleep. But still I woke in the night, checked the corners for *him*, waited until the morning light met the sill and I then waited for Vincent.

Here, I looked in the mirror, lifted my hands to my cheeks, pinched until the skin was pink.

Here we marvelled at this strange, perfect freedom. Bathing without being watched. Here we drank tea, built towers and tunnels in the sand, watched the birds, listened for their humming until they bed down and quietened.

Albie looked at me, smile hesitant, fragile as bird feathers. 'They're alive!'

'They're alive.' They were not stuffed, captured in glass.

Here we find some balance, some purchase, we settle. A year turns, summer comes again. Our neighbours are kind, soft-spoken, they welcome us into their home, their life and the cost is not dear, they do not expect press attention, reward, fresh details. They expect nothing but our company.

'Ben's got a net. He's going to catch a fish!' Albie's words breathless, excited, each one a triumph, my heart leaps for it.

'Really? A fish? Do you think he'll catch a big one?'

He nods, 'It's a big net. Can I go help him?'

I nod, smile, watch him run. 'Go, bean.'

But then I wake in the night, see him asleep, hair falling at an angle, see a ball of white stuffed into his ear. The next morning, I find the hole in the pillow, its insides bursting like cream.

In the morning, we sit on the beach, and I think what a thing to be quiet and still and thoughtless in your own body. Time moves, but I do not have to count it. I watch bodies, local people moving around us, and I do not have to worry over them.

There is salt on my fingers, and I lick it off, turn my face to the sun until it burns. I breathe and breathe, great gulps of air that feel like life.

Albie plummets down next to me, he is withdrawn. He does not smile, he refuses my arms. He has not spoken today. Not a word. Bad thoughts gather to him like birds. I can see them.

Then a gull lands beside him, its feathers bristling, its eyes like pools of oil. Albie smiles, but it is not *his* smile. It is too wide, wide as my fist. All teeth. I can see the soft red of his gums. The corner of his mouth is twitching, like there is a bug stuck under his skin.

Albie leans in close to the bird, says, 'Hello, fella.'

And I can no longer breathe this air.

🍎

The days that follow, I look more closely. He keeps the key, this old and useless thing, in his pocket, turns it in circles constantly, and I wonder how I missed it. When he rises in the night, he goes to the corner, but there is no bucket. He jumps, as if struck, goes to the bathroom.

He forgets here there is a light to switch on.

He dreams, refuses to tell me about them, but I know from the wrinkles in his forehead what they possess. If Ben knocks on the door, he will ping up, alert, afraid, and only when he sees a boy behind the door instead of a man, will he breathe.

'Bean, is something bothering you?' A ridiculous question but one that is necessary.

He frowns, sucks his bottom lip between his teeth and bites, as has become his habit. There are many things different about him now. He is quick to anger, to throw out his fists, his face boiled to a deep red. His voice will rise, higher than I have heard it before. And he will walk with a lilt on his left side, always as if a thread pulls him over. 'No.'

'You can tell me. You can tell me anything.'

His lip is bright, swollen. I want to tell him to stop, but he needs to do it. It is his comfort.

'Are ... are they looking for us? Is Teddy ... going to come here?'

'No. He's not. We will never see them again. They are gone. Do you understand?'

'But what if they do come? Will they take us back? To ... to...'

I shake my head. 'No. They won't. They are gone. I promise, bean. We're safe now. OK? They are gone. Do you know how long for?'

'No.'

'For ever.'

He nods, lets his lip slip from his teeth. This will do for now, but the fear has still not gone. For me, nor him. There is a something of them left inside us. I have explained, countless times what happened. But sometimes words are thin, until something gives them substance.

I rise, look at him, know that sessions with a prim woman in a prim seat will do little. They cannot help. But there is something that might. I take a breath, ease him for now, then I go inside our house, pack a bag, turn off the lights. We depart the island the next day. The weather is in a temper and rain falls, splashing our backs, drawing long wet tears into our coats. We leave. But already I am anticipating our return.

We arrive with the rain. It begins to fall as I take him to the outskirts of the town. To the headstones that rise like mossy fingers from the earth. To one in particular that has only a name and an age, because what more can be said of its person?

Whereas the others are polished, clean, propping fresh blooms, his is cracked, a ragged line through the middle, as if he has moved the earth, broken through. We do not bring flowers, we do not bring grief, at least not for him. We stand close to the grave but not too close – there still might be some life that wants to pinch at our legs.

We watch, we watch. We are not mourners, cheeks wet and red, we are something else: a woman, kneeling, determined palm pressed to the earth, to the V in his name, not to let the man below know she is there, but to show the boy he is gone.

🍎

The shop stands apart from the rest. The shelves have been cleared of their jars and their books and their strange faces. It is all gone. The sign has been taken down, the windows papered but for the slim cracks I peer through. Now all that is left is the shape of its name in the wood: Berry & Vincent.

I thought it would be different. Now it would be clear, clean. And yet, something keeps to the sides, a breath, moving, rumbling away inside there still. A shadow, a skim of life, and of death, and it will not be removed. I feel it.

Still.

I think of the dolls, porcelain and wax, of the men below, one moving, one not. I think of a white cotton collar, heavy with blood. I think of the box of tests I glimpsed as we ran.

I think of how he survived, the man at the bottom of the stairs.

In the beginning I wished he had not, but later, there was comfort to be had from a life conviction, from the police detective, who saw my face, whispered, 'He won't last. Not in there. Like father, like son.'

'He'll be killed?'

'And more.'

●

I see them, the proprietor and his assistant, stood shoulder to shoulder as if bound with a stitch. I feel them, lingering, like a palm pressed to a palm, its touch felt even once it is removed. Something of them lasts here. Blisters here.

Albie watches our reflections in the window. What is on his face? I cannot name it. I thought, when I brought him back to Rye, it would ease him. But there is no calm in his eyes. His hand is stiff in mine, cold, and so I rub some warmth into it, but the warmth will not stay.

'Albie. Do you see? It's empty. They've gone.'

'Mmm.'

'Go and look through the window.'

He does as I ask him. But he does not come back. He remains where he is, fingers putting oily marks onto the glass. A chill sinks teeth into my chest. I breathe, breathe. How many breaths have I taken now?

'Albie ... come back.'

His small body stands before the door. He lifts his hand, as if to open it, to enter...

'Albie!' I pull him back, fear snagging in my chest.

He looks at me with eyes like peppercorns, annoyance that stings me. Then returns his eyes to the shop. And in the window's reflection, I see him slowly bring his hand to his neck, begin to scratch, nails deeper, deeper into his skin.

'Do you have something on your neck?'

'No. No, I don't.'

I look down. My fingers are shaking. My legs too.

'Albie, you'll get scars scratching like that.'

He ignores me.

'Please. Stop.'

'No.'

And then I see it. I see my son as a man stood behind that counter, with a bent back and a bent smile. He is still as earth as he waits for customers. He does not mind the birds sifting through the air, nor does he mind the faces, the bodies, the things that are bottled, bound to this place. He does not mind them. He did as a boy.

But not now he is a man.

I see him old, older, with hair like dust, knuckles thick as bolts, his eyes black when once they were brown. I see him. Here, always. With little left over of himself, or of me. A voice in his throat that does not belong to him.

Welcome, please do come in...

I see children pass the shop, fresh and plump as fruit, holding their breath. I see quickening feet, words whispered, old rumours emerging, a new name above the door: Belling & Co.

I open my eyes. It is all gone, but there is a shiver inside my skin. Albie continues scratching his neck like a mutt with a flea. I snatch his hand away with some force. He gasps, looks at me with anger. Then he smacks his lips, and it is a crack in my ears.

My hand falls, quivering, into my pocket. My breath sticks to my lungs and black dances in my eyes like dice. I guide him down the street, this one we have walked so many times. But I do not reach for him again, and he does not reach for me.

'Albie, come away now.'

He comes, slowly, looking over his shoulder.

'Albie, look away now.'

He does not. He does not look away.

🍎

The shop stands apart from the rest, bent and misshapen. It is empty.

For now.

Acknowledgements

A heart-felt thank-you goes out to my agent, Emily Glenister, who has been a clear voice in confusing times, a word magician, and a constant support and powerhouse since day one. I'm very lucky to have you as my agent.

And another big thank-you goes to Karen Sullivan for taking a chance on my little book. It is an honour to work with you. Thanks also to the entire Orenda family: West Camel, Anne, Cole, Mark – you are all magnificent.

Thank you to my work colleagues at Waterstones for being endlessly supportive of this book and for being utter joys to know. Thank you so much to the authors, as well as bloggers and booksellers, for reading and reviewing, and for being astonishing human beings who tirelessly support others and share their love of books.

And one final thank-you to my family and friends. You know all that I thank you for.